The Lightcap

Dan Marshall

This is a work of fiction. Any resemblance to real persons or corporations is completely coincidental, except when it isn't.

No part of this work may be reproduced or transmitted in any form or by any means, electronic or mechanical, including photocopying, recording, and any other information storage and retrieval systems, except for brief quotations within a review, without permission in writing from the author.

Contact Dan Marshall at Dan@IAmDanMarshall.com

Copyright © 2013 Dan Marshall

All rights reserved.

ISBN-10: 1482725371
ISBN-13: 978-1482725377

THE LIGHTCAP

DEDICATION

To Courtney, with love.

To Katy, with remembrance.

Thank you for always believing in me.

CONTENTS

Acknowledgments   i

<u>Part One: Memory</u>   <u>Part Two: Muse</u>

Day 1   3   Suspicion   113

SV   15   Escape   123

Orientation   25   Assassin   135

The Lightcap   35   No Enemy   149

Consequences   49   Rescue   159

Election Night   61   Calm   171

Ensyn Memo   71   Storm   183

11 Months Gone   79   LaMont   193

Glass   89   Clear   211

Damen Theda   101   Aftermath   219

ACKNOWLEDGMENTS

Chronologically speaking, the first acknowledgment belongs to my mother, Judith Williams. Writing this novel would have been much more difficult had she not given birth to me. All my love to Courtney Stoneburg for being a great partner and for putting up with me while I talked about nothing other than this book for the past seven months. I owe a debt of gratitude to Robert Peate, whose work made this novel readable. Thanks to all the friends, coworkers, and strangers who showed interest during the writing process. Your encouragement was very much appreciated!

Part One
Memory

"Memory is deceptive because it is colored by today's events."
—Albert Einstein

Day 1

First days were always the worst. As the alarm went off, Adam groaned inside, remembering this was the day he'd anxiously anticipated for the past three months. Adaptech, Adam's employer, had recently merged with Brain Sync, a company that did not market or sell products to the public but subsisted entirely through government projects, private industry contracts, and licensing fees. Just over twenty years before, Brain Sync pioneered technology known as the Mind Drive, which allowed the user to control electronic devices through thought alone. In an unexpected move, Brain Sync licensed the Mind Drive to Adaptech for a reasonable fee rather than market it themselves. Having a sole license for sought-after tech, Adaptech made a killing on the market.

Adam snapped out of his early morning haze and realized the alarm still blared in his ear. *BLEEP BLEEP BLE*—klaxon ended with a thought. Seated in silence, Adam tried to clear his mind, but he could only focus on the slight hum of the electronics in his apartment. He took a deep breath and pushed himself up and across his room, grabbed a comb and worked it through his curly hair on his way to the bathroom. *Best to at least attempt a good first impression,* Adam thought, brushing his teeth with one hand and his hair with the other. He failed to maintain a rhythm, just like the game from his youth where he'd tried to rub his head with one hand while patting his stomach with the other. He gave up on the hair and focused on his teeth. No time for a shower. *If I can't have nice hair, I can at least have fresh breath,* he thought as he left the bathroom.

He put on a maroon shirt, dark grey pants, and a black vest with matching tie. This was all new territory. He hoped his clothing presented a confident front. Internally he was a wreck, heart racing beneath his chest as he stepped into the hall to begin his commute to work. He summoned the building's elevator and stood pantomiming his opening lines, lines he'd rehearsed what felt like a hundred times. "Hi, I'm Adam Redmon, manager of the Programming Division. I'm looking forward to working with you," he said, thrusting his hand into open air and shaking a phantom limb attached to an imaginary employee.

"Oh, Adam, I've heard so much about you. I bet you're the best boss ever. I'm honored to be working for you," came a lilting voice behind him.

Caught off guard, Adam turned abruptly to see the face of his neighbor Hana. She poked at the air, mocking his fake handshake, taunting smile playing against the corners of her mouth. They enjoyed giving each other hell; it was their way of being neighborly. Some traded sugar. They traded sarcasm.

"Oh, not you!" Adam joked, "I've heard about you. The higher-ups warned me that you're a troublemaker, rabble-rouser, just plain bad news." He feigned a look of dismay. "You're not going to be able to get away with any of that funny business while I'm the boss."

"I guess we'll just have to make sure you're not the boss for long," Hana quipped.

They looked at one another, and Adam wondered why she seemed so oddly serious. Her eyes were cool and detached, but then the edges of her lips turned up again ever so slightly. She grinned and said, "Don't look so pale. I was kidding."

The elevator dinged as it reached their floor. Eye contact broken, they stepped inside. Adam let Hana go first, since he'd heard recently that chivalry was making a comeback.

"Floor?" Adam asked as he selected the ground level.

"I'm going to the roof to look over some cases. I like to work with a view. Besides, I pay extra to live in a building with heated roof access, so I may as well use it."

"I'm going to the street level. Need to get to the office," Adam said as he lit the button for the roof. "You mind?"

"Not at all. The other elevator is out of order, anyway."

They stood in silence for another few seconds, trading goodbyes once the elevator opened on the ground floor.

Stepping outside Adam's apartment building was like stepping into an icy Hell, due to the razor bite of frigid wind and the noises of the city sounding like cries of the damned. He queued a playlist of *tencho* music on his dome, Japanese pop mixed with techno samples, catchy beat struck against cacophonous refrains of scraping metal, and fell into step with the rush of pedestrians as he headed toward the subway stop by his apartment. There were trade-offs to city life, but being able to get lost in music and thought while stepping in cadence with the crowd, legs on autopilot, was something Adam felt he couldn't live without. Even so, the concrete fortress of New Metra City could be brutal. Each summer felt warmer than the last. Sunlight blasted off steel and asphalt, life choked from lungs with each breath. Winters weren't any better, with frequent blizzards and increasing snowfall each season. Rising water levels and severe weather changed the landscape of the City in recent years. Parts of the island lay underwater, subway platforms often flooded, and emergency repairs to bridges and other infrastructure was more common, to the growing frustration of the stockholders. Several tunnels had closed for more than ninety days due to flooding during the past fiscal year, and there had already been more closures than at this point a year before.

As he reached the stairs to the subway stop, Adam flushed with anger when he saw that it was closed due to maintenance. *Damn it*, he thought, *between the weather and strikes and broken equipment it's a wonder anyone gets anywhere in this city*. He mumbled angrily to himself as he tightened his scarf against his neck and started walking briskly toward the Adaptech headquarters. Sixty blocks in twenty minutes. He cursed silently as he realized he was going to be late. On his first day. When his new team would be waiting. *Fuck*.

He sent a message to the office: "It's Adam. I'm sorry, but I'll be late. Unexpected subway closure. Coming in on foot." His thoughts were translated to zeros and ones, then zapped instantly to the office of the Chief Executive.

The Mind Drive had come a long way in a relatively short amount of time. Adam was old enough to remember keyboards, mice, and speech recognition, input methods that either caused irreparable damage to the nerves in the wrist, or made you appear mad as you shouted commands at your computer. Antiquated forms of interaction that were long overdue for replacement. Adam had read about neural interfaces during his youth, each article promising that the tech would be available within the next five years and that it would revolutionize the way human beings interacted with technology forever. *Marketing hogwash*, Adam thought at the time. He never imagined that not only would the tech some day come to market, but that he would be working as a lead programmer for the prestigious company that had a monopoly on selling the device.

As he dodged around slower moving groups of pedestrians, Adam thought back to the first Mind Drive he'd used in his early teens while attending a consumer electronics convention. Clunky, cumbersome, prone to error. The human mind was not known for its ability to stay on task, and the first generation of the device was panned due to its tendency to output junk data as neurons misfired in the operator's brain. To make matters worse, the device resembled a football helmet without the face mask—such a fashion disaster that it would never catch on outside data entry and academia. Detractors mockingly referred to the device as a "dome" and its users as "domers".

As with many prototypes, the next generation was vastly improved. New learning algorithms allowed greater personalization by the domers, enabling them to train the device to ignore idle thoughts and extraneous input, and built-in error correction using context-aware Artificial Intelligence was introduced. If you were walking down the street while composing a message, there wouldn't be a line in the middle that read, "Nice ass," simply because you were distracted by a passerby. The same could not be said for the first generation. By the time the current iteration, v5, had been released four years before, complaints about stray thoughts were distant memories. Now, Adaptech benefited from an almost eighty-five percent adoption rate of v5 in Metra Region, and over fifty percent in the other three Regions.

If you had any type of electronic device that accepted input and weren't desperately poor, you had a dome. Public acceptance of the technology improved as it was miniaturized, though the dome label stuck, even as the device shrunk with each release. V5 was the smallest by far, shrunk to the size of an old pair of behind the ear headphones, with a third arm that ran forward down the middle of the skull, from the back where the occipital and parietal bones fused to an endpoint where the hairline met the forehead. The three arms each ended in a small circle, about the size of a thumbnail, commonly called a bubble.

The previous version was roughly the same size, but v5 passed audio through the bubbles into the upper jawbone, below the earlobe, allowing your messages or feeds to be read to you. With v5, domes could be used for both input and output, which solidified it as one of, if not *the*, most popular consumer electronic device of all time. At that point, most people rarely ever took them off.

Hailed for revolutionizing the way humanity interacted with technology, domes also changed how they interacted with each other.

Gone were the days of phone calls and the video calls that followed them. Thanks to the dome, these were replaced with impersonal messages read aloud by a soft computer voice, affable and detached. On occasion people would send a voice message, but as more people bought domes these became less prevalent, supplanted by the more convenient Thought Transmission Messaging, or TTM. Adam referred to it as telepathy through technology, since it reminded him of the twentieth century author who said, "Any sufficiently advanced technology is indistinguishable from magic." If this was the Age of Magic, Adam Redmon was a modern-day Merlin, but instead of a wand the soft plastic of the dome granted him powers, incantations replaced by reliable computer code.

Adam could see the imposing frame of the Adaptech headquarters. This was another change to which he had not yet become accustomed. Eighteen years ago, right as dome tech was gaining wider reach on the market, Adam dropped out of Princeton against the better judgment of his peers, family, and advisers. He felt suffocated by the mediocrity surrounding him and needed to make an immediate change. He was only sixteen at the time, but had made a name for himself by developing crAIck, automated penetration testing software that used adaptive Artificial Intelligence to simulate hacking attempts from multiple concurrent vectors. CrAIck was used at that time by nearly seventy percent of companies with online presences, and helped end years of escalating lawless chaos, theft, and hacks of virtual properties. When he dropped out, Adam was courted by several companies, including three in the Top Ten, the ten largest firms in Metra Region. Adaptech neglected to recruit him for a full time position, instead offering to bring him on as a consultant.

Despite these and other lucrative offers, Adam chose to work with his friend, Jonathan Bays, who had helped code the crAIck software and was a fellow dropout. Together they created a small startup, Meshworks, and eventually released crAIck 2.0. After five years in business the company was acquired by Adaptech, a buyout enabling it to obtain the crAIck source code and a modest patent portfolio. This time the compensation package offered by Adaptech was more substantial, and included a position with benefits in their Security Software division. After more than a dozen years in that department, Adam had applied for and earned a promotion to his first managerial role.

That was how he found himself standing before the ten foot tall door of gleaming metal and glass, about to begin his first day as manager of the Programming Division for the Mind Drive v6 project. Since they had come in after Adaptech acquired their company, Adam and Jon were viewed with skepticism, even scorn. They hadn't worked their way up the ladder at Adaptech, but were brought in at a higher pay grade than many who had spent decades toiling in the cube farms, which caused friction and animosity. Jon did not deal well with the stress, eventually resigning and moving to the other side of the continent. Adam felt a pang of sadness at the thought of his old friend.

As Adam reached for the vertical bar of metal that served as a handle to the entrance of the Adaptech high-rise, he was jolted from his memories by a slap on the shoulder and an unexpected shout: "Adam! You lucky bastard! Ready for your first day as the big boss?"

He looked over his shoulder and saw the ruddy face of Nate Taylor, who'd been his manager until just a few days before. Adam smiled. "Learned from the best, Nate. Of course, I'm late on my first day. Murphy's Law and all that."

"Hell, you're a manager now," Nate chuckled. "You don't need to worry about being on time, that's for the lemmings." He pulled open the door and held it for Adam, who subtly nodded his head as a way of thanks.

"Maybe so," Adam smirked, "but I don't want those peons to get any ideas." Nate laughed. Despite their joking, Adam knew Nate was a good boss, one who was fair and cared about his employees. Nate wasn't the smartest person, but he was one of the kinder people in management, at Adaptech or anywhere else. Adam hoped his new employees would say the same about his demeanor once they got to know him. After a few minutes of small talk, Adam and Nate shook hands and parted ways. Adam wasn't a fan of idle chit-chat, but he genuinely liked Nate, even if their conversation topics never strayed beyond subjects devoid of meaning, such as sports and weather.

Adam ended up being fifteen minutes late, not bad considering the unexpected walk and the five minutes spent talking with Nate. The elevator shot to the top of the building, its doors parted and opened to a long, nondescript hallway. Looking up and down the length of it, one would never guess this was the top floor of the headquarters of one of the most successful companies in history. Adaptech was an apt name, prescient even, since it had grown in just thirty years from a small company of twenty-some-odd people to a global powerhouse with over a half million employees worldwide. There had been many challenges as Adaptech grew, including a near closure in its early history, but it had emerged as the clear leader in the field of human interfaces for electronic devices, companies that stood in its way acquired or forced out of the marketplace through backroom deals and the overwhelming strength of Adaptech's products and patent portfolio.

As in most company headquarters, there were doors everywhere. With a thought, Adam brought up the instructions for that day's orientation. "Room 4C," the androgynous computerized voice cooed in his ear.

The door was plain, with a small label at eye level that read "4C". The only indication of its purpose being the placard underneath that spelled "CONFERENCE" in bold white letters, crying out for attention, demanding the reader attend the important meeting implicitly being held just on the other side. The handle was cold in Adam's hand as he pushed down and forward and walked into a bright light, a near death experience merged with a corporate meeting. He was greeted by expectant faces, and one that was clearly displeased.

"Welcome to work, Mister Redmon," spoke the lips attached to the displeased face, which belonged to Roman LaMont, Chief Executive Officer of Adaptech. Adam had not expected him.

"Thanks, Mister LaMont," Adam said through a smile. "Sorry about being late, the subway was shut down. I'll be sure to allow enough time to account for unforeseen difficulties in the future." He tried to force back his rising embarrassment, though he knew his cheeks reddened even as he stretched out his hand in greeting.

LaMont shook his hand, then abruptly whirled to face the group and said, "Redmon here is your boss. That's the first thing you need to understand. I'm his boss. The only time you don't listen to something Redmon says is when I tell you differently. Now, let me tell you about what you'll be doing on this new project."

CEO Roman LaMont was something of an enigma. Of medium height and stocky build, he looked like someone who'd hold his own in a quarrel, but also as if he'd never be the one to throw the first punch. By all accounts, he was a shrewd decision-maker who had almost single-handedly taken Adaptech from a shop run out of four self-storage units to one occupying the most high-tech skyscraper ever built during his twenty year tenure at the top. He was not known for his kindness or approachability, and Adam had heard several stories told in hushed whispers about people who had exited the building in tears, sometimes under security escort, never to return again. Adam believed it, given what he had seen of the man. Despite LaMont's success as a businessman, he still came across to Adam as a smarmy salesman, of the door-to-door or used car variety.

Adam scanned the room. His eyes went past and then quickly back to a dark-haired beauty he had not seen before. Her hair was almost the same color as her dome, so similar Adam hadn't noticed it at first glance, until he saw the round outline of the bubble at the top of her forehead. There were only two women on his team and she was not one of them, this much he knew. He'd helped select all but two of the people that made up his group, ten culled from the best programmers Adaptech had to offer, six more poached from academia and private sector positions. He wasn't just the leader of this team; he had hand selected them. All eighteen were there, plus LaMont, and this unknown woman.

Adam used his dome to surreptitiously snap her picture and started a facial recognition search. Knowing it would take awhile to finish, he focused his attention back to LaMont, who still droned on.

"We're at the edge of total market dominance. Now is the time to leverage new technologies and acquisitions to ensure version six of the Mind Drive is better than ever, and solidify our position as the sole trusted provider of brain interface devices. This revision will be the most advanced yet, and we don't want our Chinese friends to copy it. To that end, we've brought in Miss Sera Velim, former head of Brain Sync, as Vice-President of New Products and Development." As he mentioned her name, the previously unknown woman briefly looked up from her notetab, as if to give the most subtle of greetings, a slightly annoyed look on her face, then resumed taking dictation, or whatever she'd been doing.

End facial recognition search, Adam thought. A soft tone rang to confirm his command. *Sera Velim. What in the hell is she doing here?* he wondered. A minor tritone indicated the Mind Drive AI didn't understand his query. It had been years since he'd allowed a stray thought to trigger his dome.

The rest of the day passed quickly, stack upon stack of non-disclosure and non-compete agreements signed and handed back until his wrist hurt. Roman LaMont sat in silent observation for almost an hour after his pep talk, though it pained Adam to even think of it as such. Adam made a half-hearted attempt at repairing morale, but the damage had already been done and his efforts were greeted with blank expressions and glassy eyes from those seated around the table. Adam had been so overwhelmed with signing paperwork he hadn't been able to talk to Doctor Velim. She hadn't even spoken to LaMont before she walked out in pace a step behind him, notetab held against her chest.

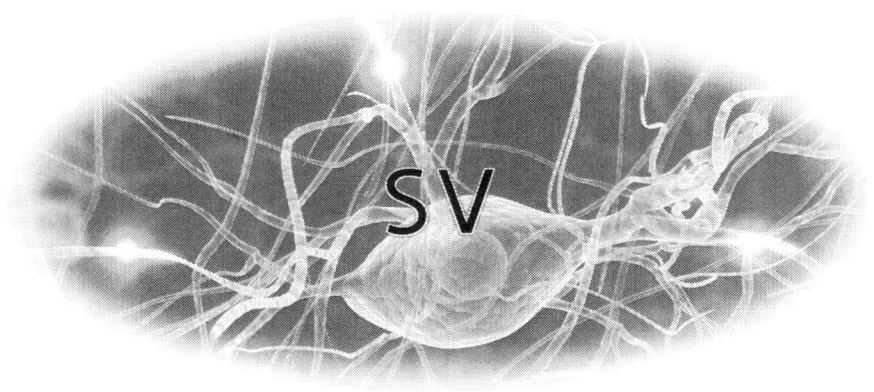

Adam had some time that evening, once he got home, to look up Sera Velim. She had been the head of Brain Sync, being thrust into the role after the sudden disappearance of Doctor Pavel Troyka over ten years before. If Adaptech was secretive, then Brain Sync was a shadow. No one knew exactly what Brain Sync did, but it had established a name for itself as the pioneer of the Mind Drive, even though it shocked the world and allowed another company to market and sell the finished product.

Brain Sync employees worked under several layers of NDAs and legal agreements. As far as anyone could tell, many employees weren't allowed to even acknowledge they worked for Brain Sync, and were given cover stories that included employment through unrelated front organizations. Despite the fact it had never put a device on shelves, Brain Sync employed hundreds, possibly thousands, of people and had lucrative contracts throughout the government and private industry. To what end, no one knew.

Sera Velim was almost as much of an enigma as her company. For instance, Adam knew of her but had never seen her picture. He was curious if there were even any out there, or if she'd somehow managed to avert leaving a mesh presence, a real challenge in that day and age. Adam's first picture on the mesh was from his early teens, taken by a cam recording people walking down a public street. The way things were then, leaving the house was a reliable way to end up as a series of zeros and ones on the mesh, unless you took precautions. There were counter-surveillance necklaces, called ramble-jamblers, consisting of a ring of high-output LEDs that cycled through the infrared spectrum, washing out any characteristics that could be used to identify or track the wearer. They were technically illegal, but were small and hard to detect so many used them.

Velim had been a doctoral student of Troyka. Some sources claimed she started her doctorate work at fifteen, but Adam had seen other evidence that placed her at an age beyond his own. Data from the mesh could be unreliable, even on a good day. When Doctor Troyka disappeared, the authorities suspected foul play or corporate or international espionage, given that Brain Sync had numerous lucrative government contracts. Foul play was officially ruled out. No evidence could be found to suggest Troyka had been killed, but he was a high profile person, and it was difficult for anyone to vanish, especially someone of his stature as an innovator and inventor.

Regardless of Troyka's fate, Doctor Velim had been his heir apparent for years, and, by unanimous vote by the Brain Sync Board of Directors, took what was widely considered to be her rightful place at the helm of the company. As a privately held organization there wasn't much public data available on its earnings, but by every indication Brain Sync's profitability had grown considerably under Velim's leadership. Though she was rumored to be caring in her personal life, she'd earned a reputation for ruthlessness in business dealings. Adam wasn't quite sure what to believe. As with most hearsay there was sure to be some level of validity, but any attempt to suss out the ratio of truth to falsehood was nothing but conjecture.

Adam had watched Velim in the conference room as she diligently focused on her notetab while LaMont spouted fiscal year sales figures, projections, and about the importance of brutally dominating the marketplace. It was almost identical, save some changes in numbers, to the growled speech LaMont had given during Adam's orientation thirteen years before. *Standard corporate bullshit. The more things change, the more they stay the same,* he thought.

He struggled to figure out exactly why Sera Velim had been at the meeting. Last he'd heard there were no plans to bring any of the Brain Sync people on board, but he also wasn't high enough up the corporate ladder to be privy to many of those conversations. She had hardly seemed to pay attention at the meeting, the entire time spent riveted to her notetab. It wasn't likely she'd been transcribing LaMont's remarks, since all meeting rooms were wired with microphones for automatic transcription. That only left two possibilities in Adam's mind: either she'd been observing Adam or his team, or she was detached and doing something completely unrelated.

Adam called up the clandestine picture from earlier and restarted the facial recognition search, hoping to find out more about the mysterious Doctor Velim. He grabbed his notetab and looked at her picture for several seconds. He found her very striking, with dark hair framing a pale face, and soft, full lips that were inviting in shape but coldly pressed together in a look of mild distaste, bordering on frustration. Her brow was furrowed, as if she were deep in thought or struggled to solve a complex problem.

Adam was also interested in Doctor Troyka, Velim's mentor. Pavel Troyka was widely regarded as one of the most brilliant electrical engineers to ever live. He built the first Mind Drive prototype by himself in his basement laboratory with off the shelf parts. Troyka was one of Adam's heroes, a mix of the engineering genius of Wozniak, the madness of Tesla, and the imagination of Turing. A force of nature, regarded as the Father of the Modern Computing Age, Troyka was considered a failure from a business standpoint since he hadn't possessed the business sense to see the vast fortune that would come from his invention, instead choosing to license the product to Adaptech.

Hundreds of theses had been written by business students on the multitude of ways Troyka had failed to gain a fortune from dome tech. Even so, the licensing fees from Adaptech provided enough revenue to allow Brain Sync to operate in the black for years while developing its next big product. Chatter started on the fringes of the mesh, speculating about the next step beyond Mind Drive. Many people claimed to have inside knowledge, but none of their stories checked out. Since Brain Sync marketed products to the military, the first guesses were along the lines of "increased sensory perception for soldiers war zones" and "elevated intellect to allow for higher cognitive function on the battlefield". Nothing ever amounted to more than wild speculation.

The device was evidently intended to provide a tactical advantage, but when Brain Sync started making inroads among the intelligence and legal communities, which could benefit from increased brain function, some claimed this new tech significantly increased the wearer's brainpower. Tales of normal people who had become geniuses and geniuses who had become gods were traded by office water coolers around the world, along with promises of a bright new age of human innovation driven by technology. Whispers of the name "Lightcap" began to echo across the mesh, but nothing had been confirmed by Brain Sync. In fact, the company publicly denied having any tech called Lightcap, but shortly after there were rumors Brain Sync had laid off several members of its research and development group. Given what Adam knew about the company, it seemed as if its leaders were upset that their shroud of secrecy had been breached by the mere mention of one of their secret projects. The company's behavior only raised more questions.

Adam, lost in recollection, did not hear the footsteps in the hall or notice them stopping right outside his apartment. The abrupt sound of knuckles rapping against his steel door ricocheted like gunfire off the wall behind his head and rudely pulled his attention back to the present. He tossed the notetab on the couch next to him and shot up, at the same time shouting, "Who's there?" It was awfully late for a visitor.

"Sera Velim."

He scrambled, piles of clothes thrown into any available hiding spot, empty carryout containers treated like cardboard basketballs and tossed along suspended arcs into the compacter. "Just a minute!" came his reply, as he put on a shirt and walked the five steps from his living room to the door.

There was a rush of air as he opened the heavy steel barricade that sectioned the rest of the world from his haven. It really was Velim. For the briefest moment he'd wondered if it might be some kind of joke, or even his mind playing tricks. Auditory hallucinations weren't without precedent, but there she stood, seemingly in the flesh and very, very wet. His eyes widened as he realized she must be freezing. "Please come in! The InfraDry is over in the corner if you want to dry off. Would you like some coffee?"

"Sure. Thanks," Velim said, stepping through the door as she took off her jacket. She laid her jacket on the arm of the couch and moved underneath a red ring, embedded and glowing in the ceiling in the corner of the room. A gentle, repeating beep increased in speed as the red ring detached and slid downward along invisible guides, slowly rotating as it descended around the circumference of her body. Adam watched as her hair dried, spots of water vanished from her dome, her torso, and her pants lightened from the color of damp fabric back to their normal hue, until the ring came to rest at her feet. Adam looked on with amusement as the puddle of water under her shoes evaporated. It wasn't often he got to watch the infrared dryer from the outside, since he usually stood in her place. The red ring quickly lifted back to its idle position, the entire process done in fewer than thirty seconds.

"Are you going to get me some coffee, or were you only asking to be nice?"

Adam nodded as a silent answer, then made his way to the

kitchen. He issued a command through his dome for two cups of coffee, rather than using the archaic buttons on his coffeemaker. It seemed strange to him, anachronistic even, that so many things still had buttons, but he supposed this allowed the products to be marketed to the small percentage of the population who weren't domers. "Cream? Sugar?" he asked.

"Black is fine. I don't have much time anyway," Sera said. She took the cup from his hand and placed it on the table next to his couch. "I need to talk to you about tomorrow's orientation. We need to make sure you're on board for the project. Roman wanted to come himself, but given the way you looked after today's orientation I thought it might be best if I came by to try and smooth things over."

"Of course I'm on board for the project. I hand-picked most of the team, and had to go through five rounds of interviews before I was even offered the position. Also, I don't know what you mean about how I looked earlier. I have no problem with Roman and as far as I know he has no problem with me."

"Whatever you say, Redmon. I just—"

"Please call me Adam. Only one person refers to me by just my last name, and he's not around anymore."

Sera stared at Adam for several uncomfortable seconds. *Is she trying to make this awkward, or does she not know how to respond?* he wondered. Adam imagined people didn't correct her often, and when they did it probably wasn't with the confidence and directness he'd offered.

"Feisty. I like that," Sera said, her dimples flashing, a hinted grin she quickly stifled. "As I was saying, *Adam*," his name offered with deference but also the slightest hint of sarcasm, "we need to make sure you understand the importance of this project. There's a lot at stake."

"Sure, I heard what LaMont said. We need to ensure we

continue to dominate the market and all that." Adam waved his hand dismissively as he said it. He wished he hadn't, because she immediately frowned.

"Look, don't parrot LaMont's corporate talking points," Velim said forcefully. "I don't need to hear about how we're going to leverage our synergy to capitalize on market forces. I'm talking about real danger from unlicensed devices. Part of the Brain Sync licensing terms stipulated that we are allowed to do random quality control checks, both at the production level and further down the supply chain. Quality control pulls on the production lines always checked out, but at the retail level we found a distressing trend. The number of counterfeit devices has been steadily rising, and our last check revealed an eleven percent counterfeit rate spread across ninety percent of retail locations. That's a real problem."

"How so? I mean, I understand from an intellectual property perspective, but Adaptech is making boatloads of money, and that doesn't seem to be in any danger even if the number of counterfeits quadruple."

Sera sighed. "It's more complicated than that. There are potential, uh, difficulties introduced if the circuitry is compromised. You're dealing with a complex piece of electronic wizardry. To make matters worse, the brain is fragile. Damages easily. When a device malfunctions it reflects poorly on Adaptech, and by extension Brain Sync. That perception isn't entirely mitigated by publicizing that the device in question was a forgery. In fact, we've been successful in keeping counterfeit reports out of the news entirely. Can't have people doubting the reliability of the brand, you know."

"Wait, what difficulties? Are you talking about a dome overloading and exploding or something?" Adam wracked his brain, trying to find any memories of mesh reports of malfunctions along those lines. He couldn't recall any. Sera looked at him as if she struggled with how to respond, or how much to tell him.

"As I said, it's complicated, and I don't have much time tonight. This is a discussion that should be had at a later time. I came to talk about Lightcap."

At the mention of Lightcap, Adam's eyes shot up. Never had a lump in his throat materialized with such speed. "Lightcap?" he asked with feigned ignorance, trying to sound as if he'd never heard the word.

"Yes. Don't play dumb."

"Okay, I *have* heard of it, but I'm not lying when I say the most I know about it is the name. I've heard so many rumors about what it actually does that at this point I'd believe you if you said it granted the power of flight and had a built-in espresso machine."

"Don't be flippant, Adam. The Lightcap is the pinnacle of Doctor Troyka's career. It's the real-world manifestation of decades of work and tens of thousands of man hours. His greatest achievement. The Lightcap doesn't give you superpowers; it makes you forget." She waited, as if expecting some gasp or evidence of shock. Adam was well-practiced at remaining stoic, a trait he'd picked up while suffering through countless lectures from his parents and advisers about how his future would be ruined without the benefit of a college degree. She continued, watching him carefully, "Of course, everything I'm telling you is covered under the NDA you signed earlier today. As far as the outside world is concerned, this conversation never happened. At the risk of oversimplification, you put the Lightcap on when you come to work. You work hard. You take it off, and then go home stress-free because you don't remember a single thing about your day. The Lightcap functioned exactly as expected in preliminary tests. Wearers reported feeling refreshed when they went home, that they were arguing less with their spouses, weren't as easily annoyed by their children, and just generally felt happier and more worry-free. More importantly, because the workers were not saddled with problems from the previous day, punctuality improved, along with productivity."

Adam sat for a moment, taking in what she had said. "Well, that's great and all, but what does any of this have to do with me or my team? We're just programmers. It's not the easiest job, but it's also far from approaching stressful. We have deadlines, but it's not like programmers are jumping out of windows due to anxiety."

She nodded once, a brief agreement with his observation. "True, but you do seem to struggle with punctuality. So far, all tests of Lightcap have been in high-stress environments that don't require much in the way of thought on the part of the wearer. War zones, that sort of thing. We want your group to be the first to give it a test run in a setting requiring higher cognitive function. All our tests indicate there should be no decrease in ability or perception. In fact, we believe there will be an increase in efficiency, since your workers won't be bothered by outside stress stimuli, such as personal issues from home."

"So wait, it makes them forget what they've done while they're wearing it, or what they've done before? What the hell is this thing?"

"You sure like asking questions, Adam. I don't have time to explain decades of research by one of the most brilliant minds ever to live—or even my own dissertation—to you. Suffice it to say, Lightcap does what it's intended to do and does it well. It was designed with the purpose of making you forget. Forget your worries from home while you're at work, forget your worries from work when you go home. Most importantly, you can't sell what you can't remember. We're pretty certain there are moles, not just in the supply chain but at the design level. The counterfeit devices we're seeing are incredibly detailed, and we believe the short amount of time between when v5 first hit market and the first confirmed forge is too short to be attributed to reverse engineering alone. This holds true for both the hardware and software ends."

Velim looked at him, giving him time to let the intricacies of corporate espionage fully sink in. She continued: "The hardware design for v6 was handled in teams, no one group having full access to design schematics for the finished product. We would've used Lightcap for them, but it wasn't quite ready for wide-scale testing. Now that the acquisition has gone through, LaMont approved expansion of the tests. Yours will be the biggest test group to date. Anyway, I have to go. Just be ready tomorrow. When we discuss Lightcap you need to come across as being on board. The people on your team look up to you, even those who've never worked with you before. You have a reputation of being solid and reliable, and we need that same sense of assurance to be associated with Lightcap in the minds of your team."

Before Adam processed everything she'd said, she picked up her jacket and was gone. The firm click of the bolt echoed with finality off the brick wall of his living room. Her cup of coffee remained untouched on the table next to his couch. He felt as though she'd created a vacuum, the air carried out with her as she left.

Lightcap, Adam thought. *I'm going to be testing Lightcap.* The geek side of Adam was excited, the pragmatist terrified.

Orientation

He slept restlessly that night, mind filled with thoughts of the Lightcap and Velim's words of warning. What had she meant when she referred to difficulties with the Mind Drive or the human brain being fragile? Domes were supposed to be read only; it was theoretically impossible for the device to affect brain chemistry or physiology in any way. That was one of its selling points. Velim must have been talking about burns or electrical malfunctions. Despite the hour he spent wrestling with these questions as he lay awake and stared at the ceiling, Adam couldn't find any other meaning behind what she'd said.

The next morning passed in a flash. Adam awoke to a soft light pulsing next to him on the nightstand. It was the indicator light on his dome, notifying him of a new message twenty minutes before his alarm was set to explode with its early morning blare. He put on his dome and the smooth, inoffensive voice read the message: "Don't be late this time. Best foot forward." It was signed "SV".

At least the pumps were working for the subway that morning. Adam nodded off in the hard plastic seat as his head bounced in time to the silver bullet car that plunged through the crisscrossed patchwork of tunnels underneath the city, an electric labyrinth playing sustained high notes broken only by the screaming music of metal on metal, wheels against rail, a *tencho* soundtrack during a robot cagematch. He would have slept right through his stop if it weren't for the balance-challenged old man who ended up in his lap as the subway car lurched to a stop a block from the Adaptech headquarters. Disheveled and soaked with the smell of stale piss and raw earth, the man pushed off Adam with mumbled apologies and then disappeared into the next car. No one else on the train lifted their eyes or paid attention. If it wasn't happening to them, it wasn't happening.

He's lucky I'm not the kind to call the Blues, Adam thought as he exited the subway car. Many people those days were quick to call the Blues if someone offended them or seemed suspicious. Officially known as the Central Provisional Authority, the Blues were a private paramilitary group that had a sole license to police the Region. They were known for their ruthless and heavy-handed enforcement of all laws, even the most minor, but particularly the ones related to public decency and decorum. Appearances were important.

Adam reached the Adaptech building, went through the glass slab door without interruption, was shot up over a hundred floors in seconds, and once again found himself at the entrance to room 4C. The placard emblazoned CONFERENCE seemed less inviting today, less pleading, as if the inanimate object had absorbed the feelings of dread he had about this day. The unexpected arrival of and conversation with Velim still had him off balance, even this next morning.

He turned the handle and pushed open the door to be greeted by unexpected darkness. *Lights,* he thought. The command was parsed by his dome and sent to the control unit for the room. The long conference table with ergonomic chairs was immediately bathed in the cool blue-white flicker of fluorescent light. He couldn't help but think about how far technology had come. Even the god of scripture had to speak the words, "Let there be light." Adam merely had to think a single word.

Lost in technotheological reverie in the conference room, Adam didn't notice as the door swung open and four members of his team entered to join him. They startled and broke him from his thoughts of self-proclaimed godhood. He quickly put on his best smile and extended his hand to each of them, typical greetings and pleasantries given by a boss who just started with a new group. Small talk about their past achievements, expectations, educational and professional backgrounds, the weather, the usual.

Adam had always been uncomfortable with that type of interaction, because he felt the conversation tended to turn into a game of one-upmanship, dueling egos trying to prove they were the best in the room, even in the world. Adam had not experienced this dynamic from the perspective of a team leader, however, and quickly noticed that each person on his team seemed to listen with rapt attention as the others spoke rather than wait for their turn so they could prove their own worth. While they made small talk, the rest of his team filed in, until all eighteen were seated around the table.

Each person there was a genius in his or her own right. Some were well-known, while others had operated in relative obscurity, staying out of the spotlight by focusing on projects which weren't considered marketable or sexy. One of them, Rahdej Singh, was the programming equivalent to a rock star. He built his first autonomous robot at the age of 12, graduated from Cornell at the age of 15, obtained his doctorate from MIT at 17, and had been on the front page of *Logic Gate,* a popular consumer technology site, a total of three times.

Rahdej was roughly the same age as Adam, and was his first choice when selecting people for the team. Rahdej had made his mark in Adaptech's Autonomous Intelligent Car division by crunching together code augmenting the AI in the self-driving cars with input data from the domes of the inhabitants. The self-driving cars already had a lower collision rate than human drivers, but with the new code allowing dome cooperation they were nearly perfect. Traveling by car had never been safer. It was this achievement that earned him a second *Logic Gate* interview. Rahdej Singh was well-known by many people for preventing tens of thousands of deaths. Not a bad thing to be known for.

"Rahdej, I'm looking forward to working with you," Adam said, worried he may sound like a starstruck fan about to ask for an autograph. Firm handshake, eye contact, impossibly white teeth. Not just because of his darker skin, it looked as if Rahdej had polished them for hours on end. Adam could see a reflection of light in them, haloed enamel flashing and moving as he nodded.

"Call me Dej. I've heard a lot about you, Adam. Honored to be under your command. Hope they're not too rough on us today." His smile really was mesmerizing.

Adam felt a bit like a deer in the headlights until he blinked and broke the spell. "Yes, we should be getting started soon," he said. Almost on cue, the door swung open and a confident form strode through. Doctor Sera Velim, looking much better than Adam felt. *She didn't have any trouble sleeping last night,* Adam thought, with more than a bit of envy.

Behind Velim was Claudia, the rotund head of Human Resources. Her body took up almost the entire width of the frame as she waddled in and closed the door. Velim took a place along the wall, near the corner, the notetab in her lap the immediate and sole focus of her attention. It seemed as if she'd dug in for another day of silent observation. Claudia took a seat at the end of the table near the door, opposite Adam, hydraulics in the chair emitting a pleading *ssst* as she settled in.

"Ladies, gentlemen, thank you so much for coming," she said. Her lips were permanently turned up at the edges, unnatural red lines locked in a hollow grin.

Maybe someone smacked her on the back as a child while she was making that face, Adam thought, and he did his best not to laugh.

"I'm here today to discuss the legal implications of the

documents you signed yesterday, specifically the medical release. There are some things that we want to make sure are clearly defined. Most importantly, you will not be using your own Mind Drives. Instead, we'll be providing prototypes for you to use. These modified units will provide some additional functions while you work on the v6 project, but you will be required to leave them in this room when you depart each day. Before we go any further, I need to remind you this is all covered by the confidentiality and non-disclosure agreements you signed yesterday. Even so, I need you to sign one last agreement," she said, which prompted many rolled eyes in the room. It wouldn't be a day at the office without paperwork.

As the papers were passed around the table, Claudia continued: "This agreement specifically covers the prototype. I am here to make sure this is all plainly and clearly communicated to you, to indemnify the company against any future claims. I'll let you read it yourselves, but to sum up what you're about to sign, it states you authorize Adaptech to take any action necessary to retrieve or disable a device should you intentionally or accidentally remove one from the premises. This is also a terminable offense, which means you will be fired without warning for removal of any prototypes or related technology, or if you attempt to modify or disassemble them. I want this to be very clear, so there are no questions or misunderstandings. Does everyone understand?" Murmurs and nods of agreement came from those seated around the table. "Any questions?" Silence. "Good. Please read and sign the agreement."

They each read over the pages in front of them. Adam skimmed them, making sure to snap a picture with his dome as he flipped through the pages. He didn't see the point in reading it then, since he knew he had no choice but to sign if he wanted to stay on as head of the project. He scribbled his messy signature on the dark line at the bottom of the last page of papers and slid them all toward Claudia. The other signed copies shortly followed.

"Now that we have that out of the way, I'll be leaving you in the capable hands of Miss Velim," Claudia said in a singsong way through the smile that never moved. She gathered the papers into stacks, gave them two sharp smacks against the table to make the pages flush, and then left, door closed behind her as if pulled by gravity.

"*Doctor* Velim," Sera hissed under her breath, quiet but still audible by Adam and no doubt several others. She flashed a genuine smile and transformed into a saleswoman as she jumped from her chair. "All right, now that we're through with the suits, let's move on to Lightcap."

Gasps escaped from several people in the room. This was most likely the response Velim had hoped to elicit from Adam the night before. He hoped she was satisfied about finally shocking someone with her revelation. He was sure that's why she'd presented it so off-the-cuff, as if she'd simply moved the meeting along to another mundane topic. The members of his team looked at each other incredulously as Velim continued: "Why did you think we were having you sign NDAs about NDAs? What did you think we were talking about when we mentioned a prototype? There's a lot of secrecy surrounding this project. Claudia doesn't even know about it, just that there's a prototype device and that the company needs to protect its interests. You'll be going through a hectic day of training today, getting acclimated with your new Lightcap and learning some of the things you'll need to know in order to be productive members of the team."

A hand shot up, belonging to Rosaria Hines, "Aria" for short. She was thirty years old, her brown skin complemented by a dark shock of hair twisted in tight curls, their natural part just off-center. Her green eyes caught most people off-guard with their piercing urgency. Adam had put up a fight to get Aria, one of only two women, on his team. She and Dej were the only two non-Caucasians in the group. Rumor had it LaMont wasn't fond of minorities, evidence that technological advancement didn't necessarily go hand in hand with social enlightenment. Dej was easy to get, since he was already under the Adaptech umbrella. Roman had not been able to resist hiring a programmer of Dej's caliber, regardless of his ethnicity, since it was another addition to LaMont's trophy case of famous coders.

Aria was someone Adam had known a long time, having worked with her while in college. Adam wanted her on his programming team not because she was the best programmer, though she was more than competent and better than a few others on the team, but because Adam knew she was tenacious beyond what many people would ever consider reasonable. Aria was a very private person, but Adam learned she'd cut her teeth as a coder while living on the streets. Using a stolen notetab and a screwdriver kit she liberated from an oblivious repairman, she taught herself to spoof the secure data connection and send a false verification packet to ATMs and automated grocery kiosks to obtain unauthorized credits and food. If necessity was the mother of invention, desperation was the father, and since Aria's parents had died when she was twelve, her substitute parents had taught her well. Adam definitely wanted someone like her on his team: a person who wouldn't stop even in the face of overwhelming and seemingly insurmountable odds.

Sera pointed and tipped her head toward Aria, acknowledging her raised hand. "Thank you, Doctor Velim. I'm Aria Hines. Can you please tell us, specifically, what Lightcap is and how it works?" Murmurs of agreement bounced off the walls. Several heads nodded up and down, which silently confirmed Aria was only asking what everyone else was eager to know. Everyone except Adam, though he was impressed Aria had been the one bold enough to ask the question outright. It did not surprise him that of all the people in the room with combined decades of academic and professional experience she would be the one to speak out. Her tenacity, her drive to answer questions and solve problems were why he'd wanted her on his team.

"Of course," Sera replied. "We will get to that shortly. I'm actually going to let Adam tell you about Lightcap and how it will be used in your project. First, I'll ask you to excuse us while I speak with him briefly in the hall." She motioned to Adam, who was trying his best to hide his confusion. He followed her into the hall, where she spun around and faced him as soon as the door had clicked closed, saying, "Well? Did you think about it? I need to know if you're on board."

Adam stopped trying to hide his confusion and responded, "I'm here, aren't I? You could've at least told me that you expected me to sell them on the idea. I thought I'm just supposed to smile and nod. I still feel you haven't told me everything."

"Of course I haven't told you everything. That would require condensing decades of resea—"

"Yeah, I know. 'Decades of research by one of the most brilliant minds to ever grace humanity.' Don't be so patronizing. I may not be a neuroscientist or have half the electrical knowhow you have, but I'm no idiot. I want to know how Lightcap works, or I'm out." Adam surprised himself with the force behind his last statement. His head felt hot.

Velim peered at him intensely, sizing him up. Adam did his best to appear intimidating, or at least to seem resolved. He was afraid he just looked as if he had poor posture. His efforts must have had some effect on her, however, because she sighed and said, "I'll be happy to provide details later. For now, all you need to know is that the Lightcap takes a snapshot of neural patterns when initialized. During the cool down period, Lightcap uses low level laser targeting to, for lack of a better term, zap memories away." She gave him an expectant look, as if to ask, "Are you satisfied?"

Adam seethed with anger to the point of having trouble blinking. A vein pulsed slightly on his forehead. Trying his best to remain calm and measured, he forced himself to speak slowly as he replied.

"You couldn't have told me last night that I'm supposed to sell them on a cranial bug zapper? You've got to be kidding me."

"It's still extremely complicated. What I've explained to you is the most basic way to describe what Lightcap does. It's AI guided, much like the Mind Drive or autocars, and emits an extremely short laser burst, measured in femtoseconds. Those come from the three modules, bubbles as they're commonly called, at the end of the device's arms. The modules on the Lightcap serve the same function as on the Mind Drive, but also add the ability to target in three dimensions to hit precise areas of the brain and emit extremely low energy laser bursts. The fourth bubble rests under the occipital ridge, and emits the last burst which intersects with the other three to provide the necessary energy to physically affect the brain. The AI calculates when to emit the bursts and controls the intersection point. When the four bursts meet, the memory at that location is gone. It's all very safe, very targeted. Again, decades of research," she waved her hands in the air while saying this, reminding Adam of his own previous gesture. "We can discuss it more in the future. Just trust me. It's safe."

Her blue eyes, solemn and intense, were already locked with his, but when she said this last line they seemed to bore through Adam. At least he couldn't doubt her sincerity.

"Fine," he said, "I'll play along, at least for now. I will need more solid ground at some point."

"Of course," Sera said, nodding emphatically, then reached to open the door to 4C. "It's a date." Adam's face felt hot again, this time due to blushing instead of anger.

Smiles. Assurances. A sales pitch, unrehearsed yet oddly cohesive. Sera and Adam discussed the Lightcap with some of the most brilliant minds in the programming field, answering questions about how the device was used and its basic function. Adam found "targeted, focused beam" was a much better sell than "cranial bug zapper". He saw Sera take a moment to enter something into her notetab, no doubt a note to the marketing team. *We're not only a focus group, we're guinea pigs,* thought Adam.

Later, he would remember this assessment.

The Lightcap

The rest of the day was a blur. There were mentions of the legal ramifications of tampering with the Lightcap and how they were not to leave the facility. It really seemed to Adam as if they were trying to drive that point home. *Never can be too careful,* he thought, sure this emphasis was made at the recommendation of the legal team. Instructions on Lightcap use were given. It was compatible with dome profiles to allow for importing personal customizations. They also discussed topics Adam found puzzling, such as wave dynamics and group movement in flocks of birds and schools of fish. After an early lunch, they were dismissed early with an admonishment to go to bed one hour before their usual time.

Before the team left room 4C, Doctor Velim informed them the next day would be their first on the project, which also meant day one with Lightcap. "It will be a long day," she added, "but at least there won't be as much paperwork involved." She smiled enigmatically at Adam.

That night, Adam had time to check the facial recognition search he had run on Velim the day prior. Zero one hundred percent results, some partials that came up to eighty percent probability; none were relevant or helpful. She really was a ghost. Since he couldn't find any good dirt on her, he decided to see what traces of Lightcap were on the mesh.

The Metamesh, or mesh, was the natural evolution of the Internet and the plethora of devices that had been developed to access it. In the old days they used to talk about the cloud, but this was more like an entire ocean, fluid and dynamic. The massive rows of server farms—still in existence, but much more consolidated and rare—were now mostly replaced by high-speed wireless nodes and flash storage embedded in almost every electronic device sold. Billions of devices, all interconnected. This created redundant nodes providing multiple paths from host to host, which allowed for rapid and robust communication, each packet routed through the circuit with the least number of hops, using any available devices along the way.

Virtually impervious to disaster or sabotage, the mesh quickly became a lawless land, teeming with unsavory characters that could use any number of methods to steal data. Since it was no longer possible to take down a specific server, as almost all data was mirrored in multiple locations, the data itself became king. New security methods and ways of thinking had to be developed to keep systems secure. Encryption experts were in high demand. Entire markets sprung up seemingly overnight. Adam himself had made his mark, along with Jon, by offering a way to run all known exploits against a specific node with the press of a button. It was, like many who had risen with rocket-like velocity, a combination of skill and absolute dumb luck, resulting in modest wealth at a young age. Right place, right time.

During the same period of time, Dej and a group of three others had developed CENTRAL (Central Entrance/Exit Node Traffic Routing Algorithm and Liaison), a new platform for routing mesh packets that required all traffic to be signed by a central authority before being passed to its destination. Combined with the software Adam and Jon had written, the mesh started to become a much better alternative to the wired internet, especially in areas where high-speed links still hadn't achieved wide penetration. Soon, entire blocks of fiber were going dark, the ease of access and increased speeds of the mesh making the idea of wired *anything* obsolete. The Internet had ruled for decades; now the mesh was king.

Adam used to joke about the mesh being the closest thing to a god he had ever known, but as he got older and gained a more intimate, first-hand understanding of how it worked, the joke didn't seem quite so funny. In as many ways as the mesh had at first been a lawless playground, it was now ruled with an iron fist. Originally, the strong encryption and decentralized nature of packet transmission made it difficult to ban any specific types of content or speech. After the CENTRAL routing protocol had been implemented throughout most of the mesh, packets had to be routed through a mesh access node. Many companies began to offer free node access to their employees, the drawback being that all employee mesh traffic was open to snooping, if an employer was so inclined.

To counteract corporate espionage once domes became widespread, lobbyists eventually succeeded in having legislation passed allowing employers to block outside mesh access within their buildings, to require workers to provide their personal passkeys to their employers, and eventually to install monitoring software on every employee dome.

It was also rumored that mesh-enabled devices could be disabled by authorities, either individually or within a geographic area. Adam had not witnessed this, but there were rumors from many different sources, enough to suggest it was at least possible.

With the way things had become, all mesh searches were logged and decrypted on command if one were suspected of something. There were ways around this system, but even those could leave oddities in traffic patterns which could arouse an amount of interest that was less than ideal. Adam knew a few ways to obfuscate his trail but if questioned he could say he was interested in whether or not any information about Lightcap had leaked to the mesh. A plausible story. It wouldn't win him any fans but it wasn't against any rules he knew of.

His query left running, Adam tossed the notetab onto his end table, stretched his arms above his head, grabbed his wrist and twisted. Pops and cracks down his spine and arms were among the drawbacks of the constant sitting and staring that came with his profession. There were ergonomic alternatives, all ridiculous looking and quite expensive, that most people did not trouble with. Bad posture was almost a badge of honor in his field, as it implied decades of time spent in front of a screen. This was, of course, taken in turn to suggest wisdom. Adam wondered at the wisdom of doing that to one's own body.

Wise or foolish, Adam needed a breath of fresh air. It was dark and cold, but his building featured an enclosed section to allow for year-round use. After he found the energy to slide his massive door from right to left along its track, he was out and down the hallway in what felt like seconds. He felt an urgent need to see the outside world, to prove it was there, or at least that his memory of it was accurate.

Feeling as if the elevator would never come, Adam bounded up the nineteen floors from his apartment to the roof. He panted with the effort, and half expected to see a vast nothingness or desolate wasteland as he exploded onto the roof, the door barreling into a swinging arc along its hinges, making an amazing racket. He was relieved to see the city, half below him and half above, its cut out geometric patterns of order against the few stars he could make out beyond the flashing screens of the floating advertisements platforms, called ad zeps, dotting the night sky.

It wasn't until he stopped gasping for air, finally recovered after his mad ascent, that he saw her. His neighbor, Hana Therdon, had been looking over the city. She turned to face him when he burst through the door, the sound of crashing metal against brick tumbling into darkness. Wearing a look of wry amusement, Hana slowly shook her head back and forth. With a slight laugh, she asked, "Do you always make a magnificent entrance, or am I just lucky to witness such a rare event?"

"Oh, you're lucky all right. Lucky to witness a moment of my neurosis. I had a panic attack or something in the stairwell. Felt as if the outside world wasn't here, or would be bombed out or on fire. I don't know why I'm telling you this."

"Because we're neighbors. Friends. We are friends, aren't we?" She looked at him pleadingly when she asked this.

Adam and Hana had been neighbors for five years, but their conversations were like those about the weather, except with more biting sarcasm. Same amount of depth, though. They dated at one point, several weeks of drinks and conversation that had not progressed beyond a few rounds of casual sex. Adam felt as if he knew her, but he didn't view her as a confidante. "Yeah, we're friends," he said, smiling. "It's fine. I just had a bit of a freak-out moment. Long day at work."

"Oh that's right, I remember you practicing for your big day as the boss. Having a tough time already? Being in charge not quite what you expected?" She seemed to sympathize as she consolingly stroked his arm.

"No, it's not that. It's just . . . I . . . I can't really talk to you about it. Sorry. I'm under seven different non-disclosure agreements. I think I even signed a NDA saying I wouldn't tell anyone I'd signed a NDA, so I'm sure I've already committed an offense worthy of death. Don't tell on me," he said with a look of resignation, his eyebrows raised.

She playfully patted his shoulder and said, "Of course not. I understand. I don't want to get you in trouble. We can just stay here and look at the City."

They did just that. Adam became lost in thought as he watched the lights from the autocars on the street below. To him, autocars were among the epitomes of the changes that had occurred within his lifetime. When Adam was a child, his father had taken him to the roof of their building at night to watch the traffic below. He remembered traffic lights, tricolored patterns commanding the flow of thousands of tons of steel and composite resin, which caused the entire chain of cars to stop and allow for perpendicular movement across the intersection. Those patterns had been replaced by lanes of dotted points of light, each threaded through the next as in a living thatchwork, passing impossibly close to another, contact never made, with thanks owed to the tech of autocars, domes, and people like Dej who had made them all talk to each other and work cooperatively.

Adam pondered the ever increasing pace and meaning of change when a soft tone emitted in his left ear. The search on Lightcap had completed. He turned to Hana and said, "I've got to run. I appreciate you being here to listen, even if I'm not able to talk much. We should get a drink some time."

"I'd like that," she replied with a shy smile.

It seemed to Adam as if he teleported back to his apartment. He couldn't even remember the elevator ride down. He grabbed his notetab and brought up the results: one thousand hits on the public mesh about Lightcap. Adam thought a command to have the results sorted and watched as they snapped into categories. More than half of the results were classified as conspiracy theory sites, hosted on nodes that forbade security software, unregulated outposts that remained set against the mostly corporate mesh that had sprung up with regulation and software created by people like Adam, Dej, and others at companies like Adaptech. Adam had no doubt he was mentioned on some of these sites. *They probably don't have very nice things to say about me*, Adam mused. He'd helped relegate them to the corners of the virtual world, barring them from the chaotic heyday they'd enjoyed. He'd ruined their party, and he knew it.

Roughly three hundred of the sites were news outlets with articles covered various aspects of why the Lightcap wasn't real or anything to be afraid of. These were mostly nodes in geographic areas marked for having a higher tendency to gossip or engage in conspiracy theories: high income, low responsibility areas. A few were low-income neighborhoods near affluent areas, apparently close enough to reap some of the benefits of prosperity. Adam pulled these up and found mostly fluff pieces with interviews of people who looked as if they were the crazies who created the conspiracy theory posts about the Lightcap. Panicked eyes, wild hair, mad scientists without authority or credentials.

Standard countermeasures, Adam thought. *Get out in front of the story, paint your opponent as a mad, raving loon, deny everything for as long as possible. Eventually people will find out, but until then you aren't going to give them any help. They'll get distracted anyway, people being as forgetful as they are fickle.* The fact the media covered it meant money flowed from someone, somewhere. Nothing aired on the news that didn't have a benefactor; no fact or fabrication was reported without prior transaction. Why would they worry about what was true when they could be making money? So went the reasoning of the media conglomerates. They had been sued several decades before by a group of concerned citizens in an attempt to force what little remained of the Fourth Estate to hold to some level of integrity. The media kings lost the first time, but on appeal the citizen group ran out of money. A series of delays kept the case in limbo until the collapse and subsequent purchase of the States by Metra Corp.

Forty years before, several State economies went under, bankrupted and gridlocked to the point of political irrelevancy. The States had been incrementally privatized over time, such that when a group of the five largest corporations pooled resources under the name Metra Corp to buy a six State region, very little changed. Regulations weren't enforced quite as often, and several of the private police forces merged to form the larger Central Provisional Authority, which provided security services for the entire Metra Region. Overall, daily life for the average citizen remained the same: poked, prodded, bought, sold, and ultimately disregarded as an individual.

After the Metra Corp takeover, the media companies being sued owned the court system set to decide the case. "There will be no conflict of interest," these companies said in a statement. "The autonomy of the courts will not be infringed. Justice, not loyalty, should be the focus of the judiciary." Talking heads with handsome jawlines and cheekbones spoke with soothing words in high definition. Who could doubt such pretty faces, such pretty voices, such pretty pictures, on the channels owned by the companies being tried?

Some people knew what was really happening, but speaking out might cost them their livelihoods. Employee protections were at an all-time low. People could be fired for wearing shoes that offended the delicate fashion sensibilities of their boss, after likely signing a contract to that effect. Say the wrong thing to the wrong person, or have a position high enough in a company to warrant a mesh auto-query, and it might attract some unwanted attention. Losing a job was the best way to end up living on the streets. Most didn't last on the streets. Adam had highly marketable skills, but others weren't so fortunate.

All of this had weighed on Adam's mind since the beginning of the day. His face was lit by the dim glow of his notetab as he thumbed through post after post on the conspiracy sites about the Lightcap. Some were outlandish, claiming with bold capital letters that Lightcap granted strong telekinetic powers, the ability to transmute lead to gold, the energy to rip a skeleton from flesh, a way to talk with the dead, direct communication with alien civilizations, or the energy to sustain a fusion reaction through thought alone. All over the map. *The human imagination will always be a dozen steps ahead of reality,* Adam thought.

Many of the conspiracy sites seemed to be doing their best not to be taken seriously, with flashing banners proclaiming alien conspiracies, or shadowy, Zionist cabals intent on enslaving the world population; long, ranting paragraphs blaming everyone from liberals to conservatives to lizardmen to poltergeists to businessmen to poor people for every problem imaginable from the abandonment of the gold standard to bunions. A few stories stood out to Adam, feasible but reminiscent of an urban legend with a cousin's friend or brother's coworker as the source. Truth twice removed. Reports of soldiers returning home, shell-shocked and crying out in the night, yelling about Lightcap and murders and plots. All unsubstantiated, none with any follow-up. Dead ends.

Adam was caught between thoughts of memories being zapped into nothingness and plots by evil businessmen to turn the world into revenue-producing slaves when he drifted off to sleep.

He found himself on the subway, same seat where he'd been that morning. Struck with a sense of déjà vu, he looked around, wondering why the car was empty. There were always passengers. His perspective shifted out of his body, and time sped up as he saw himself from outside, watching as he rocked back and forth along with the train then fell asleep, just as he had that morning. Time slowed back down, and Adam watched as the same disheveled man appeared, shuffled toward him, and fell across his lap. This time, the incident slowed almost to single frames, as if he had put a video in slow motion. His disembodied consciousness watched as the disheveled man slipped a note into the pocket of his sleeping form. As the man apologized and shoved off, Adam felt his consciousness being drawn back into his body.

There was a brief snap as Adam's point of view locked back behind his eyes, where it should be and where it belonged. Disoriented, he looked around but saw no trace of the man, not even when he jumped to his feet and ran to the door, hoping to get a better view of the adjacent car. Completely empty. He tried the handle. Locked. He could hear his racing heart thump in his ears as he sprinted to the other end of his own car. Another locked door with no one beyond. Adam remembered the note, secretly placed in his pocket as he slept. He shoved his hand into the split separating the fabric. He shook as he withdrew a tear of crumpled white paper clutched between forefinger and thumb.

There was one word, written in the bold strokes of a hurried hand.

His gaze was drawn toward the front of the subway car as it emerged from the dark underground into an impossibly bright burst of light. Then, darkness.

Adam gasped awake. He wasn't quite sure what had just happened, but it felt more real than any dream he could ever remember. He vaguely recalled being on the subway, and the man . . . the man. The note! He bolted out of bed, bare feet striking cold wood floor. The shock didn't even register in his excitement. He grabbed the jacket he'd worn that morning, matte black and secured close by strips of magnets that ran from the collar to the mid-thigh. One of the things he loved about it was that it had pockets large enough for his notetab to fit comfortably. He dug through each of the pockets, even the hidden one along the inside seam, but there was no note to be found.

After his feet finally protested too much against the unforgiving floor, he lay back down, shivering involuntarily as he got under the covers still slightly damp with the sweat of his nightmare. *Mnemosyne*, he thought. *Why do I know that word?* He turned, grabbed his notetab, and thought of the word again, this time directed at his dome. The oldest mention he could find on the mesh was from Greek mythology, Mnemosyne being one of the race of immortal deities known as the Titans. Mnemosyne was, according to the mesh, born of Heaven and Earth, the personification of memory. The most recent mention was from a software project, a venture between several corporate entities and academia aimed at mapping neurons to bits, with the intent of creating an upload of the human brain. He could not find anything linking Mnemosyne to the Lightcap, but he started a deep-scrape search just to make sure.

Most information on the mesh was easily accessible, if it was public. A deep-scrape search ran against encrypted data that was publicly available, trying to guess the passkey with a brute-force attack that included contextual clues based on anything known about the owner of the file. Many people used simple passkeys, such as the names of their pets and their birthdates, sometimes even the word "passkey" followed by "123". No matter how much technology progressed, any system was only as secure as its most careless user. People put a great deal of material on the mesh that they shouldn't, whether out of hubris, ignorance, or apathy. Since Adam knew such a search would take hours or even days to obtain any usable results, he put the notetab on the nightstand next to his bed, then fell back into a troubled sleep.

The blaring alarm kicked Adam back into the waking world. It seemed his head touched his pillow mere seconds before. He was exhausted. He blinked and was at the office, the entire morning gone like a skipped scene in a video. He remembered it if he focused, but from the detached view of an observer rather than active participant.

He once again found himself in conference room 4C, as ordered at the end of the previous day. He was seated at the head of the table, opposite Doctor Velim, surrounded by his eighteen-person team. She was speaking. "The boxes in front of you contain your Lightcaps. Transfer whatever information you need from your personal Mind Drives, but please be aware anything you load onto the Lightcap becomes property of Adaptech. Once you have finished, please put your Lightcaps in place. They will automatically turn on and initialize."

Boxes were opened with sounds of broken seals and crinkled plastic, the bags containing the Lightcaps discarded like wrapping paper at a child's birthday party. Even if there were reservations, most of these people were geeks, always excited to try out new electronic gadgets. Dej gave voice to the gasps and muttering around the table by saying, "The Lightcap looks the same as the Mind Drive, except there's a fourth bubble where the arms meet in the back." He turned the device over in his hand. "Oh, and a big etching that says 'PROTOTYPE'. That too."

"Yes," Doctor Velim responded. "That's by design. The technology is derivative, and we were able to optimize the device so that its form factor is almost identical to the v5 Mind Drive. The Lightcap provides the same control of electronics as the Mind Drive, along with extra features. Think of the Lightcap as a Mind Drive Plus."

Satisfied with her answer, a silence settled over his team as they loaded their personalized profiles from their domes to their new Lightcaps. Adam did this as well, seeing no reason to set everything up from scratch. If his employers decided to monitor his information, they'd find standard dome customizations related to thought patterns, words to avoid recognizing, and audio notifications. Nothing outlandish or illicit.

After much tinkering and several last-minute questions everyone finished setting up their Lightcaps. Adam wanted to exude confidence while hiding the pit he felt in his stomach, so he flashed a smile, said, "Alright, here we go," and slipped on his Lightcap. For a moment, nothing happened. Then, with a click, Adam was rushed down a dark tunnel and plummeted toward a bright, warm light. He exited the tunnel with great speed and basked in the comforting blanket of heated air surrounding him, his momentum slowing to a stop. He hung in place, suspended, the world completely devoid of definition, everything washed out and bathed in a soothing, opaque white glow.

Then the light was replaced by darkness.

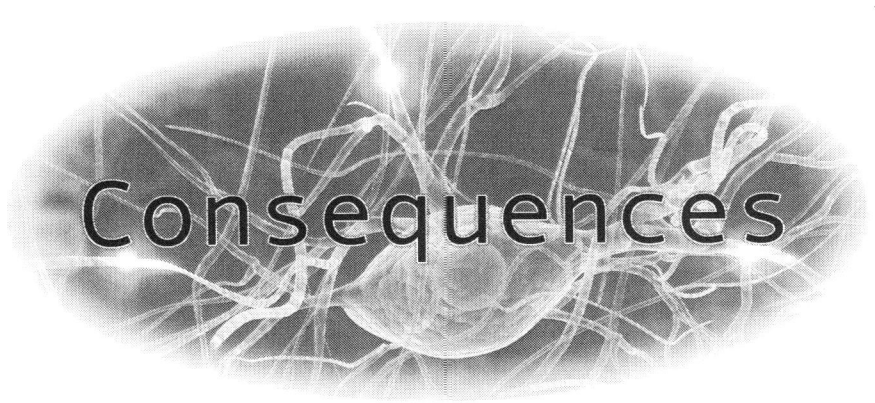

Consequences

A pinpoint of light flew toward Adam from a distant, far-off place. He felt no motion, stationary as the bright ball became exponentially larger in his field of view. He flinched as it approached to strike him. Suddenly, he was back. Same chair, same room. His arms, attached to hands holding his Lightcap, moved in downward slope toward the table, almost of their own volition. His vision and hearing felt removed, as if he were observing the world through a bubble with a slight rainbow tinge, its light refracted and split into various wavelengths. Adam's hands met the table and the air around him seemed to clear. He felt groggy, as if he'd just awoken from an unexpected nap.

Velim was still seated at the opposite end of the table. She smiled slightly and asked, "How do you feel, Mister Redmon?"

With a confused look Adam responded, "I'm a little groggy and I have a headache." He looked around and noticed no one else was wearing a Lightcap. His team faced him, their devices in front of them in two straight lines down the length of the table. "Was there some kind of problem? When are we going to get started?"

Sera laughed aloud, with several others from around the table joining her. After the laughter subsided she responded, "Get started? The day is done. The Lightcap performed exactly as expected. Exceeded expectations, actually. It has been ten hours since you last sat in that chair. The headache is expected, by the way. It should clear up shortly. Within another week or two, you won't notice any discomfort at all when removing the Lightcap. The disorientation will eventually go away too. After today, you'll unplug before your team in case we have anything to discuss. So, I ask again, how do you feel?"

Adam closed his eyes and tried to remember what had happened. *Surely this is a joke, some sort of prank*, he thought. All he could recall was the painfully brilliant ball of light, darkness, then the light again. He opened his eyes. He slowly shook his head, then remembered the clock and cast his gaze to where it sat pacing seconds silently in the corner. The clock said it was ten hours later. "I feel perfectly fine," Adam said. "The headache is gone, only lasted for a few seconds. I don't remember anything about what happened. Did we work in here all day?"

Several heads turned toward Velim. It was a question on many of the minds in the room, and they were glad Adam asked it. She took a moment to look at each person in the eyes, then said, "No. You were at an off-site facility. We can't tell you where, of course, which is as much for our own protection as it is for yours. As far as you're concerned, you work in conference room 4C. It has been appropriated for this project, and is where you'll begin and end each day. At the risk of sounding repetitive, as far as your friends and family are concerned, you work in this building, in the programming division, doing the same humdrum tasks you've done for years, whether for Adaptech or another employer. Do not mention anything about working off-site, or the Lightcap. Either is a terminable offense per the contracts you've signed. You are dismissed. I'll see you tomorrow."

She turned to face Adam and addressed him directly. "Adam, please stay for a few minutes after everyone leaves. I'd like to have a word with you."

The team filed one by one from the room, which fell silent save for the subtle swish of shoes across the floor. The carpet in conference rooms such as 4C was always atrocious. Adam's eyes traced the lines making up the carpet's garish multi-colored geometric patterns and counted the intersection points, just as he had counted the stippled dots on the ceiling of the office at his childhood school. Adam had often been sent there as a child, chastised for daydreaming or getting off-task during class. Velim reminded him of a school principal, maybe even a district superintendent—he didn't see someone of her intellect being happy running just a single school. A large, sprawling district seemed more her domain. Either way, she intimidated him, not just because of her title. It was her all-business demeanor, piercing eyes set against dark eye shadow which her pale blue irises all the more stark; her enunciation, each word ricocheting off hard surfaces, assaulting him from every angle; her posture, rigid and defined. Adam wasn't one to bow to authority simply out of obedience, but he genuinely feared her, not because he detected malice but because she seemed the sort to destroy any obstacle threatening to keep her from her goal. He hoped she would never perceive him as an obstacle.

Adam's eyes locked with Sera's as the last person departed the room, the quiet click of the door alerting them of their privacy with no backward glance required. She sat, as if waiting. Adam, confused, wondered if there was something he was supposed to say. Awkward silence made him uncomfortable, and he was already uncomfortable to begin with. After several seconds had painfully passed, Adam spoke: "I don't appreciate being made to look a fool. It's one thing if it's in private, or even in front of peers, but I have to lead these people. It's important that they view me as their leader, and instead you've made me the butt of a joke."

Sera looked amused, which made Adam angry. Just as he was about to respond with invective, she spoke in an even tone, "You have it all wrong. You weren't the butt of a joke, but a demonstration. As I told you, the people on this team look up to you, but they also need proof the Lightcap won't turn them into mindless worker bees toiling under the commands of some far-off queen. You spent about fifteen minutes here answering questions and interacting with your team. That's all. I'm sorry you don't remember any of it. You were much more personable than you're being now. I think everyone was impressed with how lucid you were, actually. There always seems to be an expectation that the Lightcap will turn you into a burned-out husk of a human being, barely functional, with monosyllabic grunts in response to simple questions and confused indifference to anything requiring deeper thought. It's not like that at all. Would you like to see?"

Adam nodded. Sera looked over to the wall, where a large screen appeared in place of the bare surface. Almost exactly to scale, Adam turned to see himself in profile along with the rest of his team, already seated and frozen. Sometimes it was disconcerting to watch someone use a dome to control a device. Even after many years, Adam still felt for the briefest of moments as if some kind of magic carried out the command. As it always had, however, that fleeting impression gave way to the knowledge and recollection that the dome's marvels weren't driven by mysticism but caused by advanced technology. At Sera's silent command, the images on the wall shifted and began to move while sound played from hidden speakers in the ceiling. The video started as Velim commanded the team, except for Adam, to take off their Lightcaps.

Adam's team members touched their heads and moved their arms downward in identical parallel movements, reminding him of synchronized swimmers. When the motion ended, their Lightcaps sat on the table in the same rows he'd seen upon his return from darkness. He watched their faces and saw traces of the same consternation he had felt just a dozen minutes before. Several of his team touched their temples and winced slightly, confirming to Adam the headache he had experienced wasn't anything out of the ordinary. He listened as the recorded Velim explained to the group that though their day had ended she wanted to give them a brief glimpse at what it looked like to wear the Lightcap. She politely asked Adam to stand. His recorded body silently stood, chair pushed back by his legs. Velim instructed the team to test the entranced Adam, to see if his mind had been muddled by the device.

They started by asking if he knew his name. "Adam Charles Redmon," came the even response. The present Adam noticed his recorded, Lightcap-wearing self provided his middle name. He never freely offered that. The team challenged him with logic puzzles and math questions, at one point even asking him to list *pi* to the hundredth digit and give the first thirty numbers of the Fibonacci series. They then asked Adam to close his eyes and touch his nose while standing on one foot, challenges more likely to come from a Blue giving a sobriety test than a group of geeks in a corporate conference room.

On the recording, Velim asked the standing Adam to sit. In the actual conference room, Adam watched, thinking his entranced self had performed better than expected. When he was sure the playback was about to end, Dej asked, "Adam, how do you feel?"

The question did not get an immediate response. The video had been recorded from an angle that made it difficult to see the expression on his face after the question was asked. He did notice his recorded form seemed to look at Velim, who gave a slight nod. "I am well," he responded.

"Yes," Dej said with an amused sigh, "but how do you *feel?*"

"I feel . . . fine." Adam conveyed no emotion. The pause was brief but obvious, at least to Adam. He couldn't help but wonder what he had thought while trying to parse the question or come up with a response. He tried to remember but couldn't. All he could recall of the experience was the blinding ball of light, as in a memory of staring into the sun.

At this point in the recording, Sera commanded Adam to remove his Lightcap. The screen dimmed and faded back to the color of the wall.

"You should remember the rest from there," Sera said. "I wanted you to see it firsthand so you understand exactly what happened. You aren't a joke to them, Adam. You're a brave hero. You all are. But your actions gave them a sense of safety your words would have never provided. Actions do speak louder, you know." She smiled when she said this last line, with a far off look on her face as if she were thinking of a happy memory from long before.

"Well, I'm a fan of both words and actions," Adam replied, each word weighed in thought before he slowly allowed it to leave his mouth. "I am curious about something, though. Why did I pause when Dej asked how I felt? The first answer I gave him was, oh, more of a systems update, for lack of a better term. When he asked again, it almost seemed as if I looked to you for a response."

Sera waved her hand in the air as if conjuring the appropriate words before she responded. "We make a concerted effort to establish the power structure before you ever put on the Lightcap. Once it's on, you're in a state that allows for use of all higher brain functions, but it also instills a sense of respect for established authority hierarchy. For instance, had the subject of our demonstration been one of your team members, they would have looked to you for guidance. Since you were the demonstrator, you looked to the only person in the room with greater authority than your own: me."

There were so many things Adam wanted to ask, but he knew doing so would only produce enigmatic explanations and riddled responses that brought up two new questions for each one answered. He simply nodded in response, thinking it best not to say anything to betray his lingering doubts. *Besides,* Adam told himself, *perhaps there's nothing to worry about.*

Sera stood. Adam did the same, having sensed her action was a cue. "We'll be having biweekly meetings throughout the course of the v6 project. This has been the first. After this, they'll be every other Friday at the end of the day, starting at the end of next week.

Due to the obvious need to protect our code, we can't go over any specifics about what has been accomplished on the Mind Drive v6 during work hours, but we can discuss overall objectives, worker efficiency, and I can give you instructions for future roadmaps."

Sera extended her hand, all business. Firm handshake, two pumps, with no indication of their previous conversations. Adam's mind swam as they exited room 4C, her heels clicking against the polished concrete as they walked down the hall. She held her notetab against her chest as they approached the elevator. Its down button lit up, no doubt triggered by command from her dome. They stood and waited in silence.

"So," Adam started as he looked at his polished shoes, feeling suddenly filled with the awkwardness of his youth. There was a spot of red-gray mud on the outside edge of the wingtip on his right foot. He resisted the urge to wipe it on something, and lifted his eyes to meet Sera's. She was looking at him with a bemused expression. He knew he should continue. "Um, I mean, do I really only get to see you every other week? I was hoping you'd be around a little more. Maybe these progress updates would be best over dinner?" He smiled rakishly.

She blinked. Twice. Once more. Adam had hoped for more of a response by that point. Measured as always, Sera said, "I think it's best if we keep our relationship professional." Her high heels once again struck the concrete as she turned with two steps and faced the elevator's large steel door, which reflected a floor-to-ceiling fun house image in its brushed metal panels.

Crash and burn. Abort, raced Adam's mind, a command he had no way to follow. It was not as if he could run away or talk to someone else. He had to do damage control. "Yeah, sure, I understand," Adam said quickly. "I wasn't trying to suggest anything, sometimes it's just hard to think under these fluorescent lights. I certainly consider it inappropriate to date a superior. For all I know you're married. Sorry."

Sera opened her mouth to reply just as the elevator beeped. Their eyes were drawn toward the down arrow that appeared in the frame surrounding the door, previously invisible dots lit like orange stars in a silver metal sky. Adam felt immediate frustration that no one had yet figured out a way to make elevators arrive faster, and he made a mental note to look into a possible solution, even to see if someone else had already tackled the problem. *No point in reinventing the wheel,* he thought. Perhaps embarrassment, rather than necessity, could spark invention.

Adam shuffled a few small steps back as the door opened in an attempt to make it obvious that he wanted her to go first. Sera obliged, and he followed. The light for the next floor down lit up at her thought, the light for the ground floor at his. After the doors closed, she turned to face him and said, "I wasn't trying to upset you, I just think it's best if we don't mix business and pleasure." Adam understood, not because of what she said, but because he was sure her eyes had moved to the left and right, along with the slightest nod of her head.

The elevator doors opened and Sera was gone. LaMont's office was on that level, and that was most likely where her new office was too. It struck Adam as odd that he didn't even know where his immediate supervisor's office was, that she'd always chosen unusual meeting places rather than show him anything of herself. He took this as another sign of her obvious reserve, and wondered whether nature or nurture gave her such a cautious personality. The elevator doors closed with a clunk and Adam's stomach rose into his throat as he was whisked toward the ground.

He probably would have appeared collected to an outside observer, but internally he was preoccupied by several different lines of thought, such as the Lightcap, Velim, LaMont, and the people on his team who trusted him to make correct decisions. He was troubled by the comment Sera made about the Lightcap leading its wearer to look toward authority figures when faced with obstacles or challenges. He supposed this was a good idea in theory, a way to make sure workers weren't sitting there listless and unproductive when they encountered a problem. In practice, he worried that a device originally pitched as something to keep work and home stresses segregated seemed to have additional capabilities and effects that hadn't originally been disclosed. Adam wondered most of all why, when wearing the Lightcap, he had seemed listless and slow, almost unaware of who he himself was. He couldn't put his finger on it. It was almost as if he'd had no will of his own.

As these thoughts tumbled around his head, he exited through the heavy door separating Adaptech from the world at large without even noticing someone fall into step behind him, pacing about three meters back. Adam's feet barely touched the stairs, his shoes issuing a rapid staccato as he bounced from street level to subway platform. When he reached the bottom of the stairs, the hairs on the back of his neck pricked. His unconscious mind perceived a sudden rush of movement behind him. He was about to whip around to face this unknown potential threat when a hand closed against his upper arm and a laughing voice said, "Calm down, Chuck!"

It was a voice Adam recognized as belonging to Jared Tinge, one of the two people on his team Adam had not personally picked. He was a competent enough coder, and Adam had worked with him before in the Security Software division. Everyone knew the reason Jared had his position was because his father served on the Adaptech Board of Directors. Adam thought of Jared as a "brogrammer", as he seemed just as likely to spend a night taking shots as he would debugging code and said "bro" far too often when talking to men who weren't his brothers. Usually Jared mushed the word into "bruh".

"Damn it, Jared, you scared the shit out of me," gasped Adam, his hand unconsciously drawn to cover his chest, his heart racing. "And don't call me Chuck. Or Charles. It's Adam." He was already angry his team knew his full name. It was because of people like

Jared that he didn't like people knowing too much about him. Certain people would always find openings to attack, or at least to use against his will.

"Sorry, bruh," Jared said, his lips drawn into a smug, dopey smile. Adam did his best not to outwardly wince. "Didn't mean to scare you. Was just making sure you were all right. You seemed a bit out of it after our reentry earlier."

"I'm fine," Adam said curtly. "And what do you mean by 'reentry'?" Adam was doing his best not to sound annoyed. He was pretty sure he was failing.

"Just checkin', boss," Jared replied. "I call it 'reentry' because I felt like a spaceman coming back from orbit. Still feel a little lightheaded. Spacey. You feel back to normal?"

Adam thought about possible long answers to such a simple question. Any sense of normalcy Adam possessed had vanished over the past several days, with talk of memories zapped out of existence and dreams of a world inhabited by Greek Titans and an odd old man. "Yes," Adam replied. "I'm fine. I suggest you focus on staying rested for our project, rather than spending too much time focusing on the details of . . . the device," he whispered the last two words, hesitant to say "Lightcap" in public, even as the bustling passengers moved in and out of the subway alcove, oblivious to the Jared and Adam.

"Good to know," Jared said. He gave a mock salute and continued: "I'm going to go home and watch election results. See you tomorrow, bruh!" He then bounded back up the stairs, seemingly eager to escape the subterranean subway station's moving throng and bad smells.

Adam tried to decide whether Jared was annoying, odd, or both as he walked into the subway car. Muscle memory and repetition took over as his thoughts turned back to all that had recently changed in his life. New position, new project, new technology. It was an exciting yet unsettling time. He still wasn't sure how he felt about it all, but he was glad to be going home for the day.

The subway door closed with a clunk reminiscent of the elevator door's. The sound brought his focus back to reality, where he was immediately struck with the sensation of being watched. Had Jared come back? One surprise like that was enough for the afternoon. Turning in a wide circle, Adam saw that no one seemed to be paying him any attention. *Nerves,* he thought, then closed his eyes, taking a minute to order his thoughts. He sent a dome command to his home control unit, instructing it to raise the temperature in his apartment by four degrees before he got home. What he needed was a good, long sleep. Adam's lanky right arm stretched against the hand rail as the subway car started its slow roll away from the station. He opened his eyes and focused through the glass door, onto the platform beyond. He saw the face of the disheveled man from his dream—only for a moment—before the man was gone.

He blinked several times, unable to believe his eyes. The subway plunged into the darkness of the tunnel.

Election Night

Adam slipped his fingers through rubber, as he pried the doors apart. They seemed to open painfully slowly to Adam, who desperately wanted out. He sprinted ten blocks back to the last stop with long strides, dress shoes striking against concrete, syncopated by the rhythmic *thwack* of his messenger bag against his back. There was no sign of the man. Adam struggled to catch his breath, hands on his knees, then drew odd stares as he tried to fill his lungs with air while spinning around to examine each face in the crowd.

After giving up in bewildered frustration, Adam started to walk toward home, wondering if he had imagined it all. He had been under a great deal of stress lately, and it had been his first day with the Lightcap. These were the only explanations he could fathom. It was either that or he was losing his mind. *Probably both,* came the thought, unbidden.

Adam's adrenaline was still pumping from his earlier sprint, so he decided not to go home. It was election night, both in the remaining States and the Corp Regions. Large crowds usually gathered at bars, playing drinking games and placing bets on how Public and Executive positions would be awarded. The election system had been modified to apply the Metra Corp Charter of Incorporation onto the Democratic framework its citizens expected, a holdover from their time as separate States under the banner of a

Federal government. In those days it had been one person, one vote, Adam knew from school. "A terribly unfair system," his teacher had said with a shudder. "Just think of how unlikely it would be for actual merit to be rewarded."

Under the New Metra Charter, however, each citizen of the Region was given one voting share per year after eligibility, with the option to purchase more shares at the current trading rate. In principle, good work was rewarded with more say in government. In practice, poor people sold their vote on their first day of eligibility, which was still the eighteenth birthday, as was tradition. The last time Adam had checked, a single share sold for two hundred credits, enough for three to four weeks of frugal meals. The rich hoarded their shares and bought many more, and had come to account for nearly forty percent of the votes cast in the Metra Region. Fortunately, the system was impossible to rig due to strong biometric security. Actual votes were still necessary to win, and anyone with enough credits could buy shares.

Alliances formed among the diminished middle class, the people who worked and lived paycheck to paycheck, along with other voting blocs such as the racial and ethnic minorities, the elderly, and the poor who retained and consolidated their voting shares. For decades before the collapse of the States, people had been urged to vote with their ballots and their pocketbooks. Now they really did vote with their money, and those with the most money got the most votes. Adam had never been political, though he still voted. Most did, since it was easy, and if they didn't vote they'd sell to someone who would. Adam didn't see the point of getting involved in things that were ultimately out of his control, especially because of the unnecessary drama of it all.

Election night had turned into an occasion to celebrate or to drown sorrows. Regardless of the outcome, there was an excuse to party, to drink, and to curse the other side, that terrible separate half of society who were too stupid to see things the "right" way. It seemed odd to Adam that most elections were evenly split. Forty percent of the votes were usually for the most pro-business candidate, who somehow convinced another ten percent or so of the voting public to go along with him or her, either through a barrage of false ads or by paying the media for positive coverage. There were many theories from many sources.

Adam headed to Hanley's, a place he'd seen featured on several ad zep screens that showed whatever spectacles were on the video nodes each night. Why watch the big game, execution, or election in the privacy of home when one could go to Hanley's, spend four hundred credits, and not remember any of it? It struck Adam that alcohol could be considered the original Lightcap, but with dangerous side effects.

A mixture of pungent smoke, warm beer, and the nasal-clearing licorice scent of absinthe greeted Adam down the street, before he saw the place or heard the murmurs of crowded conversation within. He passed a man whose back was pressed against a wall, a small glass pipe filled with smoldering white fibers pressed against his lips. He exhaled sharply through lips pressed tightly together, which made him resemble a steaming teapot. The man's eyelids drooped, his eyeballs rolling back into his head until there was nothing but white, and a dull smile spread on his face as his serotonin and dopamine levels skyrocketed. He sagged against the wall in a stupor.

Adam walked by and watched this man from the corner of his eye. Junkies were notorious for being amateur pickpockets. Adam recognized the smell of the junkie's drug of choice: Cloud. The substance had become more popular as its price dropped. First synthesized thirteen years before, Cloud looked like cotton with a slight grey tint. Cloud users could be identified by the distinct odor the drug left on their hands, a smell of burnt chemicals mixed with cinnamon. The drug produced in its users a sensation of free fall, adrenaline and euphoria combining in a head rush lasting an hour or more, depending on dose. For some, taking Cloud was a social activity like drinking, but there were many who couldn't control the urge to use the drug frequently.

One thing Adam found interesting about Cloud was that reports indicated it seemed to affect the function of the domes, to the point that the small print in the Mind Drive v5 instruction manual specifically warned against the use of Cloud while operating the device. As far as Adam knew, this marked the first time a user manual for an input device warned against using a specific drug. Many brilliant minds were working on understanding the physiological mechanisms that hindered dome functionality among heavy Cloud users, but the prevailing theory was the drug had the side effect of weakening connections between neurons in the brain, making it harder for domes to get readings.

He doesn't really seem to care about not being able to use a dome. They probably still put buttons on things because of people like him, thought Adam. He couldn't help but feel people such as this junkie were holding back society by creating undue drags on social services. They just needed a bit more self-control. Then again, most used vaporizers for Cloud, exhaling nothing more than a small puff of odorless smoke. The junkie must not be able to afford one, as cheap as they were. Adam felt a brief pang of sadness at this thought.

A bouncer stood at the door of Hanley's, face forward, arms crossed against his bulging chest. The bouncer gave Adam a perfunctory once-over, then tilted his head back, providing a silent signal that Adam could enter. The wooden door with its lone rounded window swung open and stopped against the wall with a hollow *thunk*, the din of the patrons inside seeming to double in volume as he stepped across the threshold. From left to right he scanned the room, a large open space with screens mounted on nearly every available vertical surface, casting light made of flashes of color. This place was made for consumption and excess. Despite feeling very out of place, he couldn't deny there was an almost palpable energy in the glowing room.

Groups of people stood in the packed bar so they could see as many screens as possible. Adam found a table in the corner affording him a view of the vast room, and he attempted to send a drink order from his dome. He immediately heard a minor tritone, along with a soft voice stating, "No command unit found for this establishment." It had been a long time since Adam had been to a bar that wasn't Mind Drive compatible. It had also been a long time since he'd been to a bar.

As he was trying to remember the etiquette for ordering a drink, a tiny woman materialized, seemingly from nowhere. She was so small Adam had thought at first she was a child, but as she moved closer he realized she was a small woman. The waitress stopped chewing her gum long enough to ask for his order. "Scotch. Old aged. Rocks," he replied. Adam may have felt out of his element in a place such as Hanley's, but he could still order a drink with confidence. He'd practiced this when he was younger, thinking he could impress a waitress who was the focus of his youthful infatuation. She had not been very impressed; truth be told, she had not seemed to care at all. He still liked scotch though.

The diminutive current waitress disappeared into the crowd and returned several minutes later, carrying a large glass of brown liquid that washed around two dueling spherical ice cubes. "Twenty credits," she said as she chomped, her mouth decimating her gum. He gave her thirty, feeling both generous and thankful she had appeared when he needed her and retrieved his drink so quickly. Adam picked up his glass, slowly swirled the scotch in it and looked around the bar. Most faces were turned with rapt attention to the bar's screens, which showed animated maps of the Region, each precinct lighted with blue or red depending on which candidate—the one who was pro-business or the one who was very pro-business— was leading or had won.

In some cases only a few ballots had been counted, which led to them reporting absolutely nothing, saying things like, "Too close to call," and, "This is just a projection, only two percent of the polls have closed." Someone had evidently decided these statements sounded better than, "We have nothing to report." The news could never stop, even if there were no stories to cover, because it would cause a drop in ratings. Actually, the news stopping would itself be news. Anything was more interesting than dead air.

Adam watched each screen briefly, more interested in how people responded to the news than the news itself. Groups of patrons cheered or wailed, then he noticed a group that had occasionally done the opposite. Words were traded, and in some cases the thick-necked bouncers stepped forward with menacing faces, unspoken warnings of their potential intervention. Already an excuse to party, politics had become an excuse to brawl. "If you can't beat your opponents in the tally, beat them in the streets," was the motto of many. The bouncers were there to keep beatings from occurring, for the sake of the bar's insurance policy, not any sense of obligation to customers.

Adam couldn't help but chuckle. He took a pessimistic approach to politics. He'd always voted for the candidate who seemed most likely to lose a few minutes of sleep if he or she were to accidentally run over a small, defenseless animal. There wasn't always a candidate who met that criteria, however, so sometimes Adam would have to pick the one who seemed the least interested in using an elected term to pad a bank account. One election, Adam couldn't even figure that out. He ended up going to a voting center that year, forgoing his usual method of mesh vote. He stepped into the booth, closed his eyes, and picked one at random. He had considered not even voting for the briefest of moments, until he remembered his mother and father would have been very disappointed, had they been alive to see it.

After Adam's first vote, his father took him out for dinner and a drink, hugged Adam, and said, "Voting is a way to have a small amount on impact of larger things in the world."

Ray and Monica, Adam's father and mother, died a little more than two months later in an autocar accident. Adam, with the benefits of age and wisdom—including more than a bit of cynicism—now thought his father naïve about the nature of reality.

Adam sat in the bar and took another swig of his drink. He reflected that despite his wisdom, cynicism, and knowledge of the nature of reality, the election campaign that year had been particularly troubling. He had voted weeks before via mesh. The choice that year was an easy one, between the incumbent CEO and his challenger, a man who had cut a swath of destruction through the corporate world as an executive at TeleVice, the largest media company in the Metra Region.

Money bought and paid for both candidates, corporate stooges to their cores. People were, after all, voting for the executive head of the second largest corporate Region in the World, after the Cascadia Corporation, which owned the former west coast of the United States and a few other contiguous properties. The elections that night took place in the Regions of Metra and Cascadia, the Confederated Republic of Texas—Confederacy for short—and what was left of the United States, a conical shaped chunk of land starting northeast of the District of Columbia and spreading west beyond Colorado.

The media companies operating in each region had some degree of crossover between board members, as if forming a Venn diagram of influence and power, overlapping areas containing the richest of the rich who made money off everyone else. Having four major elections all within the same night created an ideal situation for ratings. Election night became the most watched video event of every fifth year. Even those who had sold their votes liked to watch, to be caught up in the excitement of the crowd, to be parts of something.

Adam worked through four glasses of scotch and quietly watched as race after district race was called, trying to guess which group of patrons would grumble or celebrate. He looked back to the large screen in the center of the room and saw the talking heads on the screens preparing to announce the results from the executive races. These results always came last, to provide a climatic end to the foreplay of smaller challenges. Up for re-election were the CEOs of Cascadia Corp and Metra Corp, and the Presidents of the United States and the Confederacy. Money was the deciding factor in all regional races, not just the corporate leadership positions. Politics had been awash in dirty money for years. In the Corporate owned Regions they were just more open about it, considering it a necessary evil.

The screens had shown each incremental update, "With seventy-eight percent of stations repor—no wait: seventy-nine!" Numbers traded back and forth, one candidate robbed of the lead by another. The crowd was frantic, brought from ecstasy to agony and back every few minutes. The first race announced was that of the CEO position for Cascadia Corporation, whose incumbent won reelection. The second race decided was the President of the Confederacy; a staunch pro-business challenger unseated the sitting President, a theocratic isolationist with dreams of kickstarting Armageddon. The third was that of President of the United States, who drew attention due to nostalgia and a small amount of pity. The incumbent's challenger lost, failing to make an effective case for his economic recovery plan. The status quo remained for the most part unchanged. Adam was satisfied, if not affected in any way by these results.

A silence fell over the crowd. The newscaster, with his expensive suit and well-coifed hair, dramatically turned to face the camera. With agonizingly slow delivery, the man recited his opening lead into the election results for Metra Corp, as elbows jostled and necks craned to get the best view. *Does the act of observation affect the outcome?* Adam wondered. *No*, he thought to himself as he downed the last of his scotch, *there are no such things as quantum elections.* The patrons groaned and cheered loudly in response to the results. The exceptionally business friendly candidate, Tim Montery, had unseated the current CEO, Paul Dewey, who had failed to generate profit at a quick enough pace. The current CEO had focused instead on using a portion of the excess to reinvest in infrastructure and pay outstanding debts, acts for which he had now been punished.

The screen cut to the smug face of the victor, Tim Montery, who began delivering his acceptance speech. The energy of the crowd in the bar started to remind Adam of the cold pressure before a sudden rainstorm. He got up about the same time the first punch was thrown, by an angry, red-faced man who bounded to a cheering man and punched him in the face. The surprised victim fell back. At the same moment his friends pushed away from the table and converged on the attacker. The attacker's mates were just a step behind. *This is a quick storm,* Adam mused. *Glad I was paying attention.*

Adam was halfway to the door by the time the fight had begun to ripple through the crowd, a shockwave of destruction sent from the center of the room. He was hit by a bottle, but it bounced harmlessly off his bony shoulder and back into the crowd. *Thank goodness for unbreakable glass,* he thought. Adam's lean frame was able to pass unhindered between people, and he made it to the door just as the bouncer from outside became aware of what was happening. Adam reached the door right as the bouncer opened it, a look of surprise on his face as he served as unplanned doorman.

The bouncer's wide shoulders took up almost the entire width of the door frame, leaving just enough room. "Thanks!" Adam said as he slipped through, but the bouncer was gone, his attention already turned to the riotous crowd threatening to overrun his burly fellows. If the team of ten bouncers weren't able to quell the crowd's chaotic energy, the Blues would be called. Adam wasn't a fighter, so he had no desire to stay. Due to his distaste for the Blues, he was doubly glad he made it out with minimal incident.

Adam felt his heart racing again, but once he was outside in the cold air the pounding subsided. His every exhalation visible, he pulled his jacket collar up around his neck, then stowed his hands in the warm wool of his pockets. Adam heard gunshots in the distance, signifying a protest, a celebration, or just a murder. He enjoyed the crisp air during his walk home, icicles forming in his nose with each breath. His feet had trouble with some steps toward his home due to the alcohol.

Adam eventually stumbled into his apartment, and the soft sheets called to him. He brushed his teeth and drank a glass of water in an attempt to rid his throat of the taste of scotch, then fell into bed and sleep almost at the same moment.

Ensyn Memo

"Adam," came a soft voice. The voice seemed familiar, but he couldn't place it until it continued and he recognized it as his dome AI, saying, "Please make sure you are ready for the presentation this morning." Then, "Signed by Nate Taylor."

Did I fall asleep with my dome on? I didn't think I was wearing it, he thought. Something about sleeping while wearing the Mind Drive made him more tired than without, and his eyes struggled to adjust to the beam of light that shone through his apartment window. He expected some degree of a hangover from the night before, but he felt clear-headed as he sat up in bed and stretched his legs against the floor. He yawned and scratched his shoulder.

Presentation? Adam thought with a shock. It had taken him several minutes to parse the message, and he was alarmed when he couldn't recall anything scheduled for that day. He focused his attention to his dome, thought, *Please refresh my memory regarding today's presentation*, and sent the message to Nate, hoping for a quick reply.

Despite having plenty of time before he was due to work, Adam thought it best to go in early. If he had to present something, he would need time to prepare. The street outside his building was quiet, the city slowed by the stillness of early morning. Instead of his usual *tencho* playlist, that morning he opted to listen to the sounds of his shoes against the sidewalk and the silence of near-empty streets, something he didn't often have the chance to experience at the normal hours of his treks to and from the office.

The tempo of his falling feet matched the beat of his pounding heart as his thoughts drifted between his new role and that day's forgotten presentation. He was perturbed, not only because he had no recollection of any pitch, but since he couldn't figure out why the message came from Nate Taylor, who had been his boss for years before Adam's recent promotion.

As Adam reached the subway on his way to Adaptech, a soft tone rang in his ear, followed by a smooth voice reading Nate's reply: "Yes, for the Ensyn project. Didn't you get the memos? Several were sent."

No, he thought, sending the response.

Nate replied quickly. "Don't put me in a bad spot, Adam. I'm really counting on you for this. Can you come in early so I can brief you?"

One step ahead of you. I'll be there in just a few minutes, he thought in response.

"Good," intoned the soft voice in his ear. "Meet me at my desk." Despite the even tone of the dome AI reading the message, Adam detected frustration from Nate.

The subway brought him to the stop near Adaptech shortly after he received Nate's message. He ran a mesh query for Ensyn, wanting to be as prepared as possible once he reached the office. As he exited through the train's open doors, his query's initial results came to his dome.

Three quarters of a century before, several companies raced to replace the keyboards, mice, and screens that had dominated computer interaction for the preceding decades. New interfaces were developed, large and miniature touchscreens incorporating gesture input—two, three, and four fingers used to draw intricate and specific patterns—to perform desired tasks. Eventually lasers replaced screens, lasers that fired directly into the retina, overlaying virtual data atop the data absorbed by the senses from real world. Though they had been heralded as new and novel ways to interact with computers, the touchscreens led to worker fatigue, arms raised instead of planted firmly against desks while typing on keyboards, and heads-up displays quickly led to collisions for pedestrians and drivers alike. No one could accept such a state of affairs for long. A public-relations nightmare resulted.

Audio came to be accepted as the safest medium by which to transmit data to users on the go before the Mind Drive debuted, which smoothed its pathway to success. A domer could transmit video signals wirelessly to a nearby notetab or vid screen. Adam felt thankful for this as he made his way up to the ground level, his eyes closed, his hand trailing along the icy cold railing bolted into the wall of the stairwell.

The voice in his ear read the first result, an About Us page from the Ensyn Energy public node. "Ensyn Energy was founded by Doctors Freeman and Graeme. Originally specializing in biomass petroleum, the company diversified into other areas after an investment of capital from Luminus Industries, eventually bringing a high yield solar panel to market incorporating energy production via photosynthetic biomass. We are now providing electricity to seventy percent of the Region and growing. We at Ensyn Energy are happy to serve and to provide the technology powering our lives."

Typical PR speak, thought Adam. Other results filled his dome with stories about how Ensyn had used past-due utility bills to obtain liens against debtor property, foreclose, then rent it out at twice the rate—sometimes to the original occupant. Those unfortunate enough to make the transition from mortgage holder to tenant were typically forced to get another job or even indenture the mortgage to their children, payment for keeping houses in families funded by economic bondage passed from one generation to the next. Adam felt a wave of disgust and revulsion at such predatory practices.

Adam didn't have time to sort through most of the reports, but he saved the search to study it in greater detail later. He went inside the Adaptech building and up to Nate's floor, taking two stairs at a time with little effort, unusual for him. The security department, consisting of Adam's old colleagues, was a handful of floors from the ground. A typical corporate cube farm, each homogeneous grey wall blending into the next. Adam walked down three rows, then turned to the right and went to the end to seek Nate.

Adam had been many times to Nate's desk, the largest one at the end, a perk of managerial excess. Truth be told, there was an extra square meter, not much difference for a man of Nate's girth but enough to cause envy in many others. The extra desk space at both ends, most of which was taken up by stacks of paperwork and memos, provided enough room for an extra picture of his children. Nate Taylor was a family man, and a family man was a good company man.

Adam was surprised to clear the cubicle wall and see an empty workspace where Nate usually sat. No chair, no light, not even a vid screen. Boxes covered the inoffensive geometry of the carpet, stacked under the curved plastic desk and out into the center, leaving just enough space for Adam to kneel down at the desk in front of them. He opened the closest box and was surprised to see stacks of lined and printed. Almost all records were digital due to ease and cost. Paper was uncommon and indicated a particularly old or important document.

Adam felt a spontaneous wave of respect and stopped looking at the papers, instead pushing aside his confusion long enough to send a message to Nate. He thought, *Where are you? I'm at your desk. Did you move?* After waiting several minutes for a reply, his curiosity overcame his patience and he started to thumb through the documents. The first he pulled was a court judgment of a foreclosure filed by Ensyn Energy, but it included notes from the corporate attorneys, scratched words in the margins suggesting Ensyn had influenced the decision by acting through a Metra Corp proxy controlling that particular district court. Each case Adam flipped through showed similar behavior, odds stacked against homeowners from the beginning.

He opened a box containing pictures and field reports from an Ensyn plant outside Boston, a reclamation facility for processing sewage sludge into biomass to be later refined into petroleum. An accident had apparently resulted in contamination of drinking water sources, and Adam even found evidence suggesting a blackmail had occurred. Several of the pictures showed a woman and a man with a ring whispering to one another in the quiet corner of an elegant restaurant. Two more with the same pair entering an ornamented hotel. Any investigation was over before it started, and it seemed clear to Adam this was a result of bribery, not justice being served.

In the last box Adam found financial documents. These records showed Luminus Industries had become a Metra Corp shell company over twenty years before, a fact hidden from shareholders of both organizations. After its significant investment, Luminus controlled Ensyn Energy, and bank statements showed dividends from Enysn had been diverted into offshore accounts instead of disbursed, millions of dollars of profits siphoned off and gone forever. Stealing from stockholders was one of the most heinous financial crimes in Metra Region, punishable with up to several decades in a hard labor camp. Whoever knew about these documents would take action to keep them from coming to attention, whatever the cost.

Adam wasn't sure what he was experiencing. Nate still hadn't answered him. Five minutes had already gone by, or had it been ten? Twenty? Adam had no idea how long he'd been digging through boxes. He queried his dome for the time. Minor tritone, command not recognized. He tried to access the messages from Nate. The sound repeated. He stood and took two steps outside of the cubicle, fingers against the bubble under his right ear in a vain attempt to improve the recognition. No commands worked.

He turned and stepped back toward where the boxes had been. He was shocked to find that the floor had disappeared. His left foot passed through the plane where it expected to find purchase, the rest of his body following close behind. Adam fell rapidly down a dark, hollow cylinder until a round light appeared in the distance below him, painful and brilliant, directly in his path. He closed his eyes instinctively as he rushed toward the surface, but his eyelids did nothing to block the terrible pain as the intensity increased.

When Adam was sure he could take no more, the light vanished into darkness. He opened his eyes and at the same moment inhaled so sharply that the back of his throat felt as if it were being raked with a stick. After Adam blinked several times he noticed a taste in the back of his throat, raw and earthy, almost a smell. He found himself on his back, his head against his pillow, at home with his arms at his sides. He reached up and found he was not wearing his dome. He saw it next to him on the table by his bed, beside his notetab, where he had apparently left them, though he couldn't recall doing so.

Not wanting to aggravate the headache he felt forming at his temples, Adam grabbed the notetab and pulled up the page about Ensyn his dome had read to him in the dream. Adam shuddered as he read the words on the screen:

"Ensyn Energy was founded by Drs. Freeman and Graeme. Originally specializing in biomass petroleum, the company diversified into other areas . . ."

Adam looked up several court cases he remembered from the dream and they all seemed to exist. He wondered what that meant. He also wondered how deeply he should investigate, worried his search might raise a flag of suspicion in some data-mining algorithm scanning for illicit mesh activity. Adam confirmed enough details from the boxes in his dream to imply that the rest of what he had seen in them was also true.

Are those documents real? Adam could not help but ask himself as he lay staring at the ceiling. The last time he'd dreamed about paper it turned out not to exist, and he had no idea why this paper would be any different, except the things he'd seen referred to actual places and events. The documents—documents he didn't possess and couldn't prove as real—also showed corruption was coming from the top down, through Metra Corp and its subsidiaries. *Are the boxes really at Adaptech in Nate's cubicle,* Adam wondered as he lay in bed, *or was that symbolic imagery of an authority figure?*

Adam finally fell asleep in the beginning of the morning, three hours before his alarm was set to pain him. He went into work early the next day to go straight to Nate's desk, only to find it was where it had always been, arranged exactly as he remembered it from when he worked in that department. There were no boxes in sight. All he found was Nate Taylor, as pleasant as ever.

"To what do I owe this occasion?" Nate asked with a look of delight. "You really should come to visit more often."

"I know, I know," Adam said, holding his hands up in a gesture of surrender. "I'm a terrible former employee. I didn't really want anything, but I had a weird dream and you were in it. In the dream, you sent me a memo that I never got, or at least never read. I came into work early so I could figure it out, but when I came to meet you at your desk it was gone."

"Gone? Hmm," Nate said, rubbing his chin. "Not that I know of. Still here every morning when I come in. Was there anything in place of my desk?"

"No," Adam lied, not wanting to discuss the contents of the boxes with Nate or anyone else. "Just an empty desk."

"Ah," his former boss said shrewdly. Adam felt Nate knew he was lying. As if providing him a chance for honesty, Nate asked, "Well, what was the memo about?"

"Ever heard of Ensyn Energy?" Adam asked. "It was something

to do with a presentation. I never found out if we were giving a presentation *to* Ensyn or *about* Ensyn. I never even saw the actual memo."

Nate shrugged and gestured to a stack of papers at the far edge of his desk. "Tell me about it. I'm pretty sure some of the memos on the bottom pre-date your tenure at Adaptech. It's hard to keep up sometimes."

Adam chuckled. "Even worse as a manager, as I'm sure you know," he said with a wink. "I just had to check it out. Sorry to bother you."

"Not a bother at all, Adam," Nate said. "Thanks for coming by. Don't wait so long to visit next time."

They shook hands and Adam went to room 4C to begin his workday.

11 Months Gone

In the week after the election there were scattered riots, most of them small and spent within a period of several days, but the newly elected government had not marked the end of civilization, contrary to the most dire predictions of the loser's supporters. Eleven months, gone in a blur, had put the Regions in more precarious positions. Cascadia Corp's CEO started his third term and continued the aggressive expansion east that had been the hallmark of Cascadian policy for the past two decades, in sharp contrast to the Cascadian Charter goals of "Peace and Prosperity through Unity".

The Confederacy had ousted its president, an elderly, devout man who had spent the last three five-year terms focused on religious doctrine, setting up what he believed to be the dominoes that would one day fall and lead to the return of his warrior deity. While he focused on scripture and prophecy, the citizens of Arizona voted by an almost four-to-one margin to adopt the Cascadia Charter and escape the dismal economy brought about by the President's lack of fiscal responsibility. The remaining voters in the Confederacy had approved a rising star from the business class, a bespectacled man whose squinting eyes suggested a shrewd approach to governance. The would-be preacher-king had been replaced by a smooth-talking, smiling suit who promised prosperity through increased dealings with the Cascadia and Metra Regions. The United States had continued their economic free fall, ceding more territory to their geographic bookends on each coast, reportedly pulled under by the costs of their social programs and fiscal mismanagement. This stood in stark contrast to the prevailing attitude in the Corp Regions, where financial solvency was the primary goal, along with the acquisition of profit, the poor viewed as inconvenient baggage. The consensus in the Corp Regions was that the poor deserved their lot in life due to bad decision-making and laziness, at least according to the media. Otherwise, why would they be poor?

The newly elected CEO of Metra Corp, Tim Montery, had formerly been the head of operations for TeleVice, a media conglomerate with holdings in all Four Regions. Mister Montery was one of the people who lived squarely in the middle of the intersecting spheres of power and influence in the continent's society. He was rumored to have an influential voice among the other media powerhouses. There were no rules demanding financial disclosures or barring conflicts of interest, and Montery hadn't freely offered any information. An outspoken advocate for corporate expansion, Montery said the fiscal irresponsibility and religious fervor of the United States and Confederacy, respectively, were impending dangers to the citizenry, dangers that could only be protected against by strict adherence to management and profit, the benefits of which were obvious. Montery had argued during the campaign that the problems plaguing the Four Regions occurred despite strong business growth, not because of it, and that an increased market capitalization, along with ever-decreasing social programs, represented the only long-term path to widespread prosperity.

Cora Slate, young but known for business acumen and her ability to say no to all requests, said to include declining her mother for a kidney, was declared Vice CEO. Slate's defense was that her mother was feeble and would be so even with a new kidney. The old woman had a limited ability to offer any financial recompense for the body part, Cora's father having left his considerable fortune to his protégée and only child. Cora had established a reputation that inspired equal parts of reverence, fear, and hatred. Her beauty awed only half as often as her ruthlessness. Many said she inherited the trait from her father, the sort of man who would leave all his money to his daughter just so his estranged widow would die in rags.

Montery selected Roman LaMont as his Executive of Commerce, a prestigious position many viewed as a stepping stone to Vice CEO, then CEO. LaMont chose to remain as CEO of Adaptech, not wanting to abdicate any of his hard-earned influence for a cushy Metra Corp executive position. He had, however, immediately started to use his new title and power to funnel money to Adaptech and himself, slowly at first but more with each passing month. Most of his time was spent at Metra Corp headquarters. He only appeared via video node on the rare occasion when something at Adaptech absolutely required his attention.

The Metra Corp Board of Directors, fifty representatives from the various precincts, elected to represent those who had given them the most votes, ratified the results. It seemed to Adam those who gave the most votes were always the rich. Voter demographics aside, there was a certain degree of self-interest, as most of the current Board members had already purchased significant numbers of votes, and could cast that significant number for themselves when the elections came. And so the pattern repeated.

Wars were different in those days, enlightened as they were. Virtual attacks on capital, hostile takeovers in digital realms that increased and decreased conquered territories without loss of life, had replaced battles wrought with bombs and bloodshed. Most people didn't care which Region held their citizenship, so long as the Region's politics appeared stable and enabled them to acquire personal wealth. Regardless, a decades-long propaganda campaign had promoted a decidedly pro-corporate attitude among the citizens of Metra Region, many of whom believed without question or evidence that an acquisition by the United States or Confederacy would leave them destitute and begging for scraps in the streets. The media had convinced these citizens that corporate governance provided an easier path to wealth, trumpeting several success stories involving newly acquired citizens or immigrants. As a result of this targeted campaign, many inhabitants of non-Corp Regions had pushed for lower taxes, loosened regulations, and the abolition of remaining social programs. In some cases they had even petitioned for a corporate takeover, Arizona being the largest and most recent. With border zones expanded, market cap increased.

Adam was aware of all this in an abstract, passing sort of way, as were most Corp citizens. The media played up the elections as prime-time soap operas, with ad zeps flashing node addresses and times for debates and other election coverage. People tuned in and were drawn as moths to flames, or paralyzed deer in headlights, he wasn't sure which. As important as everyone claimed elections were, they were forgotten almost immediately after as the news marched from one cycle to the next. People cared then didn't, the 24/7 world and its glut of distraction preventing passion from being sustained. Commercials broke in every four minutes no matter the program, sometimes *within* the program via product placement. The entire world had become a product placement opportunity.

It was difficult and ultimately depressing to think of the world in such stark terms, so Adam tried to avert doing so, instead attempting to lose his thoughts as he stared into the smooth, patternless ceiling above his bed. He knew if he were cornered and forced to confess his views, he would admit he despised almost everything about the world that had provided him with material opportunity and felt as if no one talked about anything important, interesting, or real. Most people he knew primarily talked about the dividends they were after, or the insipid drama shows, sports stars, or the cameras following the real lives of the most despicable people in the Region. These were people who would be in jail if it weren't for the ignorant masses watching them on the video nodes. It made Adam upset when he thought about it too much. Why didn't most people give a damn about anything important?

Regardless, Adam didn't have room to complain, and the people in his field were more quick-witted than most. As intelligent as Adam's colleagues in the past seemed to be, they had not usually talked about anything of depth while at work. The weather, new gadgets, amusing mesh videos, and their children or pets dominated pre- and post-shift encounters in the halls, the elevators, the cubicles and after-work gatherings. With the Lightcap project, he didn't remember any office conversations, if they even occurred. Despite his inability to remember events during work hours that might give him a sense of accomplishment, Velim praised his performance as head of the project in each biweekly meeting and his colleagues treated him as a leader in each monthly meeting, bolstering his confidence as a manager. Room 4C, with its long conference table, became a place he associated with pleasant interactions and contentment. Things for him were better than they had been in a long time, long enough that it made him feel old to think about it.

Velim had seemed withdrawn since their last encounter in the elevator. She was cordial during their meetings, even lavished him with praise on occasion, but never anything beyond business, no acknowledgment of their previous encounters, and certainly no more late-night visits to his apartment. Adam did have late-night visits from his neighbor Hana, since they began dating again two months after he started on the Lightcap project. For some reason, he had begun spending more time on the roof, even sitting in the covered room on cold nights, and they started having long conversations about nothing necessary, which became conversations about their pasts and aspirations. Hana surprised him one warm night by grabbing his collar and pulling him in for a kiss, cutting him off mid-sentence during a story about a college prank. Adam was caught off guard but not at all opposed, their clothes barely half off by the time they fell into bed after stumbling through his front door, years of pent up tension from flirting in the laundry room and elevator and hallways released in the span of a sweaty, feral night of hair-pulling and bicep-gripping bliss. It had been better than he remembered.

They had fallen into a comfortable rhythm, each with their respective apartments. His bed had mostly become hers, with the rest of her belongings safely stored in her own abode. She'd even run down the hall to brush her teeth and shower in the morning. Adam liked the arrangement, conversation and a warm bed. She was flexible both physically and intellectually, able to carry conversation on a variety of subjects, would spend the occasional night in her own bed and had never stolen any closet space from him. Hana worked as a lawyer for TeleVice, so she would occasionally have to travel, sometimes even to other Regions, leaving Adam with the solace of solitude. Adam found the occasional absence did make his heart grow fonder of her, though he missed the fresh fruit smoothies she made for him while he worked on freelance projects or read the news and conspiracy sites. He was an information junkie, which she tolerated, if only because it gave them new topics of discussion beyond rehashed personal anecdotes or anything that would be taken as offensive or transformative. He liked her enough.

Each day at Adaptech started to blend into the next, each week into the next, each month into the next, punctuated by the occasional weekend, and those were sometimes filled with freelance work, personal projects, and the rare day-long crash, a seeming side effect of long days and late nights bent over a notetab. The disorienting dreams, headaches, and exhaustion were things of the past, which left only the boring monotony of life. Lately, even the biweekly and monthly meetings had seemed like carbon copies, the same words rewound and spoken again in slightly different arrangements, tongue against teeth more practiced than spontaneous, letting him daydream about other things, his mind stuck on repeated thoughts about the futility of trying to change the status quo.

Adam began to feel like a sellout, with all the self-loathing the label entailed. For the most part he didn't think about it, instead choosing to enjoy his status as a manager at one of the most stable companies in the Region; and the beautiful woman who slept in the crook of his arm almost every night, her warm breath playing across his neck with each deep fall of her breast. What more could he possibly want? There were plenty of people who would kill to be where Adam was. With Hana sleeping beside him, he listened to the news, his dome softly whispering in his ear. Things were mostly calm, expansion and acquisition reflected in small market gains over the past several months. People were generally in a good mood, and even those who usually wore the most sullen faces around the office had a bounce in their step much of the time.

The issues they had all first experienced when getting used to the Lightcap—the headaches, disorientation, and restlessness—were all gone, replaced with appreciation for the days free of politics and problem-solving. Those aspects of corporate life certainly still existed, but were played out in a dream state and not remembered. Every three months they were given a psychological evaluation, apparently to determine how well the tests were going, how well the subjects were adjusting to what could only be considered an unprecedented work experience. Velim had given him an overview for the team after each evaluation, assuring him they were all performing better than expected. He had observed the team, too, watching with interest as they met jovially each morning, then—seemingly whisked through time—back in their seats nine to ten hours later, where they talked and laughed about their plans for the evening and the weekend. No one took work home. Even if they'd had the desire to obsess over the details of the v6 programming they wouldn't have had the ability, which made this the least stressful project Adam had ever worked.

Adam slipped out of bed. Hana gave a muted groan as her arm fell from his shoulder to the soft pillows and sheets. He tiptoed around the room, silently slipped clothes over his slender limbs, and pulled taut the strap of his messenger bag against his jacket. His door screeching was not enough to rouse Hana from her slumber, wheels sliding along rusted tracks, echoing off brick walls, as Adam left the apartment and started his day.

Adam's commute had become second nature as well. The subway pumps, finally fixed, had worked for a near-record number of days in a row. Adam slept more soundly most nights now that his life had settled down, and he used the time on the subway to catch up on world events, local news, and market forecasts. He still scanned the crowds on the platform sometimes, his eyes narrowed and attention focused, hoping to catch a glimpse of the unkempt man, though he didn't even know why. Adam had not seen him since the night of the election, and he'd recently started to wonder if he suffered from an overactive imagination. The man could simply be an externalized phantom representing the apprehension Adam had felt about his changing life. He didn't think someone was playing a joke on him.

Even still, he could not help but look every time someone bumped him, as the bodies bounced left and right with the subway along its track, and to shove his hand into his pockets in a frantic search for a note slipped in secret. His sudden glances always ended in disappointment, hands drawn empty out of pockets, no notes ever found. *Why am I even looking for these things?* Adam would wonder. *They can't possibly be real.* He began to wish he could target his Lightcap on his memories of the man and the note and erase those as well as every other day's programming work.

The repetition Adam felt for almost an entire year on the Lightcap project broke after an otherwise ordinary day. At the end of the day, all the team members took off their Lightcaps in separate rooms. This struck Adam as odd, but he assumed it represented an extra layer of security for the v6 software they were programming, preoccupied with thoughts of his dinner date with Hana as he left work. The next morning Adam became actively alarmed.

Adam sat at the head of the conference table in room 4C. After the team sat down, two absences glared at the rest. Every day Velim had filled the seat opposite Adam, but that morning she was gone. The other absence, a seat to Adam's left and four away from him, was that of Damen Theda, a fresh-faced young man who was eager to prove himself a capable member of the group. Damen was not the sort to shrug off work. Sometimes Adam had wondered if even the loss of a limb would cause Damen to call in sick, as he seemed so dedicated, yet he and Velim were absent for the first time on the same day. An uneasy silence settled over the group as the clock moved past seven. Eyes shifted between the two empty chairs, noses sniffling and throats clearing preludes to the question on everyone's mind. The seventeen team members remaining occasionally looked to Adam, who had nothing to offer beyond what they already knew.

Finally, after five minutes of anxious silence that felt like hours, the door and frame parted to reveal Sera Velim. Her demeanor was unchanged from the previous morning, even as her eyes scanned the room with no acknowledgement of their missing colleague. She began her usual morning routine, giving updated figures on company earnings and market reports. Aria Hines raised her hand, but Velim did not notice it for several minutes as she read aloud. When she finished reading, she looked up but did not respond to the silent request.

Aria took Velim's lack of response as approval to speak. She stood and asked, "Where's Damen?"

Adam saw a look on Velim's face that could melt paint, replaced in a split second with a consoling smile, as if she were a mother about to tell her children their family couldn't afford any holiday presents that year. She said, "Oh, he didn't tell you? He mentioned he was going to send you all a message. He accepted a position with a company in the Cascadia Region, effective immediately. He didn't inform us until after his shift yesterday, though he did offer to give a proper notice. After consulting with legal, we declined and parted ways amicably. We were sorry to see him go, but we understood his motivation, given the lucrative offer he received." A plausible but unlikely story, Adam felt. Velim's nails ricocheted off the glass table, *tinktinktink*, which made him wonder if she was agitated or just annoyed. After she finished speaking, her eyes took on a glazed look for a moment, most likely while issuing a silent command to her dome.

Aria fell back into her seat with a sullen look and an almost imperceptible sigh. Adam, along with everyone else in the room, knew Velim hadn't been completely honest. They also knew she wouldn't offer any more information. Velim continued with her recap of recent Adaptech performance, then asked them to put on their Lightcaps and begin their day.

Adam experienced a moment of hesitation as he put on the cool plastic device, its three enveloping arms resting casually at points along the back and top of his head. He wondered what would happen if he refused to wear it, then shuddered at a vision of himself as a poor beggar. Adam decided the transgression would not be worth its potential penalty. As he pressed the arms down, he felt them expand, two around the sides, ending just under his ears. The third arm slipped slightly past his hairline onto his forehead. He felt the arms click, making a sound which he had heard hundreds of times, and once again fell into the familiar ball of light.

Glass

Everything was blue. The whole world had taken on the hue of the sky, viewed through a fisheye lens. For one heart-stopping moment, Adam was sure he had been thrown from an airplane in the upper atmosphere, as he perceived reality rushing toward him like a fastball thrown by a vindictive pitcher. It dawned on him at the last second, as impact seemed inevitable, that he had just removed his Lightcap. Adam snapped back to the room, like a rubber band pulled tight and then released, and looked up to see a screen displaying the image of LaMont where Velim usually sat. He noticed Damen's chair was still empty. Concerned looks on the faces of those who remained told him Velim's suspicious story was still in their minds. Though she had met with them over eight hours earlier, it felt as if she had been with them mere minutes before. As if summoned by their return, the screen brightness increased and LaMont's mouth began to move.

"Ladies, gentleman," he intoned with all the trustworthiness of a snake-oil salesman, "I understand there were some questions about the sudden exit of Mister Theda this morning. I thought it prudent to be here when you, uh, came back to us, to answer any questions or address any concerns you may have."

Never before had Adam been able to hear the heartbeat of another person, but he was fairly certain he could hear seventeen other hearts as they raced, his own leading the charge. No one dared speak. It seemed several people had even stopped breathing for fear their exhalations might draw attention. Many fidgeted or averted their eyes, not wanting to be drafted to ask a question or be addressed in any way. LaMont had that effect on people even before he had been named Executive of Commerce, third in command of the entire Region. Adam figured he himself was the one with the least to lose by speaking, since he had worked for Adaptech the longest, and he also knew it would be difficult though not impossible to replace him.

Adam stood and addressed the two-dimensional video feed of LaMont, framed in the thin black plastic line surrounding the screen. "Mister LaMont, we do appreciate you taking the time to address our concerns. While I can only speak for myself, not the rest of my team, it seems out of character for Damen to leave so abruptly. I can understand why he may not have the time to send a personal farewell to each person, but it troubles me no one found it necessary to notify me in advance of someone in my group abruptly leaving. Also, Doctor Velim seemed quite content to ignore Damen's empty chair until one of my employees asked her about it. Why is that?" Adam didn't want to call Aria out, even though LaMont probably already knew who it was.

Adam had found unexpected boldness, his statements delivered with a steady voice and confident gaze at LaMont's face. The executive, however, seemed unaffected, his smile frozen in place as Adam finished his question. LaMont regarded Adam for several long seconds, silent, which caused several in the room to stir uneasily. An unexpected laugh from LaMont, deep and genuine, broke the tension. They could only see him from mid-tie up, but Adam imagined LaMont's hands were clutched against his belly. As the laughter subsided, he wiped an eye and said, "You geeks always put so much thought into everything. Damen Theda was a great employee for the time he was with us. But he's also a young man: rash, spontaneous, thinks he knows everything. No doubt he's romanticized his new job and location. It's not as if he's the first young man in his twenties to make a spur-of-the-moment decision. It was as much of a surprise to us as it was to all of you. Now, regarding the way Doctor Velim handled it, I accept some responsibility for that. I set her agenda, and she is beholden to it. I should have told her to add in something about his departure. I can assure you such an oversight won't happen again."

Several faces in the room had adopted LaMont's amused demeanor, infected with his laughter and confident explanations. Adam did his best to appear satisfied, but he wasn't as convinced. He had always viewed LaMont as the sort who would shake with one hand while reaching around with the other to stab in the back. Duplicitous. Even as people like LaMont were held up as role models in society—and Adam did envy him in certain ways—he knew there were no significant amounts of decency or honesty within him, that there was only acute self-interest. The belly laugh had marked the first time Adam could recall seeing anything from LaMont approaching a genuine sentiment.

LaMont surveyed the room from the limited angle of his video feed, seemed content his answers were well received, and went on, "I know it's painful to have someone suddenly depart, even now that you understand what actually happened and why Damen chose to leave without saying goodbye. In times like these, it's important to maintain team unity and morale. To that end, we've rented out Glass for the evening. Dinner and drinks are on me. Just don't get too wild." This last line was delivered with a comical wink, prompting nervous chuckles from around the table. LaMont finished with, "Go on and head over there. When you get to the bar, just tell them Roman sent you. They're expecting you. Adam, please stay behind. I'd like to speak with you."

As the room emptied, stray glances shot in Adam's direction. The mood had been improved by Roman's information about Damen's departure, even more so by his offer of food and spirits. In all the time Adam had worked at Adaptech, he could not recall a single meal or drink given even at a discount, let alone freely. LaMont was known throughout Adaptech for his frugality, so it struck Adam as not only noteworthy but of singular significance. Why would LaMont behave so strangely?

The room quieted as the group left, until the door shut behind the last person, audible even to LaMont over the video feed. He asked for confirmation: "Are they gone?"

When Adam nodded affirmatively, LaMont's eyes narrowed and he continued, "Doctor Velim has said nothing but good things about you, that you are beyond any expectation of competency and resourcefulness, and that you are among the top fifty minds in your field. I only say this because I want you to understand that if you were anyone else, you'd have been out on your ass after that little stunt you pulled. I want to be very clear. If you ever treat me that way again you're done."

Adam's eyes lit up with shock and his mouth started to open in reply.

LaMont continued: "Stop. Don't speak. Again, it's important this sinks in. I am not speaking in metaphors or hyperbole. If you disrespect me in front of anyone that way again, I will personally come down there and terminate you myself. Do you understand?"

Adam gulped. *Is LaMont talking about my life or my job?* he wondered as a chill passed down his spine. There was a part of him that wanted to extend both middle fingers, rebellious and proud. There was a bigger part that enjoyed having a place to live. The bigger part won. He slowly nodded his head.

"I want you to say it out loud. Do you understand me?" LaMont spoke his words with a measured intent.

Adam croaked, "Yes, sir. I understand." With that the rectangular screen in room 4C turned off, the light and colors fading into blackness.

Adam made his way to Glass slowly, thoughtfully, and took the opportunity to mull what Roman had said. He felt fortunate this was only the fourth interaction he'd had with LaMont in the entire time he'd been employed by Adaptech, his first being after his new hire orientation, when LaMont had shaken his hand and wished him the best of luck as a new employee without even looking Adam in the eye. The second was during his final interview for the position to head the v6 programming division, when LaMont appeared disinterested and asked questions that could have come from a book titled *Logic Puzzle Questions for Interviewees*, none of which were relevant to the job. The third was LaMont's terrible excuse for a pep talk given during the Lightcap project orientation. Adam's three previous brushes with LaMont had left sour tastes in Adam's mouth, but those tastes were nothing like the current one.

Adam thought this might be the right time to update his resume, certain there had to be other positions and companies out there that didn't come with the ego and cult of personality surrounding LaMont. Adam ultimately dismissed the thought the instant he remembered Adaptech offered him an opportunity few other companies could: to work with and develop cutting-edge technology. At his heart, Adam was a geek. He would have taken a position with less pay and more stress if it allowed him to work with technology not yet publicly available. He could never say that out loud, at least not to most. Instead, when discussing his work at Adaptech he mentioned the salary and company name, which impressed most people, before he brought up that he also enjoyed helping create the technology that drove society's progress.

Adam made his way from the subway exit near the bar, lost in thought and not minding his steps on the wide, empty sidewalk. Most residents in this neighborhood were too affluent to walk anywhere, which allowed him to progress without interruption, eventually ending at the entrance to Glass. He had only been a few times before, always in the summer, so he did not expect the difference in ambiance provided with the glass roof in its closed position, dusted with a light layer of snow sparkling in the moonlight, thousands of glimmers added to the already white-dotted night sky. Most on the v6 programming team had already had the time to down a drink or two, and now enjoyed relaxed conversation and free food. Adam made it halfway to the bar before Dej noticed and left a table with Aria and several others to intercept him.

"Hey Adam, how'd it go with LaMont?" Dej asked, beer in hand. It seemed not to be his first one of the night.

"Nothing I can't handle," Adam replied as they arrived at the bar. He faced the bartender, finger held up to Dej requesting patience, their conversation paused, and said to the man behind the bar, "Aged scotch. Rocks." He turned back to Dej and continued, "I'd rather just forget about it. Some people will always find a reason to be angry or to remind others they're the one in charge. I'm not talking about anyone specific, of course. I do hope none of you think of me that way. I make an effort to be approachable as a leader. Honestly, in terms of sheer talent, I think there are a few coders on the team who would be better at this than me." Dej was one of those people, but Adam did not want to come across as playing favorites.

Dej smiled, understanding implied through blinding white teeth. He raised his pint glass and said, "To Damen." The *clink* of pint and tumbler glasses echoed off the glowing blue walls surrounding the bar, then faded into the murmured conversation from the rest of their group. The sound caught the attention of Aria, who turned and noticed Adam and Dej standing together. She excused herself from her table, sneaked up behind Dej, and slipped her arm around his shoulder.

"I hope this handsome man isn't bothering you too much, Boss," she said a little too playfully, her head leaning toward Dej's neck. Adam was amused by her intoxication, having never seen her in a position of such vulnerability, her entire face lit up with overt affection. He had known her for almost two decades, but he wasn't sure he had ever seen her teeth when she smiled before that moment. There was a clause in their employment contracts prohibiting romantic involvement between members of the team, but Adam was not one to pry. They both seemed drunk, and he felt no obligation to make assumptions about the nature of their relationship. Adam was happier not knowing the details. Plausible deniability. He'd had over twenty meetings with Velim, and she'd never raised any protest about the performance of either Dej or Aria. That was good enough for Adam.

Dej, however, suddenly appeared several shades lighter as the blood rushed out of his face. He seemed tipsy, though not on the same level as Aria. Dej was sober enough to realize she had just got very comfortable with him in front of the head of their department. Dej froze, his mouth opening and closing a few times, his words dead at the back of his throat before his tongue and lips had a chance to cooperate. Adam enjoyed Dej's discomfort and Aria's abandon for several seconds, while doing his best not to laugh aloud. Finally, he brought his hand down to Dej's shoulder with a muffled *thump* and responded, "No, Aria, it's fine. Dej and I were just having a toast in honor of Damen's next adventure. Not a bother at all." He looked to Dej, who gave a sheepish grin, his teeth still distractingly white even with the color drained from his face. Aria's deep green eyes filled with happiness. Adam smiled, winked at Dej, and continued, "You're both clearly very drunk, so I'm going to let you enjoy that, along with the hangovers in the morning. I'm sure you won't remember any of this."

As Adam stepped away from the bar, a soft sound played in his ear: the notification tone to alert a user of a new message. He noticed the conversations around the bar faltered momentarily, indicating strongly that the rest of them had received the same message. It was from Damen. They all started listening to it at roughly the same time, their discussions placed on hold.

The soft computer voice read the message in his ear. "Hey,

guys, sorry for leaving without saying goodbye. I just landed in Cascadia Province and got a chance to send a message. The position I was offered was too much to turn down, and they said they could only give it to me if I could start pronto. It was really great working with you all, at least I think it was, from what I can remember. Best of luck to you guys, come out and visit some time if you're able to get a travel pass." Adam saw relieved expressions circle the bar, punctuated by shaken heads. He heard small bouts of laughter and the occasional comments on the frivolity and the short-sightedness of youth, expressed with a mixture of condescension and envy. The existing feeling of enjoyment in the room turned to outright celebration, with glasses tipped and refilled several times over.

Adam made his way around the room, stopping at each table to talk to the programmers, who were more cheerful than he had ever seen them. He made small talk with them, an act he found difficult but necessary, especially in a leadership role. He remembered once hearing that the higher up one was in an organization, the more diplomatic one had to be. *Apparently LaMont missed that memo*, Adam thought, imagining a stack of memos on LaMont's desk several times taller than the stack on Nate's. As they talked, he was again reminded of the lack of substance in their conversations, words traded over things as pointless as their chosen sports teams, the bitter winter weather, how the bitter winter weather affected their commute, how the bitter winter weather affected their utility bills, and the popular dramas on the vid nodes. It had been this way at every work gathering he had attended, but the past gatherings he had attended had the added benefit of discussions of shared office experiences, experiences Adam and the other coders had been robbed of, thanks to the Lightcap.

The group lasted late into the night, nursed scotch Adam's only constant companion as he spent the better part of the evening moving from table to table, chattered irrelevancies giving his mind time to reflect on Damen Theda and the rest of his team. The message had been written with Damen's style, but two aspects of the story didn't sit well with Adam: Damen's sudden departure and the convenient message containing much of the same language Damen used in daily conversation. It was also signed with his passkey, which really only proved the message had been sent from his dome, not that Damen himself had sent it. *If not Damen, then who? And why?* Adam wondered, not sure why he even doubted Damen authored the message. *What more proof do I need?* Adaptech had always been good to Adam, and he had no reason to doubt what he had been told. People changed jobs, even abruptly, all the time.

Adam felt a moment's anger with himself for not being able to be happy for Damen, for not being able to shake his persistent thoughts that conspiratorial shadows lurked in every corner. The last of his team departed Glass with waved goodbyes and loudly spoken admonitions for safe travels, which left Adam seated alone at a table, the city spread out before him, sparkling from his vantage point on the roof. As he finished his drink and stood up to leave, Aria and Dej reappeared, and Adam realized he hadn't seen them for at least the past half hour. He had some idea of what they had been doing, but he thought it best to let it go, as the memories of their earlier awkward conversation were still fresh in his mind. He rethought his assumption as they drew closer, based on the frown Dej wore and the puffy skin around Aria's stark green eyes. She had definitely been crying.

"Adam, we need to talk to you," Dej said worriedly, looking to Aria. "We think there might be more to the story. About Damen, I mean." Dej still looked slightly drunk, but he had the sullen face of someone who had been at least partially sobered by reality. They all sat down at Adam's table.

Aria sniffed and said, "I was immediately suspicious. On the first day of the project, Damen and I walked to the same subway station after work. You know I'm not a big talker, but Damen definitely was, and he gave me the short version of his life story. He was so excited to be working for Adaptech, especially because he mentioned dreading having to move out of the City or the Region to find work. His mother was ill, and his family had sold almost everything they owned to keep her in a facility where she could get the care she needed."

Adam thought about what Aria said. He didn't know Damen well at all, having talked to him for the longest unbroken stretch during his hour-long interview when he was being considered for the project.

"Well, it sounds like the offer he had was enough to get him to leave. I understand wanting to be close to family and your parents. If mine were still around I'd want to be able to see them too. Maybe he decided the money was worth moving to the Cascadia Region," Adam offered.

Aria shook her head slowly from side to side, looked down, and answered, "That's what I thought at first, too. Maybe it was just about the money, but I also don't know how much more he could have possibly been offered at another company. I don't know what Adaptech is paying him." Her eyes flicked to him as she said this, non-verbal recognition that they were prohibited from talking about compensation by their employment contract. "But I do know it's expensive to migrate to another Region, especially a corporate one. Expensive enough Damen would have to be making about thirty percent more than what I'm making just to make it possible, let alone worth his while. I have over ten years of professional experience. Damen was fresh out of university. The math just doesn't add up." She clutched a glass of water and stared down into it, distressed.

Adam worked to suppress a frown. As manager of the project, he was privy to compensation data. He struggled with whether to tell Aria that Damen was paid slightly more than she, thanks to the racist, misogynistic LaMont, who hadn't even wanted to bring her on board in the first place. Adam had to negotiate with LaMont to pay her twenty-five percent more than LaMont wanted and considered it a minor miracle he had succeeded. As it was, Aria was the lowest-paid member of the team for no reason but LaMont's prejudice.

Aria didn't give him the chance to divulge anything, however. "Also, I—" She looked to Dej, who tightened his arm around her shoulder and nodded, as if to let her know she could tell Adam. "I ran a trace on the message that supposedly came from Damen. Sorry, I know that's not allowed, but I couldn't help myself. I had to know. It definitely came from his dome, but I couldn't find any kind of geotag on it at all, which makes it impossible to prove where the message originated. It seems odd that Damen would go to the trouble of hiding the origin of a simple farewell message." Adam was surprised Dej and Aria would trust him enough to bring their concerns to his attention, but he chalked it up to his demeanor of integrity and as a byproduct of the courage he had shown by standing up to LaMont earlier that afternoon.

They sat with the air suspended in silence between them like a crossbow pulled back, about to fire. Adam finally said, "I appreciate you letting me know. I'll do my best to find some answers. You need to be careful about who you tell, even talking about it between the two of you, especially at work. There are ears everywhere." This last line was punctuated by his raised finger, circled in midair.

Being overly analytical had its downsides, and Adam was intimately familiar with the majority of them, particularly the downside of paranoia. He spent his entire trip home lost in thought, attacking different possibilities from all angles. Hana was gone on a business trip, not to return until the following week, which allowed him to continue his pondering uninterrupted from the comfort of his flat. Adam went through his evening routine from muscle memory, teeth brushed and flossed without any conscious thought, sheets pulled back, bed occupied, and finally fell into a restless slumber, the scent of sweet musk stuck in the back of his nose.

Damen Theda

Adam opened his eyes. His hands were clasped in his lap. He faced a screen filled with line after line of code. He did not recognize the bare cubicle, with nothing more than a desk, a chair, and the screen in front of him. The walls of the cubicle, beige and unremarkable, were tall and topped with a translucent white dome to let diffused light enter from above. Disoriented, Adam reached up and felt two smooth surfaces encompassing the back of his scalp. A third bisected the top of his head and ended in a round circle on his hairline. The arms met in a fourth circle under his skull's occipital bump.

This was his cube at the Lightcap project, Adam was sure of it. He turned to look at the code on the computer screen, but it was jumbled, washed out by a glow seeming to emanate from everything around him. *This must be a dream*, Adam thought. He noticed a squiggled line added to the ones already on the screen. *That's interesting*, he thought, and another line appeared.

Adam suddenly heard cries of desperation, sounding far off and muffled like the screams of a jet engine passed through several thick walls. He slid open the opaque door separating him from the larger room and stepped into a row of a cube farm, each cubicle like the last, their bubbled tops giving the appearance of a room full of eggs in a large, open carton. Adam walked down the walled row.

"Hello?" Adam called out to the seemingly empty area. The word died shortly after it left his mouth, absorbed by the beige carpet lining the cubicle exterior walls. He pulled open the doors of several cubes to find each one empty, save for the same types of desk, screen, and chair that had been in his own.

Adam heard another cry, clearer and filled with pain, rather than the desperate anger of the last one. The sound of shuffled feet truncated with a dull thud followed, coming from one of the cubes. Adam raced to throw open door after door, finding nothing behind them but the desks, chairs, and screens displaying the same blurred chunk of code he had seen in his office. Adam made it to the last row of cubicles, where the first door he opened revealed a man slumped against the floor, Lightcap lying next to him.

Adam turned the man over and discovered with horror the face of Damen Theda. Dark red blood flowed from his nose and mixed with a milky fluid from his ears. Damen, still alive, shook slightly. More blood slid down the side of his face with each blink of his unfocused eyes. "HELP! I need help!" shouted Adam, the sound of his voice muted against the enclosed walls of corporate solitude. Adam heard rushed footsteps and the sound of heavy boots on thin carpet as two men rounded the corner. Blues, uniformed with batons dangling from their hips, hands readied on the holsters of their pistols. One rushed to Damen, the other to Adam.

The man tending to Adam pulled him from the cubicle and spun him in a circle, and as his eyes flicked to the Lightcap a look of relief spread across his face. The other man, the one with Damen, said, "This one woke up. His device is off." Adam turned at the sound of the voice and watched, unable to intervene, as the Blue drew his revolver and pointed it at Damen's forehead, its barrel resting where the Lightcap's front bubble usually lay.

POP.

Adam jolted awake, his bed sheet stuck to his chest with warm sweat. He clutched at his heart as tears formed in the corners of his eyes. He shook his head and tried to convince himself it was only a dream, even as he felt that what he had just experienced had the distinct footprint of a memory, similar to a long forgotten moment from childhood brought back into hazy recollection by a smell or sound. He jumped out of bed, making it to the bathroom just as his stomach expelled his dinner and scotch in fetid chunks against toilet water, sounding like gravel thrown repeatedly into a deep puddle.

The cement floor of his bathroom was cold and rough under his hand. Adam pressed the back of his head flat against the textured grey wall. His chest heaved with breath caught in choked gasps as he wept. Aria and Dej were right. Adam sat this way until his senses returned and the throbbing at his temples subsided. At some point, he pushed off from the floor and got to his feet, livid and filled with thoughts of righteous retribution. He would find those responsible and bring them to justice. He would slay entire legions of men, with his bare hands if necessary, if it would avenge the young man who had died while under his charge. But first, he needed proof there had been a crime.

Finding Damen's address was easy enough. He was a registered voting shareholder, and voter registrations were public information available to anyone with a connection to the mesh. Though it was meant to assist in political fundraising, it allowed Adam to find his destination without accessing Adaptech's employee database.

Minutes later, his clothes hastily thrown on, Adam was out the door and gone. He had never been to Damen's but was fairly confident he could find the apartment, as he now had the address and a passing familiarity with the neighborhood. Adam pushed open the front door to his own building and stepped out into the freezing knives of wind and snow that buffeted his exposed skin. He walked with purpose, his footsteps echoing into alleys and off cars surrounding him. He was still angry, but as he walked his reasoning mind caught up with him. *It was just a dream*, he thought. *What else could it be*? His mind went back to the dream from almost a year ago, with its empty subway car, mysterious old man, and above all a note slipped into his pocket that did not seem to exist in reality. Then there was the Ensyn memo, pages upon pages of paper found in Nate's cubicle that may or may not exist. Why would this dream be any different from the others?

Adam wandered through street after street of row houses for what felt like hours, his resolve waning, until he came to a familiar cross-street that gave him a bearing to his destination. After checking the address, he walked around both sides of the building looking for any signs of life, but there were no lights or noise to suggest anyone was awake. Adam wasn't sure of the time, having rushed out of his apartment without grabbing any devices or checking a clock, but the silence surrounding him suggested the middle of the night. Damen's apartment was on the right side of the first floor of a converted row house, now a fourplex, that looked as if it were a thousand years old. Adam quietly walked up to the window to the left of the front door. He tried to open the window but failed, its wood solidly lodged in its track, layers of paint added over decades bonding the boards together.

He had similar luck with the side window, which opened an inch, stopped, and stubbornly refused to go back into place or up any further. He climbed the fence barricading the back yard and met the same resistance from the window adjacent the back door. Adam considered going back home, then felt emboldened by the privacy provided by the high fence and the lack of light in the back yard. *At this point, I have to know,* he thought as he picked up a smooth rock in the garden, cold and heavy against his palm. He turned it in his hand, feeling its weight and shape before throwing it in a tight, straight line at the window. It struck with a crash, broken shards flashing reflected moonlight as they fell. Adam heard glass sprinkling on metal, accompanied by the slide of rock over cheap linoleum. A dog barked in the distance, but there was no other indication his actions had alerted anyone. Adam walked up the steps to the back porch while wrapping his jacket around his arm, then cleared the remaining pieces of shattered window away and climbed through. *As efficient as any professional burglar,* he thought bitterly.

Adam's eyes struggled to adjust to the lack of light. He climbed over the sink and dropped down to the floor, boots crunching with each step, grinding slivers of glass into dust as he made his way farther into the flat. Pale moonlight and neon colors from far-off ad zeps came in through the window, providing enough light for him to see that the room was completely empty. A set of saloon doors separating the kitchen from the rest of the house emitted a long high-pitched shriek as he parted them. He stepped through into another empty room, his eyes playing tricks on him as ghosts danced in shimmers of light coming in through the window. Adam walked from one corner of the room to the other to satisfy himself that nothing was nothing there. The building heater kicked on, permeating the room with the scent of burnt bark.

Damen's apartment consisted of four rooms: kitchen, bedroom, living room, and bathroom. All were empty, with the exception of a toothbrush on the back of the top shelf in the bathroom medicine cabinet. The toothbrush was odd but did nothing to solve the mystery of Damen's disappearance. Adam couldn't find anything suggesting foul play or a rushed exit. *And why would I?* he wondered, and felt his face flush with embarrassment for breaking and entering an empty apartment in the middle of the night.

The floorboards creaked as he made a second pass through each room, tracing his hands along walls and windowsills as he searched for any type of clue. Adam jerked his head toward the front of the house at what sounded like a jiggled doorknob, but it was just the venetian blinds swinging against the window frame, moved by air from the heating vent. *I need to get out of here,* he concluded.

Adam made his way back to the kitchen, walked toward the window and began to climb over the sink, positioned to make his exit, when he noticed faint writing scratched on the frame under the lip of the windowsill. He moved closer and squinted to see the letters under the dim moonlight.

It read "ms = no enemy".

Adam had no idea what this meant. He delved into the darkest corners of his memory to remember anyone he knew with the initials MS, or what the phrase "no enemy" might mean. The letters might have been written long before by someone other than Damen as a notation or inside joke. He did not want to misinterpret these letters as being related to Damen's abrupt disappearance if they were not. Adam remembered his visit there was the result of a nightmare, and he grimaced at how foolish he was. He had left his home in the middle of the night, wandered around until he found what he thought was Damen's apartment, broke a window to get in, and then walked around the empty rooms several times in an attempt to uncover . . . what? A conspiracy? A nefarious plot? Evidence of foul play? Yes, evidence of foul play, at least. Adam could not shake the suspicion there had been some.

All Adam had found were empty rooms, a lone toothbrush, and nonsensical letters etched in a wood window frame. He thought back to the solemn conversation with Aria and Dej, their earnestness, their minds sincerely convinced that Damen had met some evil end at the hands of . . . someone. No one quite knew for sure. Maybe Damen just wanted to make a clean break, or to not suffer through awkward conversations with coworkers, forced laughter, and small talk with people he'd likely never see again.

But the dream had seemed real: the color of the blood, the urgent anger in the first cry he heard, the desperate sorrow in the second. The sound of the gunshot still echoed in Adam's mind, the copper smell of blood and gunsmoke. Adam thought back to the dream from almost a year ago of the empty subway car and the disheveled old man. It dawned on Adam that his dreams might not be the most reliable source of accurate information. He began to wonder the odd dreams might represent. Apprehension? Fear of death or being forgotten? Adam didn't know, but as he emerged from the broken window in the full moonlight, visible to anyone who might have been looking, he felt the full embarrassment of having committed a crime based on a dream.

He felt downright sheepish by the time he got home, the cold walk back to his flat filled with silent curses and self-criticisms. He hadn't brought his dome or wallet, so he had no way to call or to pay for a ride. Adam walked with his collar tightened around his neck, his head down as if to gird against the strong wind, which seemed to change direction with his every turn, slowing his progress. His path from point A to point B took him through some parts of New Metra City he would not normally care to visit even in the daytime. On one block, Adam was sure he walked past a Cloud house, the distinctive cinnamon sweet scent of the drug mixed with the burnt chlorine smell of its ignition. Silent figures watched him from the front porch as he passed, their narrowed eyes following from right to left until he was gone from their sight.

Adam's heart nearly stopped when he pulled open his door and saw the back of a long-haired woman in his living room. He flinched as she abruptly spun around to face him. It was Hana. She rushed him and jumped, her arms wrapped around his shoulders, her legs around his waist. He hadn't expected that, and let out an involuntary "oof!" as she slammed against him. They both almost fell against his door, but Adam caught his balance for both of them in time.

"Holy shit! There you are! I was so worried about you! Don't you know it's the middle of the night?" she sobbed, her words strung together without thoughts of spacing or breath. Her lips pressed against his neck, her face bent down to the side under his jawline. Adam thought he felt a warm tear as she pressed her cheek against his. Hana unlocked her legs and stepped back down to cold floor, releasing his neck to look at him, her eyes suspicious. "Where were you? I just got back in and I was going to come surprise you, but you were gone. It's almost four in the morning." She continued probing his face with her eyes.

A refreshed mind could have probably created a better excuse, some kind of believable story. Adam's mind was anything but refreshed. "I-I couldn't s-s-sleep. Went for a w-walk," he stuttered, his body's way of protesting both his exhausted state and the chill he still felt down to his bones. Adam shivered and pulled his jacket pulled even tighter, its stitched seams near splitting. He willed warmth back into his numb fingers and toes. When he felt his chattering teeth wouldn't provide percussion to his speech, he added, "It was colder than I expected, and I got lost." He praised himself internally for appending something plausible to his excuse.

Oddly, Hana didn't seem to doubt him. She hugged Adam again, his chin resting on the top of her head, both their gazes directed to his left. His wallet and dome sat on the kitchen counter, within eyeshot. Adam saw them about a split second before Hana did. His stubble gripped her long, dark hair as she pulled away, her eyes raised to meet his.

"Why didn't you take your wallet or your dome? At first I was worried you were with another woman," Hana said. "Now I'm just worried. Is everything all right?"

Adam cursed his haste. Besides being inconvenient, his lack of foresight now made his story much less believable, since Hana and anyone who knew him for more than a day knew he wouldn't go anywhere without his dome. She had even joked before about how Adam would face a moral dilemma if a fire broke out in his apartment and he was forced to choose between rescuing her or his precious device. From what Adam could recall, he had given her a sarcastic response, telling her it was absurd even to ask such a question because he could always buy a new dome. "But now that you mention it," he had said, "I do really like the way it fits against the back of my head, and it would take some time to break in a new one." She had punched or slapped him, he couldn't remember which.

"I'm fine," Adam responded, trying to exude confidence in a statement he didn't believe to be true. "I promise. I know it may be hard to believe, but I need you to trust me. I was having a hard time sleeping. I had this crazy dream and I had to go check it out. I can't really tell you more than that." His eyes turned down with this last sentence. He wanted to tell her, but he knew it wouldn't be right to involve her in his paranoid delusions—not to mention it would be a breach of his employment contract if he were to tell her why he went to Damen's that night. The truth was not his friend, he reflected sadly.

Hana's lips squeezed together and her brow dropped to provide Adam a look of disapproval mixed with frustration. She pressed: "Is it something with work? I would like to know why my boyfriend wandered out in the middle of the night without taking anything with him, even a coat appropriate for the weather, coming back here shaking uncontrollably with purple fingers."

Adam sighed. Hana was right, of course, but he didn't feel he could or should get into it with her and wasn't really sure what to say to get her to drop it. "Yes, there are some things stressing me out at work. I can't really . . . talk to you about any of it," he said, almost saying he couldn't remember, catching himself at the last minute. "I wish I could, but those non-disclosure agreements . . . I could lose my job." He hoped this would end the discussion, since she was very proud of the prestige and wealth that came with their careers. "Besides, you're a lawyer. You know how it is."

Hana didn't look completely satisfied, but she did look as if the prospect of dating an unemployed man did not appeal to her. Doing his best to steer her thoughts down that path, Adam said, "The fact I've even told you it's related to my job probably breaches some agreement. I really should stop talking about it. Please trust me, I'm fine. I just had to check on something." He delivered these last lines with a flat voice and even eyes, in an effort to imply that he was genuinely scared. She relented, then withdrew shortly after to her own apartment. Adam sighed once she left, frustrated with himself for acting like a freak and with Hana for coming back from her trip early, that night of all nights. He already felt like an idiot, and having to answer her questions did not alleviate that sentiment.

With a groan, Adam collapsed onto his bed. He could still taste the scent of burnt bark from Damen's furnace. He briefly wondered why the scent stuck with him before falling asleep.

Part Two
Muse

"To feed your muse, then, you should always have been hungry about life since you were a child. If not, it is a little late to start."
—Ray Bradbury

Suspicion

Adam closed his eyes and, one odd sensation later, his alarm went off. Monday was waking him again. Despite his odd dream and reaction to it, another weekend had departed, blurred and mixed with every other moment from the past year. That morning's subway commute contained no old man or flashes of false memories and culminated in the same rocket trip to the top floor of the Adaptech high-rise, the same solitary walk down the hallway to room 4C. The conference table, the faces seated in the same places, made his life feel monotonous yet cyclical. Adam felt he could just relax and let the flow of his routine carry him without any effort on his part. It was just easier to let go. What did he really need to do, if everything at work was unknown to him?

Adam was shocked out of his stupor by the face of Velim, who sat across the table from him when he removed his Lightcap at the end of the day. No one else was in the room besides the two of them.

She smiled and said, "Hello, Adam."

"Hello," Adam said. "What am I doing here? Where is everyone?" He motioned to the empty chairs.

"Well, there are a few things we need to discuss," Velim said, her hands clasped in front of her, all business. "But first, I have a question for you: did you go somewhere early Saturday morning?"

Adam took a deep breath, then another. He wasn't sure how much Velim knew about his activities, but the fact she was asking meant she knew something. He needed to tread carefully, because if he told her a provable lie things could become very complicated. "No, I didn't go anywhere, but I did leave the house." He hoped this half-truth would be enough for her, but her raised eyebrows and expectant eyes prompted Adam to continue. "I couldn't sleep, so I went for a walk. I left some of my things at the house, and I got lost." He paused. "I don't mean any disrespect, but none of this is your business. Why are you asking me these questions?"

Velim looked amused. "Adam, you don't understand. *You* are our business. Well, your mental health is, anyway. We're asking these questions because we have a vested interest in the function and utility of the Lightcap product, the security of the v6 code, and your ability to lead the project. Is there anything you think we should know? Have you noticed any odd thought patterns lately? Hallucinations? Have you *remembered* anything?" She delivered her last question with an accusatory tone, or so it seemed to Adam. *You're just being paranoid*, he told himself.

"No to all," he said with an exasperated sigh. "I'm done answering these questions. It bothers me that you would insinuate I am somehow causing issues with the project after giving me nothing but glowing reviews and feedback up to this point. If what I was dealing with was any of your business, or involved your caps and domes, I'd tell you. I'm leaving now, unless you have any more questions."

"Make sure you do tell us," Velim said calmly. "May I remind you that part of your contract states you must tell us immediately if you believe the Lightcap is causing any issues. I have a vid meeting with LaMont from his office at Metra Corp. You're dismissed."

Velim turned her attention to her notetab, no doubt entering notes about her conversation with Adam. As he got up from the table, the video screen started to materialize against the white of the wall. He left quickly, not wanting to see or talk to LaMont, still annoyed from when the CEO had threatened him at the end of the week before.

Adam made his way down to the ground level. As he exited the building, its giant door trailing behind him as if pushing him out, he saw Aria standing about twenty feet to his right, pressed against the side of the building. She saw him at the same time, then summoned him with a small jerk of her head. As he walked up to her, she started to turn and said, "Let's walk. We should probably get away from here." They threaded through the rush-hour crowd, becoming part of the throng of people walking down the street. Several blocks away from Adaptech, Aria whispered, "What was that about? Velim making you stay after, I mean."

"I have no idea," Adam said, annoyed. "She asked me if I left my house early Saturday morning, which I did, so I admitted to it. She already knew the answer. I think it was a test to see if I'd be honest with her. Then she asked me if I had noticed any odd thoughts, or if I've been seeing things." They walked on in silence for a few paces. "She also wanted to know if I've remembered anything," Adam said, wondering if he should tell Aria about his strange dreams or excursion to Damen's apartment in this middle of the night.

"Well, have you? Been seeing things or hearing voices or remembering stuff, I mean?" Aria looked concerned, as if she had wondered the same thing about him.

"Damn it, no," Adam said. "Have I been acting strange lately? I don't feel any different." He tried not to take his frustration with Velim out on Aria. Aria was next to him. Velim was not.

"No. Sorry," Aria replied. "Just asking. I'm worried about all of us. For a project that's supposed to be stress-free, I feel pretty on edge. You seem to be going through something similar." Her concerned look remained, but Adam understood it now. She wasn't just concerned for him but for herself. Probably for Dej too. She changed the subject. "I can probably guess the answer, but have you found out anything about Damen?" They continued walking as Adam formed his answer carefully.

"No. Not on the mesh, and there hasn't been any public activity on Damen's dome since last week." He stopped short of telling her he had gone to his house. "I'm not sure what that means." They walked on, oblivious to the crowds of commuters around them.

"Adam, can I trust you?" Aria asked. Her question caught him off guard with its urgency, as if she were bursting with a secret. He nodded in agreement. She continued. "I went to Damen's house last night, after it got dark."

"You *what?*" Adam exclaimed, his eyes bulging. "I said I'd look into it. I can't have you going off and doing things that could get you—and the rest of us by extension—in trouble." His expression softened, and he chuckled, "Now that we got that out of the way, what did you find?" He did not mention he had been there the night before.

"Nothing," Aria said in helpless frustration. "Absolutely nothing. The back window was broken, so someone else may have been there before me. I spent four hours scouring the place from top to bottom, until I heard footsteps on the ceiling above. The upstairs neighbor must get up early for work."

Adam thought about how best to phrase what he wanted to ask Aria, but he knew he would have to give it away to get what he wanted—it was all or nothing. He sighed and asked, "Did you see the toothbrush or the letters on the windowsill?" Aria looked at him with suspicion and accusation on her face, or so Adam thought. He answered her next question before she had a chance to ask it by saying, "Yes. I was there. I'm the one who broke the window."

Aria gave him a look she had never given him before, of either respect or incredulity. Her next words erased his doubts about her intent: "Smart *and* you have balls. I'm surprised. Don't take this the wrong way, but Dej and I had you pegged for a company man at first. I mean, I've known you long enough now, but not well, you know? And with this being your first time in a manager gig—I just figured you'd be all gung ho to prove yourself to the suits. But I saw your face the day Damen disappeared. Dej and I talked about it, and decided you were an honest guy. We were already going to talk to you about Damen, but when you showed up at Glass several shades lighter after talking to LaMont, that sealed it up. What did he say to you, anyway?"

Adam took a minute to decide he was going to tell her the truth. Given what he had already admitted to her, he knew he would be in considerable trouble if she planned to turn him in to Adaptech. He also admired her for the things she had been through, things that would have broken most people, and that clouded his judgment a little. He decided he didn't have much to lose at this point. "He threatened to fire me. Well, he actually said he'd end me, and I'd be done. I'm pretty sure he was serious. Don't plan on finding out, even though he was probably just blowing smoke or having a bad day. LaMont doesn't really matter. I've only had to interact with him a handful of times in over a decade. What I'm really interested in is what you found in Damen's apartment. Didn't find, whatever. I was only there for maybe half an hour. Also, you didn't answer my question: did you see the toothbrush or the letters under the windowsill? There also should have been broken glass from the back window in the kitchen."

Aria shook her head. "No, I didn't. Now you have me wondering. I was thorough, and there wasn't any broken glass. I had nightview glasses with me, and I was wearing heavy boots. I would've seen it or heard it cracking when I walked. I checked all the windowsills too. As far as I could tell, the place had been scrubbed. What were the letters under the windowsill?"

Adam and Aria discussed the mystery as they moved on the sidewalk, as if products on an assembly line of pedestrian momentum, their warm breath visible in small puffs that disappeared into the chill air. Adam enjoyed being able to talk to someone about the situation, even if he couldn't shake the feeling there might be some penalty for it down the road. After they had walked for what seemed like a hundred blocks, they reached Aria's apartment, in a dingy building with rusted siding in a forgotten part of town—one of the neighborhoods where even the Blues seldom ventured. Adam remarked to himself that Aria was most likely the wealthiest person on her block, even as one of the lowest-paid people on his team. Her modest home was certainly a step up from the dumpsters and stairwells she had slept in when she lived on the streets. He tried to picture Aria steering clear of Blues and regular citizens, most of whom would kick and spit on a beggar before giving her any credits or food.

Not that Adam could see Aria as a beggar; she didn't seem the sort. Aria was too proud, too resourceful for begging, he felt. At the moment, he was impressed by the thick steel of her front door, along with the barred windows protecting an immaculate if understated interior. She guessed his thoughts. "Hey, you didn't exactly rescue me from poverty," she said. "I did that myself. There's a reason I live here. The rent is cheap and I'm out of the way of nosy neighbors and bored Blues. You have any idea what it's like living in a posh burb as a woman of color? Plus, I get to spend money on stuff like this." Aria opened a closet door, then pounded its inner wall with a closed fist in a triangular pattern. This caused the wall to break its invisible seal and move back softly on hidden hinges to reveal a surprisingly large secret room.

Dej, inside the room, turned to smile at them. "Hey, guys." He looked at Aria, pointed at his dome, and said, "Thanks for letting me know you were bringing a guest."

"No problem," Aria replied. "Did you get the transcript of our conversation?" She walked over and sat next to Dej on a swivel chair, then turned to look at Adam, as if to say she knew he wanted to demand an explanation, but would have to wait another minute before doing so.

"I did, thanks."

"Maybe you should answer Adam's question," Aria smirked at Dej, as she tilted her head in Adam's direction. "He's probably wondering why I'd broadcast our conversation over the mesh, through Adaptech's servers." Adam nodded, feeling faint.

Dej smiled broadly, his teeth nearly blinding Adam, contrasting sharply with the dim light in the room. "So, I've made a few modifications to our domes. I've written code to enable device-to-device transmission. There's a pulse wave sent out over mesh-enabled devices, like radar, as a way of seeing what devices are within range and measure the shortest amount of hops to the destination. I found a way to use that protocol to deliver targeted messages, text only, very low bandwidth, to a specific dome. If I install the software on your device, you'll be able to send and receive messages. Matches to your neural pattern, too, so if someone steals your device they won't be able to access the hidden program. Best part is that it uses the pulse wave to map the shortest path from device to device and leaves no trace on the nodes used for transmission."

Adam was impressed, but he also wondered what the penalty would be if they were caught. Of course, he had already done enough to ruin his career and get blacklisted, at least in Metra Region. Adam figured he didn't have much more to lose at this point. He also couldn't shake the feeling that something terrible had happened to Damen, or forget the images of something terrible happening, no matter how many times he reminded himself his main source of evidence was nothing more than a dream. *Maybe I am crazy,* he thought, though he doubted insanity would serve as a defense if they were caught.

His thoughts of the trouble he could get into caused him to miss Aria's first few words, as she said, "... to get our hands on one of those prototypes. Just to see inside it, try and get a code dump. I don't give a damn if I get fired and sued back into the gutters. I measured and marked off small dots on my fingers with a pen so I could get the dimensions of the Lightcap as we handled it each day. I'll use my 3D printer to create a replica of one and leave it in my bag in room 4C when we go wherever it is they take us each morning. When we get back and take them off, I think I can get clearheaded soon enough to drop mine before putting it on the table. If not, one of you will have to cause a distraction. I'll switch the real Lightcap for the fake, then bring it back here where we can try to figure out exactly what in the hell it does. Dej has something else you'll be interested in."

Dej seemed excited for this one, as if he had saved the best for last, or was finally allowed to tell a long-kept secret.

"We copied a dozen terabytes of data from an archive on LaMont's storage node," Dej revealed with a look of pride. "Had it for over a month now. It's encrypted, but I've got a brute-force crack running on it, so we'll see. It had connections logged from Metra Corp and Adaptech headquarters, so there could be anything in there. You want a copy? I can transfer it to your dome when I load the point-to-point messaging software. If we all coordinate it might cut down on some processing time."

Adam's eyes widened. He briefly considered turning them in and using his having done so as a bargaining chip to have his own transgressions forgiven, but he had too much respect for Dej and Aria to do that. He also knew there was more to this story and that it would be difficult to uncover on his own. Something about the far-off look on Velim's face, the way LaMont had responded to his questions about Damen's disappearance with threats of termination, and the deliberate deflections about how Lightcap actually worked made him want to know what the device was really doing to them all.

Adam, Aria, and Dej agreed to work on cracking LaMont's encrypted data, and Aria made a note to double check the measurements before beginning work on printing a Lightcap replica. They decided it would be best to wait until the next post-shift meeting in three weeks' time, in case Aria didn't come to her senses quickly enough to drop the device while lowering it to the table. This gave them extra time to make contingency plans.

Adam felt excited as he made his way home with Dej's new point-to-point messaging code and terabytes of LaMont's encrypted data loaded on his dome. He walked quickly from Aria's neighborhood and caught the subway, the trip back to his flat full of worry and exhilaration, glad to finally feel the promise of answers, even if those answers meant throwing away everything he had worked to achieve. Adam had spent years at Adaptech working toward making a name for himself, but if LaMont and his fellow administrators could get rid of Damen, what would stop them from doing the same to him or anyone else on his team?

Adam got home well past dark and stumbled through his door, shaking his frost-bitten limbs to move his blood. He changed out of his work clothes into warm wool pants and a long sleeve cotton shirt, then brushed his teeth. He had just finished when there was a quiet knock at the door. Hana looked up at him and smiled when he opened the door, her expression one of apology. After their conflicts, she would usually be upset for a day or two, then request or grant forgiveness, depending on the situation.

She leaned in, kissed Adam on the cheek, and half whispered, "Hi. I thought I heard you come home. I just wanted to see you and apologize for getting upset a couple of days ago. It's not my place to push or to pry, and I definitely don't want to get you in trouble." Adam invited her in, and she sat down on his sofa. "Speaking of which," she continued, "you're home awfully late. Long day at the office?" This time her question seemed to hold nothing more than casual interest, as if making conversation.

Adam was caught by surprise. He had expected Hana to tell him she had forgiven him, not to apologize for her actions. He said, "It's no big deal. I'm not angry or anything. I just have to be mindful of staying within the bounds of my work agreements. I didn't have a long day at the office, I just went out after work." He sat down beside her on the couch.

"Were you with someone? Where'd you go?" she asked. This disturbed him.

"I went out for a drink with Dej," he said, doing his best to sound unconcerned, knowing a lie was better than the truth. He could not tell her what they had talked about, but she had shown signs of jealousy in the past, so Adam thought it best to leave out any mention of Aria. Dej was also one of the few people whose name she knew. Everyone knew Dej.

Adam was surprised she didn't push it further. Instead she asked, "Oh, and were you home earlier today? I thought I heard you, but when I came over no one was here."

"Nope, wasn't me," Adam replied. He momentarily wondered if someone had actually been in his apartment earlier, but he dismissed the possibility. She seemed to believe him. They laid down together and Hana drifted off to a quiet sleep. Adam lay awake, his nose still tickled by the musky scent in his apartment, wondering what he had got himself into.

Escape

Groggy, sleep-filled eyes opened. *Was Hana here last night?* Adam wondered. He had lost track of time. He reached over and felt nothing but cold sheets. He struggled to recall the sequence of events making up the past several weeks, but each cycle of night and day blurred into the next, like cream stirred into coffee. *Speaking of coffee,* Adam thought as he got out of bed, rubbing his face and eyes.

Another morning trek began with an elevator ride down to the ground floor, Adam's feet pushed forward step by step with motivation which seemed to come from nowhere and lasted just long enough to bring him to the subway car. The slow back and forth rocking of the car threatened to lull him back to sleep. Just as Adam's eyes were about to succumb to gravity, the subway car screeched to a long, slow halt. His stop and another day at work lay ahead of him.

The conspiratorial agreement he had made with Aria and Dej caused him tremendous anxiety, though they hadn't yet done anything. Adam's notetab was still running at home, as it had been for the past several days, cycling through millions of different combinations of words, letters, and phrases in an attempt to crack the password needed to decrypt LaMont's data, but the code remained unbroken.

Dej's hidden messaging system had provided novel pleasure at first, but this soon wore off as the threesome quickly found their conversation topics exhausted. None of them cared to emulate the news nodes by reporting nothing at all. The knowledge the system existed was still a comfort, though, and gave Adam the solace of knowing he was not alone.

As Adam entered room 4C, he was greeted by the gazes of his entire team. His eyes immediately went to Aria and Dej. They gave him no special greeting, no secret winks or knowing nods. They barely acknowledged him. Aria's eyes lifted from her notetab screen, quick enough to miss had he not been paying attention. Dej gave a brief smile, and then was back to his animated conversation with Jared Tinge about sports, including insults traded on the nature of the sexual tendencies of the other team's players, complete with insinuated relations of a maternal nature.

Adam did not remember having seen such joviality in room 4C. He had never excelled at social interactions, so it was possible he hadn't noticed or had been too distracted by his own thoughts. Regardless, the happy noises of conversation immediately stopped when the door swung open to reveal Sera Velim, with Roman LaMont a half step behind her as they walked into the room. LaMont's face carried a huge grin. Adam could not recall ever seeing him look that happy. Velim looked tired, her expression difficult to read. They both took a seat, she at the head of the table, he off to the side. LaMont's eyes lost focus as Velim addressed the room.

"Good morning, team. Today we will be doing some physical and neurological assessments while you're under Lightcap. We wanted to let you know ahead of time, since you may experience some slight aches and discomfort after your shift this evening. We didn't want you to worry. Are there any questions?"

Several heads shook. An uneasy silence stagnated the room. Adam raised his hand. Velim's eyebrows raised in response, as if she was surprised anyone would ask a question, particularly him. He decided not to wait for her acknowledgement and asked, "What kind of tests? I can't speak for anyone else in the group, but I get a physical twice a year, so why is this necessary?"

Velim was quick with her reply, as if she had rehearsed the canned response this exact question. "Well, of course we expect you're all taking good care of yourselves. Wouldn't want to bring undue hardship on the company by increasing our health care costs, would you? If you take a look at the employment agreement, you'll find a major aspect of the Lightcap testing is making sure it doesn't cause any issues with brain chemistry or physiology, or have deleterious effects on other systems in the body. We've performed psychological tests before, as you know. Today's test will include a physical component, so we wanted to be proactive about dealing with any questions you may have about the process." Her expression was blank as she said this, indicating no emotion. When Velim finished, she looked at LaMont.

LaMont stood up and barked, "All right, let's get started. We've taken the liberty of providing comfortable athletic shoes for each of you, so your performance won't be inhibited by dress shoes. Retrieve them from under your seat and put them on." After the group complied, LaMont continued. "Great. Put on your Lightcaps."

The last memory Adam had of the day was the sight of his arms lifting the Lightcap past his head. Then there was nothing but darkness.

Adam was sure his head had been split in two. He brought his hand to his forehead in response to the white-hot pulse of pain shooting from the top of his head to the bottom of his neck with each beat of his heart. He could feel that he wasn't wearing his dome or Lightcap. Adam's eyes worked to focus against the dim light and numbing pain in the center of his head. He realized he was at home, in his own bed. He also heard sounds of water against metal in his kitchen. He swung his legs off his side of the bed and sat up, only to gasp in pain as his head protested against the sudden motion. He gave serious thought to laying back down.

Several deep breaths helped Adam to gain his sense of balance, strength, and purpose, and he pushed off the bed. His body almost immediately crumbled back into the soft comfort of the edge of his mattress. Adam, caught off guard by the vertigo, regained his balance and stood up, bracing his arm against his dresser for support. Eventually he made it into the kitchen, and found Hana cutting vegetables as a pot of water boiled on the stove. She smiled at him and said, "Hi, honey. Feeling better? You were a ball of sunshine earlier." She playfully slapped him on the arm when she said this, and the pain that traveled upward from where his neck met his shoulder caused Adam to wince. Hana turned back to the vegetables, the knife in her hands tapping as it connected with the cutting board, green onions and carrots falling into sliced rows.

Adam tried to mask his confusion and responded, "I don't remember any of that. How long have I been here? Did someone bring me home?" Even as he asked, his vision dimmed. Then there was a bright flash and he was between two men, their arms secured under his own, his weight carried by their strength. Adam's feet scraped against the frayed carpet in the hallway outside his apartment, unable to move under their own power. Just as quickly, he was back in his kitchen hearing Hana's voice echoing off his brick walls.

" . . . Came home, said you were tired, then lay down. You seemed really upset, so I thought I'd make your favorite meal while you napped." Adam noticed the smell of baking chicken. Hana had never apologized by cooking for him. Even as the scent of dinner filled him with hunger, Adam caught another odor in the air, pungent and familiar. He could almost taste it. Hana distracted him from trying to place it by saying, "Dinner will be done soon. Normally I'd ask you to make some drinks or set the table, but you're in rough shape. Why don't you sit down?"

Adam's legs still wobbled, his head still throbbed in agony. He didn't require much convincing. Adam sat at his dining room table, his head down, and rubbed the back of his neck. Then he experienced another flash. This time he was in the hallway outside his apartment, being dragged across the threshold by the same muscled men. Hana was there, watching as they brought him in. She followed behind them quietly as they took him into his bedroom and dropped him against the mattress with a loud *thunk*. The sound in his mind brought him back to reality.

"You're sure no one was with me when I got here? Did I talk about anything other than being tired?" He asked while rubbing his forehead.

With his head down, Adam thought his voice might have been too muffled for Hana to hear. He wanted an answer, even though he was sure she planned to stick with her story regardless of the truth. He turned to his right to ask again, so she'd have a better chance of hearing him, just in time to see her grim face and a glint of light from the knife in her hand. Hana seemed lost in thought for a moment, then lunged at him. He shoved against the table on instinct, turning away from her, which pushed his chair against her and broke her momentum. Adam's aching body screamed at him, but he was able to knock her off balance and deflect the blade with the chair, save for a cut down the back of his right arm. He immediately stepped behind her and wrapped his arms around her protesting arms and torso. Hana raged and flailed against Adam, trying to kick him and hit his face with the back of her head at the same time.

"What are you doing?" Adam cried, his mind caught between shock and pain.

"You remember," Hana gasped, her small frame struggling to break free from his bear hug. She still held the knife in her right hand, but Adam evaded her attempts to dig its point into his hip. "You're not supposed to remember. Just give up—they're already on their way."

Blues! Adam thought. It had to be Blues, just as with Damen. He was fairly certain the outcome would be similar, or undesirable in any case. He had to figure out a way to deal with Hana then get the hell out of there. As Adam struggled to come up with a plan, Hana dropped, having lifted her legs abruptly while his arms weren't prepared. She hit the floor and rolled, but came to a rest sprawled out on her chest, unmoving. Adam kneeled down to turn her over, aghast. When he did so, she grabbed his sleeve. The knife's handle stuck out of her lower ribcage, its blade angled upward into her. Blood poured from the wound onto her clothes and his dining room floor. She hadn't accounted for the weapon clasped in her dominant hand. *Why?* Adam wondered, horror-struck.

Hana blinked her eyes rapidly as her mouth opened and closed, but little sound escaped beyond a gurgled sigh, low and weakening. Adam had planned to incapacitate her or knock her out; he hadn't wanted to kill her. Her hand on his sleeve was losing its grip. He watched as the light behind her eyes faded and her blinking stopped. It was then he noticed writing, etched into the plastic bubble resting beneath her ear, reading "PROTOTYPE" in small letters. Hana was wearing not a dome but a Lightcap! He pulled it off and shoved it in his pocket.

At least we don't have to make one now, Adam thought, *but if she was telling the truth, the Blues are almost here.* He rushed to the window and looked down to the street, but saw nothing more than the usual traffic. *They must want to keep this quiet,* Adam thought. *Can't have people asking too many questions.* He ran into the hallway outside his apartment and turned into the main passageway. The stairwell door was just beyond the elevator. He was almost halfway there when the elevator dinged. *Shit,* he thought. He was right by Hana's door, which he tried frantically. The door yielded, and Adam pushed it back against its frame quietly, holding his breath. His heartbeat rushed in his ear, its downbeats filled in by the clomp of heavy boots—two sets as far as he could tell—passing by Hana's door.

As soon as the Blues passed, he inched the door open. When he saw them turn the corner toward his apartment, he threw open the door and sprinted past the elevator toward the staircase, doing his best not to make noise. As Adam reached the stairwell door, he heard men shouting. Giving up secrecy, Adam threw the door open, slamming it against the wall. He took the steps two, three at a time, his bare feet against the concrete floor, his hands gripping the cold steel of the railing. When he was halfway down each flight, he leapt over the railing to the next floor down, halving the number of stairs in each set. He heard rushed footsteps on the stairs several floors above which indicated he was not yet safe. Nameless Blues pursued him, intent on his capture or worse. He needed time to think.

Adam made it to the ground level, his frantic and desperate descent ended. His feet found purchase against the smooth tile in his building lobby. He flew through the front door out into the street, happier than ever before to live in a part of Metra City boasting an active night scene. He heard the stairwell door bang against its concrete walls and shouted voices echoing after him. Adam took a hard right, headed straight into a crowd of people, his shoulder down and pointed ahead, battering through the group, its cries of outrage failing against his deaf ears and panicked mind.

Crouching low to the ground, Adam made his way through the moving pedestrians in a zigzag path intended both to hide his location and avert collisions. His neck and arm continued to throb, but he decided his stiffness was preferable to a gunshot wound. The Blues caused a commotion behind him as they worked their way through the crowd. One block ahead lay the entrance to the subway. Adam kept as low to the ground as he could while still jogging toward the station. He made it down the steps and hopped the turnstile, knowing the cameras would capture his image as he cleared the horizontal bar, then jumped into the nearest subway car as the doors closed in what felt like one swift motion. Adam turned around to see one of the men chasing him, his partner no doubt still at street level. The man wore a long, dark jacket, and had his hand in his pocket, most likely wrapped around the grip of a gun. The man threw his head left and right, his eyes scanning every face within range. As the subway car screeched away from the station, its wheels on rail, the Blue turned back toward the stairs, appearing to give up.

Adam finally felt safe. He also felt as if he had run for hours, but in reality he had been sitting at his dining room table just ten minutes before. His heart still raced, but it slowed as his adrenaline lost its hold. He became more aware of his surroundings as he observed the people in the car. They were all lost in hushed conversations, in contrast to the detached aloofness Adam usually observed. Electronic games and domes, the typical distractions of city life, sat in pockets unused in a uniformity Adam had not seen before. He strained to hear the muted words of the passengers, most of which were lost amid the noises of the subway as it barreled down its designated path.

Only snippets of conversation were audible. Words like "Blues", "assassination", and "affair" popped out against the background. Though the people around him were quiet, he could tell from their nervous energy and facial expressions he had missed important news. Hana's Lightcap was in his left pocket. Adam considered putting it on so he could read news reports from the mesh, but he was afraid the signal might be traced. He also recognized the importance of maintaining control right now. Thinking of the Lightcap with disgust, Adam decided he never wanted that contraption on his head again, no matter the circumstance. He also reflected that his career at Adaptech had effectively ended.

Being an information junkie was terrible in times like these. Adam struggled to appear detached while he secretly tried to listen to the discussions going on around him. They all clashed together, making it impossible for Adam to follow any one track. Twenty different voices inundated him on the same subject, with words mangled against one another. Unable to contain his curiosity, he got off at the next stop, the soles of his feet slapping against wet concrete, discarded gum, and other trash, taking the stairs two at a time until he emerged at street level. Adam was glad to see an electronics store half a block away, its screens and notetabs behind the storefront window facing out, tuned to feeds from various mesh nodes.

A crowd had gathered around the shop, its eyes aimed at the screens. Adam silently considered the communal response to tragedy, that people were standing together even as they separately processed what had happened, to be the one good thing to come from bad events. Adam chose one of the feeds to watch, a screen containing the overly painted face of a blonde talking head. The precise movements of her lips implied well-spoken words, but Adam had to be satisfied with reading the captioned text, as the audio could not pass through the thick window of the shop.

"We have been able to confirm Tim Montery's body was found in a suite at the Waldorf-Astoria hotel," the text under the woman's grave face read. "We're still attempting to get answers about who else may have been in the room. For now, Metra Corp appears to be in the hands of Cora Slate, though initial reports indicated there was a second victim in the room, originally identified as Miss Slate. A spokeswoman for the Central Provisional Authority denies Montery or Slate was in the room. We'll have more updates as this story develops."

As the crowd murmured, Adam felt none of the shock he would expect to feel upon surprising news. Montery was dead. Slate too. He wasn't sure how he knew, but there wasn't a shred of doubt in his mind. The pain in his back strengthened, reinserting itself into his consciousness as a blast of light blinded him. Adam staggered back and sunk to his knees. Half of the crowd turned to look at him, the other half still lost in the dim glow of the screens as everything faded to black.

Adam's vision was set forward, off into the distance. Everything was clear, though he was not focused on any one thing in particular. Unlike before, he had no sense of autonomy, but was instead propelled, inch by inch, along a predetermined path. He progressed down the immaculately appointed hallway, willing himself to stop, only to be answered by the continued sound of his footsteps.

An armed man stood outside an ornate door, guarding its woodwork with his stone face and sidearm. As he gave Adam a knowing nod and opened the door, it dawned on Adam that the man was guarding what was behind the door, not the door itself. Adam's feet carried him through the open door and into the room beyond. He could see two figures asleep under white sheets, creating a rhythmic rise and fall as they breathed.

The man was on his back, the woman on her side, her right arm draped over the man's torso. Adam was shocked to recognize them as Tim Montery and Cora Slate. Soft smiles lingered at the corners of their mouths, exhausted and euphoric. As Adam's eyes were set forward, he saw motion in his periphery: his right arm was lifting of its own volition, his hand grasping the handle of a knife. Adam, a prisoner behind his own eyes, watched as his arm and hand again moved without being commanded, plunging the knife into the necks and chests of the slumbering forms.

Short cries and protecting hands erupted in a brief eruption of movement. The knife quickly dispatched these, slamming down again and again until the motion ceased. Blood ran and pooled everywhere: on Adam's hands and arms—he could taste it in his mouth. Blood spread on the white sheets and turned them a deep red. The bedroom door opened, and Adam saw the same armed man. The man's hand motioned and Adam's feet moved, again without any intent on his part. He tried to speed them up, slow them down, stop them; no matter what Adam tried his feet continued their path of progress, across the room, out the door, around the corner.

Adam snapped back to consciousness, groggy and lightheaded. He opened his eyes to see several people standing over him, their expressions ranging from worried to annoyed. No doubt they thought he was a drug user or a drunk. He struggled to his feet, his head and body crying in protest at the movement.

"Hey look, it's HIM!" a voice, seemingly disembodied, shouted from somewhere in the crowd. Adam tried to find the voice's source, but his eyes instead came to rest on one of the vid screens, where the feed displayed his face along with a caption imploring viewers to message the authorities with any information. "Someone message the Blues!" It sounded like the same voice, but Adam didn't wait around to find out. His feet pushed against the rough pavement, his arms wrenched away from prying hands. He again used the pedestrians to his advantage as the bloodthirsty cries of the crowd faded further away from him with each hurried stride.

Adam needed to make it to a safe place. Aria's was the only location he could think of which was both close and safe, unless they knew she was involved. He'd have to take the chance. Adam's head still throbbed with every movement, making it difficult for him to think. He needed a minute to gather his thoughts and figure out the safest way to reach Aria's, since his face was plastered all over the video nodes. People would be looking for him.

Several bags of trash rested against the wall of an alley to his right. Adam stacked the bags in a way that would shield him from the views of passersby, leaned against the brick wall of the alley, and slid into a seated position behind the trash. He took several long, deep breaths, willed his heart to stop trying to burst from his ribcage, and thought about his very long day full of unexpected surprises. Adam's ears buzzed; his arm was still tender and bleeding; his bare feet felt both hot from running and stone cold against the cracked cement of the alley.

At this moment, after struggling and losing adrenaline, Adam's body finally gave out. He was filled with horror as he realized he had murdered two people earlier that day in cold blood. Between his aches, pains, and sorrow-filled sobs, he missed the sound of approaching footsteps until they scraped to a halt directly in front of him.

"Hello, Adam," said a man's voice, emitted from a face bathed in shadow. Adam looked up and thought, *Too late to run. This is it. I'll die in this alley.* The man leaned down, a ramble-jambler in his hand, the side of his face illuminated by a line of light carried in from the street. Adam had seen the man's face in his dreams and on the subway. The disheveled old man spoke again: "Come with me, it's not safe here."

As the man placed the jambler around his neck, Adam once again fell into unconsciousness.

Assassin

Adam first became aware not of a painful or blinding light but a dull pressure. He next sensed his own heartbeat, ticking as a metronome he felt obliged to obey, to follow. He noticed his arms hurt, one more than the other. Adam winced as he reached over to feel the wound, sealed in gel that would dissolve as the skin regrew, where Hana had sliced him with the knife. The cut was deeper than he had originally realized.

Adam's eyes opened and a pattern came into focus, drop ceiling panels reflecting the light in the room. Breathing hurt. His clothes were different, made of soft linen. Memories rushed back to him. Hana had tried to kill him. He remembered her face, stern and emotionless with blade in hand, intent to end his life. Is that what he looked like when he had murdered Cora Slate and Tim Montery? Adam could remember killing them. Not clearly, but well enough to know it was true.

There were footsteps in the hall. Adam considered trying to flee, but there wasn't any fight left in his body. The door opened, soft light from beyond spilling through in diverging lines, split by a shadow. The man stepped into the room and closed the door. Adam watched him reach over and twist a knob. The light on the ceiling responded with more intensity against the walls, which brought the man's face into focus.

Adam recognized the eyes from pictures, but nothing else. The ears, lips, nose, and even teeth looked different, but the eyes had the same fire in them he had seen in records and footage. The man looked neat and proper, cleaned up since their first meeting on the subway. The man's frame was shorter than and not quite as wide as Adam remembered. Then again, Adam reflected, the old man had sported a beard and several more layers of clothing the last time their paths crossed. Adam recognized him: Doctor Pavel Troyka.

"I'm glad you're awake, Adam," Troyka said as he sat next to the bed. "There's a lot to talk about. You're probably aware Tim Montery and Cora Slate were killed yesterday. Yes, you did it." Adam flinched when the elder man said this, and tears began to form at the corners of his eyes. Troyka continued, "It wasn't anything you could control or stop. In fact, without the low level doses of Cloud I've been giving you, you wouldn't remember any of it."

"You've been giving me drugs?" Adam asked, alarmed. "Why would you do—" He stopped, silenced by Troyka's raised hand.

"Yes. In your toothpaste, deposited via syringe. It was the only way to dose you every day, or close to it. I'm lucky you have good hygiene, or else I would've had a much more difficult time finding a way to get doses of Cloud into your system. It's been known for awhile that it can interfere with the dome's ability to get a solid neuron read, but it also counteracts Lightcap's hold over memories to some degree." Adam's mouth gaped open in surprise.

Troyka stopped to take a breath. Adam sensed he would have to be proactive if he wanted to ask questions, since Doctor Troyka was a professor and could easily slip into lecture mode.

Adam interrupted, "I understand, at least to some degree, why Cloud could interfere with the dome and its neuron scanning, but how does that affect the memory component of the Lightcap? Also, why do I only remember some things? And the Lightcap still seems to work and accept commands when I wear it. I'm guessing it does, anyway, or else I'd probably be dead—like Damen."

Troyka said, "I heard about Damen. I'm sorry I couldn't do more to help. I gave you very low doses of Cloud, but daily. The amount was minuscule, just enough to undo the trauma on your neural pathways caused by Lightcap." He shrugged. "It's, well, sort of complex. I mean the answer to why you remember some things, but not others. To put it plainly, the relationship between Cloud, the dome, and the Lightcap is not well understood."

"You didn't make Cloud?" Adam asked, wincing with pain. He had been convinced Pavel would tell him he had developed Cloud as a secret countermeasure to the Mind Drive device he had unleashed on the world.

"Not at all," Troyka answered. "I wish I had. It's a novel compound, unlike anything I've ever seen in the realm of pharmacology. No one knows exactly why Cloud affects the brain the way it does. There is actually much debate as to whether Cloud was intentionally designed to interfere with the domes, or if it was just a happy accident." He paused. "Either way, that's why the Blues have ramped up drug-enforcement actions lately, with a special focus on Cloud. LaMont knows the more Cloud spreads, the more difficult it will be to control the populace with Lightcap."

Adam again interrupted, "About Lightcap, Doctor Troyka—"

"'Pavel', please. We live in dangerous times, my friend. We are in constant peril. There is little need for formality."

"Sure. Pavel. So, Pavel, about Lightcap. Doctor Velim was light on details. She said the Lightcap takes a snapshot of the brain, and then uses targeted lasers to zap memory clusters before it's removed, erasing all memory of the time it was worn. At least, that was my understanding. I'm just a coder," Adam said.

"Ah yes, Sera. I will answer your questions, which will hopefully give you some insight into the behavior and actions of our dear Doctor Velim. First of all, forget everything you've been told about

Lightcap and how it functions. While Lightcap does have a deleterious effect on memory, it is not as targeted as you were led to believe. I'll do my best to explain succinctly. When I first developed the Mind Drive, our early testing showed it created a sense of docility in many people, seemingly a side effect of the electrostatic field created by the device. It appeared to cause lowered inhibitions, making the mind more open to suggestion and subliminal input. I was looking for a way to advance our technology," Pavel said, shaking his head wistfully, "not to control people or make them weak-willed. It took me over a year to find an effective way to counteract that unintended consequence. This was early in the development, decades ago. I tried my best to bury the notes and research about this effect, but there are still a few people alive who remember, and probably a note or datafile somewhere.

"I left Brain Sync because of LaMont. Don't think this acquisition was recent; there was pressure as far back as fifteen years ago. He sent men to kill me, then got his hands on Sera. Maybe he had even before that. Who knows? At this point, Roman LaMont is probably in control of a significant amount of capital, along with Sera," said Pavel, his voice betraying anger.

"How is he in control of Sera?" Adam asked, as he slowly lifted himself up to a seated position. His arms and back complained, but it felt good to see the world horizontally again, even as his stomach lurched and threatened to revolt.

Pavel motioned at him and said, "Be careful. You still have drugs in your system. Curanol, which mixes with the gel in your wound to promote faster healing and skin growth. Also makes you a little drowsy and nauseated. LaMont's in control of her because that's what the Lightcap does. It's the fully realized potential of the Mind Drive tech, plus some other vile stuff LaMont's lab goons came up with. They're smart, but they have no ethics, no humanity. Just 'progress'. I don't know exactly how it works, but I have a guess. I found the one in your pocket. Sorry. Curious mind, you understand.

I haven't had much time to look at it, but the best I can gather is that it significantly amplifies the hypnosis-like effect exhibited by the early builds of the Mind Drive. It doesn't erase memories so much as it traumatizes the brain into forgetting. The reason you're remembering the really terrible things first is because most of the time you probably *were* doing mundane tasks—at least many of you. Sitting in cubicles and throwing code, or whatever you call it these days.

"The device seems to have multiple levels. One makes you very obedient to commands while allowing for higher-level autonomy to carry out those directives. The other end of the spectrum allows for total body control. Wireless command in and out, maybe even some sensory pass-through, allowing the person in control to feel what the receiver is feeling? It's hard to say without further study. The device you had is only a receiver. I imagine LaMont has the control device. His might be the only one, or there might be multiple. The control unit likely allows the wearer to control any person using a Lightcap that is connected to the mesh." Adam felt increasing shock and horror turning to outrage with every new word Doctor Troyka spoke.

"I've tried to get to Sera," Pavel continued, "but she's well protected, as is LaMont. I've got someone on the inside. You know him. Dej Singh. Of course, he and Aria are now an item. They weren't sure if you could be trusted, but I told them I had good a feeling about you. I'm worried about their safety, but they haven't been dosing with Cloud, so they don't remember anything. I still don't like the thought of them being there. We need to bring this to an end and get them out. On the plus side, Aria won't have to try to pull off that absurd stunt you all planned, thanks to the Lightcap prototype you had when I found you."

Adam wasted no time, taking the pause as an opportunity to break in. "Yeah, don't thank me, thank my dead girlfriend. It was hers. I took it from her right after she tried to kill me. Are you telling me she was under control? Directly? Or was she just following an order?"

Pavel shook his head, a look of sadness on his face. "I'm sorry. I'm not entirely certain. I would imagine it depends on conditioning. If you put a Lightcap on a soldier and tell him to kill someone, that's not going to require direct control. If you order him to kill his own mother, it most likely would. Depends on the soldier, I guess," he said with a chuckle. Adam didn't laugh, the memory of blood on his hands much too recent to allow him to appreciate gallows humor. "For an office worker, you could tell them to file papers, or, in your case, debug code, but you would need to take them under direct control if you wanted them to assassinate someone, or something equally out of the ordinary. The human brain is still a mystery in many ways, even with all our advancements, but it seems as if the Lightcap can turn anyone into a mindless drone, remotely controlled. I can't begin to express the sorrow I feel over these events, how my invention is being perverted and abused," the old man finished with a sigh.

"But what's the point?" Adam asked, his legs now planted against the floor, requiring deep breaths to calm the shock of pain at his vigorous movement. "Control? They're already in charge of everything. Money? They already have more credits than a man could spend in a lifetime. Why do this?" He was genuinely baffled, his horror aside.

Pavel looked down. Adam almost spoke again after several long seconds with no response. The old man said, "Greed is a curious thing. Some men are content with nothing, while others seem bent toward acquisition beyond measure. We know more about the brain than ever but still know next to nothing, and even less about the human psyche. I've often wondered what drives some men to their evil deeds, but there is no understanding madness. It consumes you, becomes you. I have no idea why LaMont is doing these things. I only know he must be stopped.

"Dej and Aria are still on the inside. We'll need to get them out, and then find someplace safe. We'll probably have to leave this Region. I have some friends in the United States who can probably find a place for us, somewhere out of LaMont's reach."

"Wait," Adam said, "What about Velim? We have to get her, too. Think about what information she might have, or what might happen to her if we don't take her with us. There's no way I'm leaving her under the control of that psychopath LaMont."

"Adam," Pavel responded, with a tone that would normally be appropriate for delivering an apology, "I don't think it's possible. She's too well protected. Even if we could get to her, I'm not even sure she'd be able or willing to go. She might be damaged from long-term Lightcap exposure, or may just be on LaMont's side, after having spent—"

"No, I know that's not true," Adam said sternly. "She always had a Lightcap on. Thought it was her dome, but it makes much more sense now. There's no way I'm leaving her behind. We need to figure out an escape plan that includes her. Bonus points if we can take care of LaMont." Pavel looked thoughtful, as if he could sense Adam's determination.

"I can't promise anything," Pavel said. "We'll have to run it by Aria and Dej. Without them there's no way we can even think about Velim. Otherwise it'll just be you and an old man." He laughed. "Because of Aria, we know they take your group from the Adaptech building to Metra Corp headquarters every day. She risked her life by wearing a hidden tracking beacon, courageous as hell. Dej was able to get some reconnaissance drones in the air, registered as meteorological survey aircraft through a front organization. Thanks to his efforts, we know LaMont has your team loaded into a JMR-Heavy chopper for the ride to Metra Corp. The roof of the building opens, allowing the craft to land inside. After that the programming team is taken one floor down, where they spend the rest of the workday. We can go over all the logistics after Dej and Aria get here, but I am of the opinion, if you want to try to rescue Velim—"

"I do," Adam interrupted.

"—Our best way into Metra Corp is to stow away on the chopper. There are four cargo holds where we can hide. It'll be a damned cold ride, but it shouldn't fly so high that we'll have trouble breathing. The highest we've observed them get is about five thousand feet."

Adam could scarcely believe what he was hearing. *What sort of things is LaMont making us do each day*? he wondered, then asked Pavel, "How do we know they'll still be making daily runs?"

"Their projects continue without you, Adam," the old man said with an amused look. "You are not as indispensable as you have been led to believe." As this sank in, Pavel continued: "Once we're in the landing bay it's only one floor down, which beats the alternative of trying to get in from the ground and somehow make it to the 180th floor without attracting attention. Now that LaMont's in charge of both Metra Corp and Adaptech, he's got even more power behind his plans. We think he intends to bring Lightcap tech to market within the next year, and use it as a way to bring the populace under greater control than ever before. Since there are almost no regulations now, and LaMont controls the company tasked with enforcing the few that do exist, he won't have much trouble getting the device to market as-is." Pavel's words ended just as a loud knock came through the air. "Excuse me. Stay here, just in case."

He sat in thought for a moment as he listened to Pavel's footsteps, which grew quieter as he made his way away from Adam's location. There was a long moment when Adam could hear nothing, his breath caught in his throat, his ears strained against the tense silence to pick up whatever was going on beyond the door to his room. Adam couldn't tell if the sudden sound of voices he heard was excited or angry. A loud slam came next, and he concluded there were only two possible types of visitors: friends or foes. Adam decided he had nothing to worry about if they were friends, and if they were foes they'd find him soon enough. He jumped to his feet, as much as he *could* jump given his thrashed and exhausted body, and cautiously made his way through the door into the hallway. The voices became much clearer. They sounded familiar.

He turned the corner to find Pavel's back facing him. Aria's eyes flicked to Adam first, drawn by his movement. Dej saw him a split-second later, and pushed past Pavel, bounding across the room in three steps and throwing his arms around Adam's shoulders. Adam almost toppled from the sudden impact, but Dej's strength kept them both upright. Pavel turned to see what had caused Dej's excitement. Aria watched them, an amused look on her face. Dej nearly shouted, "Sorry, Adam, didn't mean to almost knock you over. We were so worried when you weren't there yesterday at the end of your shift. Sera was gone too. LaMont briefed us today via vid feed. He said you suffered a 'mental break', were wanted for questioning, and that we should all be on the lookout for you!

"We saw the news reports yesterday on Tim Montery and Cora Slate, and that you were a wanted man. Then the reports changed, saying Montery was dead but not Slate. They changed it again today, this time saying Slate was also dead and there had been an attempt on LaMont's life as well. I think they've given up on finding you. They're now reporting Jared Tinge as the prime suspect, after he was captured while trying to assassinate LaMont," Dej said.

"Jared?!" Adam exclaimed. "He's an idiot, not an assassin. Not even an idiot—just not the brightest."

Aria chimed in: "Yeah, we were surprised too. Anyone who knows him wouldn't buy it for a second. They caught him red-handed, though, trying to break into LaMont's office. He had a gun and everything."

"LaMont," Adam said, "is the one behind all this. He's the one who put Jared up to it, probably to make it seem as if he was being targeted by the same person who killed Montery and Slate." He looked at Dej and Aria as he said the names, not seeing any indication they knew it was him. Pavel, standing behind them, shook his head slightly to let Adam know they were unaware. Adam continued through gritted teeth, "Speaking of which, I need to tell you something. I am the one who killed Montery and Slate. They were having an affair, and I murdered them in their hotel room with a knife. I remember it. Well enough, anyway." Dej and Aria stared at him in horror.

"What?" Aria practically screamed. "You killed the CEO? And the Vice CEO?"

"We've figured out what the Lightcap does," Adam said. He glanced at the old man who gave him a slight nod of encouragement. "Well, Pavel told me his suspicions. I wasn't in control of my body, but I still recall the important details. The Lightcap lets LaMont drive people. The only thing that makes sense is that I was under LaMont's control. I don't see him giving anyone else the ability to control his Lightcap puppets. The benefit of framing Jared for the assassination was twofold, giving LaMont a way to deflect suspicion about his own involvement, since he stands to benefit the most from the sudden and concurrent deaths of Montery and Slate, plus it satisfies the need of the public to have a scapegoat. Speaking of punishment, what happened to Jared? Is there any way we can get to him? He gets on my nerves, but I'm not going to let him suffer for a crime he didn't commit."

Aria looked defeated. Dej's face looked as if he had been punched in the gut. He said, "We tried, Adam. We looked at the different options for getting him out. They already convicted him. Since he was caught in the act with several witnesses, LaMont had a press conference last night, saying justice will be swift so our Region stays strong and unified. He said that unless an example is made of Jared, others may try to take matters of politics into their own hands. There's an execution set to take place in about an hour, scheduled for broadcast over the vid nodes."

"We have to stop them. I can't let Jared die," Adam said, his hands balled into fists. "Especially since this wouldn't be happening to him if I hadn't escaped."

"You're right, Adam," Aria replied. "It wouldn't be happening to him. It'd be happening to *you*. I don't mean to be rude, but you're far more valuable than Jared Tinge. You're more valuable than a dozen Jared Tinges. At least we know we can trust you. Well, now we know. We were pretty sure before, but your credibility became unquestionable after they tried to kill you."

"What happened with that, by the way?" Adam asked. "You and Dej never mentioned anything about Doctor Troyka, or about any of the other stuff you were doing." He turned to Pavel. "And you. Why not just come to me directly, tell me about what was happening, and try to get me on your side? Instead you break into my house, secretly drug me, almost get me killed, and have apparently been stalking me for what, a year? I thought I was losing my mind."

Aria and Dej both looked at Pavel. "I'll start," Troyka said, "since I am the one who originally reached out to Dej. I have known for some time that LaMont has been planning something. I had no idea what it was, and I knew if there was any proof I was still alive, he'd send someone to kill me. I needed someone on the inside. I had a short list of people I thought could be trusted, a list that included you, Adam. In the end, I was able to find some traces Dej left on the mesh—well hidden but not completely erased—suggesting he would be open to the risk. You were far more of an unknown element. I started dosing you with Cloud almost a year ago. I thought it would be a way to independently find out what sort of person you are and to provide a way for you to independently come to a conclusion about what was going on at Adaptech. I had a pretty good idea of what effect it would have on you, but no way to know for sure. For that, I apologize. It was not my intention to use you as a test subject, but it was done out of necessity. If it is any consolation, I did not share my suspicions about the true extent of the Lightcap's powers with Dej out of concern for how the knowledge would affect him. Dej and Aria got to know one another enough that he knew she could be trusted. We talked about bringing you in, but we didn't know how to do it in a way that wouldn't tip our hand. That night at Glass, after Damen had gone missing, was their way of feeling you out, making sure you were the type of man who'd choose to do what is right instead of what is expedient. They took a great risk, and fortunately it paid off."

Adam looked at Dej, who broke into a half smile. Aria suppressed her grin and just shook her head. She said, "Yeah, I consider myself a good judge of character. I knew you were all right, maybe even approaching decent. After we had given you enough information that you could've turned us in but didn't, I was sure."

Adam felt more than one emotion. He was angry at Pavel for using him as a lab rat, annoyed Dej and Aria hadn't trusted him more quickly, and upset Jared had to pay the price for something he—no, LaMont!—had done. He stretched his back, feeling the usual pops and cracks along with pain but also more limber and filled with the desire for justice. *LaMont will pay for this*, Adam thought. *He made people do terrible things, and we have to make sure he will not have the chance to do it again, or to see Lightcap to market.*

After much discussion, they agreed to watch the execution of Jared Tinge. High-profile executions garnered high ratings on the vid nodes, typically attracting the most consistent audience numbers, a tendency the advertisers loved. Who could turn down a sure thing, a guaranteed money-maker? The media did their best to demonize the convicted, as sympathetic victims getting murdered by the state weren't good for ratings. Instead, a network would list the crimes of the sentenced party, like a vengeful god judging sins before the entire world.

They turned it on right before the act to see a clip of one of Jared's ex-girlfriends insinuating he emotionally and physically abused her. They changed to another feed and caught the tail end of an investigative report on the Tinge family suggesting a political motivation to benefit the Tinge name. Adam muted the sound.

Solemn quiet settled over the room as the image of Jared appeared on the screen. He was calm, almost serene even, as he stared into the camera. Adam noticed the telltale bumps under his ears that suggested he was wearing a dome. A Lightcap, most likely. The camera angle switched to a profile view and confirmed Adam's suspicions. That would explain the vacant look on Jared's face: he was evidently calmed by the mind-warping effects of the Lightcap. The camera stayed on Jared for several minutes, no doubt while a list of charges was read. Dej grabbed Aria's hand. Pavel gripped the arm of his chair, his knuckles white.

Adam watched with them as the needle plunged into the waiting vein and a countdown timer appeared on the screen, ticking from twenty to zero with cold consistency. They watched as Jared's eyes focused against infinity and his eyelids succumbed to gravity. They observed a flutter of his eyelashes at the end, a last attempt to fight inevitability, then stillness.

Jared Tinge was gone.

No Enemy

The next several days passed slowly. The safe house where Pavel lived was a half-dozen blocks from Aria's place, deeper into the ghetto where the Blues seldom ventured. The first few days were tough on Adam, as he recovered from his physical injuries and suffered slight withdrawal symptoms from the last year of daily Cloud doses. Pavel lent him a notetab, but Adam had to use a keyboard for the first time in ages, his fingers angered by constant movement, his wrists pained with daily abuse. He was frustrated by his slow typing speed, especially if Pavel was using a notetab in the same room, the rapid-fire *tack tack tack* of his aged fingers expertly landing against its plastic keys, making Adam feel even less competent. The old man refused to use a dome, distrustful of the very device he helped to create.

Doctor Pavel Troyka proved to be an odd fellow, brilliant but mad. Adam and he had long conversations while Dej and Aria were gone, talks on topics ranging from the latest discoveries of the large particle accelerators in Europe to economics, history, the nature of consciousness, and where tech like the Mind Drive and Lightcap went wrong.

Five days after his panicked escape, as Adam was on a notetab looking up information on LaMont that might aid their attempts to crack his datafile, Pavel and he got on the subject of Damen and how his unexpected loss had been the catalyst that forced Adam to finally acknowledge there was more to the Lightcap project than they had been told.

"What do you think Damen knew?" Adam asked Pavel. "I had a dream where I watched him get shot in the head. It felt incredibly real, but I'm not sure at this point what was real and what I just imagined. Aria didn't even see the same things I did when she went to his house. Were those things there, or did I imagine them?" Adam began to doubt everything he thought he knew.

"Yes, Aria told me. The toothbrush and the message etched in the window. What were the words again?"

"It said 'ms = no enemy', in all lowercase letters. Do you have any idea who MS might be?"

"I know many people with those initials," Pavel said thoughtfully. He sat with his fist against his chin, his elbow on his knee, the classic pose of a thinker. "Several companies, too. As far as I know, none of them is involved with Adaptech, Metra Corp, or the Lightcap in any way. If we're able to decrypt LaMont's datafile, it might contain information about this MS person."

"Do you remember the day you ran into me on the subway?" Adam asked. At this point, he wasn't sure if he had made the entire thing up, if it was some sort of false memory stemming from his cryptic dream.

"Of course. I made sure you didn't miss your stop," Pavel answered. Adam felt relieved his memory of the event was at least partly rooted in reality.

"Did you slip anything in my pocket?"

"No. At least, not that I recall."

"That's what I thought. I was having such strange dreams. Some things I knew were memories, but others seemed more like symbolism, or subconscious interpretations of what had happened in my life recently. Does the name 'Mnemosyne' mean anything to you?"

Pavel furrowed his brows in frustration. "Not really. I know it's a name from Greek mythology, but it doesn't bring up any specific memories or lead me down any particular course of thought. With a name like that, I'd be remiss to forget anything referencing it."

"What did you say?" Adam said, his attention heightened by Pavel's words.

"That I don't know the name, other than from Greek myth—"

"No, no," Adam broke in. "The last part. About being remiss to forget something referencing such an uncommon name," Adam said. His words spilled out rapidly, measured speech overruled by his excitement. "Remiss. MS. What if the first part of the letters on the windowsill weren't initials but a title? I seem to recall Claudia the HR drone and LaMont both referring to Velim as Miss, not Doctor. She had a Lightcap on but must not have been under direct control, because she looked annoyed at LaMont and even made a point of correcting Claudia. Maybe Damen learned something he shouldn't have?"

Pavel was quiet for several moments, eventually responding, "I don't think so, Adam. After Aria and Dej told me about Damen, I checked up on him. I found that he had been arrested as a juvenile for a number of things, including drug use. His father spent the family's life savings having this fact expunged from the public record so his son wouldn't be blacklisted and could get into college. Damen stayed out of trouble after that, but if I had to guess, he was back to using Cloud and that caused problems with his Lightcap."

"So how did he know about Velim not being an enemy?" Adam asked.

"I would imagine he did not. Aria didn't see those letters, and she spent hours scouring Damen's apartment, looking for anything that might be a clue. She found nothing. Adam, I don't mean any offense by this, and I feel it necessary to apologize because my actions may be partly to blame, but do you think it's possible you imagined the letters, just as you imagined me slipping you the note on the subway? My intent of giving you low doses of Cloud was to counteract the havoc Lightcap was wreaking on your brain, but there may have been unintended side effects. The things you remember might be actual memories mixed with artifacts from your unconscious mind. Things you worry about, things from your past, anything. Even something you overheard once without realizing it."

For a moment, Adam considered that Pavel might be right, that it might all be some kind of figment of his imagination, his mind playing tricks, or dementia brought on by Lightcap, despite how real it all felt to him. Adam had spent days trying to crack the passkey LaMont used to encrypt his datafile. He had read hundreds of different articles on LaMont, glowing pieces describing his deep respect for capitalism, his business prowess, his keen sense of negotiation and acquisition, even his love of history, his favorite book being the biography of the founder of the Region, Preston Pennington.

Something occurred to Adam. He asked Pavel, "Do you think there's a possibility of the Lightcap misfiring? I mean, if LaMont is directly controlling someone, is it possible he could pass through more than just intentional commands, such as stray thoughts or subconscious fears and desires?"

Troyka scratched his head, pondering Adam's suggestion. He replied, "Well, it's *possible*, I suppose, but not the most likely answer. Occam's Razor suggests the least convoluted explanation is likely the most plausible. I know it's hard to think of yourself as someone with a compromised mind, but I'd like you to consider that at least part of these dreams, visions, whatever they are, may be rooted in physiological damage to your brain caused by the Lightcap, Cloud, or both. I am sorry to have to say that, of course, because I may be partially responsible."

"No, I *know* the most reasonable assumption is that I've lost, or am losing, my mind. I know it sounds ridiculous, but there's more to it. I don't know how I know," Adam said, embarrassed to resort to emotional pleas since his logic had failed him, "but I need you to trust me. I'd never heard the name Mnemosyne before that dream, I know that for a fact. It didn't even register with me, not until I looked it up on the mesh."

"Well," Pavel said, "if you really feel that way, what do you think it means? Mnemosyne, a name on a piece of paper slipped into your pocket during a dream. Your dream about company named Ensyn, memos and boxes of paperwork that may or may not exist. Then a phrase, 'ms = no enemy', which you think refers to Sera for no reason at all, etched into a windowsill but gone the next day. Visions? Hallucinations? Prophecy? This is the real world, not some loony cult or vid node drama," said Pavel. His voice raised a little by the end, his breath grabbed in gulps. He turned around in his chair, grabbed his notetab and said, "I can't believe I'm even entertaining this thought. Preposterous." His fingers flew over the keys. "See? No luck with Mnemosyne as the passkey. LaMont's datafile remains encrypted."

Adam hung his head and said, "I know. I already tried it. Spent hours just sitting here trying different things, anything that came to mind. I looked up everything I could find on LaMont. I tried his ex-wife's name, kid's name, alma mater, nicknames, pretty much any mesh trace of him I could find. Nothing. Hey, let's try 'ms = no enemy', or 'Ensyn memo', some variations of those."

The sounds of spring-loaded keys bounced against walls as they tried all the permutations they could conceive of the letters—different capitalizations, arrangements, character substitutions, but it was no use. LaMont's datafile would not open. For all they knew the passkey was a hundred characters long, random and impossible to guess. Pavel turned and said, "See? I hate to break it to you, Adam, but the dreams and things you saw weren't real. They didn't actually happen. Just because you see a random assortment of let—" Pavel stopped short and a perplexed look spread across his face as he poked his finger against the air as if spelling something out. He continued: "Letters. They're all the same letters, just in different arrangement. It would appear," his eyes jumped to Adam, "there is an anagrammatic aspect to your visions, something we were not aware of until now. The mind is powerful, but I don't think this can be attributed to randomness. *If* what you say is correct, and that's a very big 'if', then a misfire from LaMont could come across as scrambled. An unintended side effect. Hmm." He paused. "I might owe you an apology."

Adam took in what Pavel said and contrasted it with what he knew of LaMont, his family life, the schools he attended, the kinds of things that might inspire or drive him. There was a moment when everything fell into place, his memory brought into sharp focus by an article titled "Titans of Capitalism" he had read about LaMont's meteoric rise to the upper echelons of business, following and surpassing the footsteps of his father and the generations before him.

"I have an idea," Adam said, spinning around to face his notetab. Pavel watched curiously as the younger man's fingers slowly tapped against the keyboard. "Our conversation about what motivates people like LaMont got me thinking, along with an article about his family being leaders of capitalism. Titans. Mnemosyne was a Titan too, but none of the variations of her name worked. There was a part of the article that described LaMont's family as 'belonging to money'. Let me see . . . " His hands finished their slow dance across the keyboard and then stopped, one finger held perilously above the enter key. He held his breath, then pushed down against the plastic, its click echoing against the walls. His eyes rose to meet Pavel's, a smile on his face. "Got it! 'Money's Men' was the passkey. He could've chosen something more difficult to guess. His hubris was his undoing."

Pavel's eyes were bright, elated, as his notetab screen was filled with the information contained in LaMont's datafile, sent from the decrypted file on Adam's machine. "Adam," he said, "there are terabytes of data here. Who knows what it contains? It could be useless, or it could have the schematics of the Lightcap control unit itself. This should keep us busy for some time." Pavel pressed his lips together and wheeled around to look at Adam. "There are also, ah, implications about what this means—your receiving the anagrams, I mean. There might be *more* information in your head, whispers of LaMont's wandering mind sent across the mesh to yours. More importantly, I now agree with you that we need to obtain Sera. The things she might know could prove to be invaluable."

When Dej and Aria came over after work that night, Adam and Pavel shared the contents of the decrypted datafile with them, explaining how they had happened upon the passkey. The couple up to then had not been pleased by the idea of rescuing Velim, unconvinced as they were that she was trustworthy or worth saving. When Adam told them his theory of how he knew LaMont's passkey, and that he had never seen Sera without a Lightcap, they agreed to help rescue her.

"We are now twice as likely to succeed," Pavel joked. "Of course, the likelihood was only a fraction of a percent before."

We're still statistically screwed, Adam thought wryly.

The quartet spent the next several days wading through LaMont's data. He was a digital hoarder who would have had stacks of papers to the ceiling had he not been born in the electronic age. While the enormous amount of information may have proved useful if they had had time to sort through it all, for now it just made their task daunting, all the more because they didn't dare sending the data over the mesh, even encrypted, for fear of interception along the way. Fortunately, between Pavel and Adam, along with Aria and Dej in the evenings, they were able to find some useful information. There were login credentials for the Adaptech and Metra Corp networks, blueprints, meeting notes, helicopter schedules, Lightcap schematics, and a lot of source code.

Aria found some information on the JMR-Heavy choppers used by Metra Corp. They'd been purchased at a bargain price from the US government, which divested itself of much of its former military might as a last-ditch effort to avert bankruptcy while losing several States around the borders. The United States subsequently sold additional land rights to Cascadia and Metra Corp, then lacked the manpower and force required to quash the secession of several of the Southern cities to the Confederacy. This military clearance sale worked out well for Metra Corp, netting the Corporation several acquisitions to bolster its air, land, and sea fleets, necessary for protecting the border and its domestic interests, at least that was the story from the media.

The choppers used for the daily trip between the two skyscrapers had several cargo holds, just as Pavel said, and Aria also found files to confirm that the flight plan never took them above five thousand feet—along with the schedules of the guards and pilots. Even more helpful were the diagrams for the Lightcap, complete specs for the outside measurements, with some information about the internal components such as the mesh radio and neural interfaces. LaMont's datafile allowed Pavel, Adam, Dej, and Aria to start planning.

Four runs each day carried supplies back and forth between the Adaptech and Metra Corp headquarters. Aria and Dej would go over in the passenger hold during the first run, along with the rest of the v6 team. The second run, the lightest, would allow Adam and Pavel to go over in a relatively empty cargo hold, but it wouldn't get them there until two hours after the first run—two hours during which Dej and Aria would have to hope not to be discovered while figuring out just what had been happening for the past year.

The Lightcap Adam took from Hana proved to be a worthy challenge for Pavel. The old man spent over a day trying to figure out how to open it, his micro-spudger poking along hidden seams until he found the proper sequence to release the internal clamps. The plastic halves of the Lightcap's front bubble separated with a click. "Eureka!" Pavel cried, his fist struck against the air, a boyish grin on his face. Dej was excited to do a complete code dump of the device, to start looking for potential weaknesses or hidden functions. More things to keep them busy.

Several days later, Dej said he had an announcement to make. He seemed to be trying to suppress a grin or keep a secret. The others turned their attention to him. "So, I've been looking through the Lightcap code, working with the Doc on some of the hardware, and I think we might have found something really big," he said, nodding to Pavel.

The old man jumped up as if on cue. He said, "Right, so I found the radio module that allows the Lightcap to connect to the mesh and receive commands. More importantly, after I found it, Dej here found a way to shut it down."

Dej's smile flashed brilliantly against the dim light of the room, seeming brighter than the lamp. Pavel looked as if he wanted to high five himself or give himself a few hearty pats on the back. Adam, glad to see his friends joyful, regretted having to break their reverie of self congratulation, but he had to ask one question.

"That's really great guys, but doesn't the Lightcap just make them go into a docile mode or follow pre-defined commands in the event of a connection loss? I'm not trying to take away your moment of glory, but won't it just mean a bunch of office workers just sitting there, or at worst writing code?"

Pavel jerked his thumb at Dej, who clapped his hands together and said, "Adam, so glad you asked!" He had clearly walked right into a set up, a way to allow them to draw out their presentation and build suspense. Dej continued: "The Doc was a huge help. As you said, what's the point of shutting down the mesh link if they're just going to zone out or follow some sort of commands given in advance? So we looked at different sections of code, and it seems there are different emotion calls that are made. The AI software translates that to physical areas in the brain, which are then agitated by the Lightcap to induce the desired response.

"I'm fairly certain I isolated the call for utter panic. Sheer emotional mayhem. We're going to hit them twice. Send the command to make them all lose their minds, hopefully causing complete chaos, and then send another command to disable the mesh radio. I think the device will still control the worker in chaos, going off the last order received. The effect will last as long as the device is worn. It's not ready yet. Maybe in another day or two," Dej concluded, hands in his pockets. He seemed to glow with pride at his success.

The group felt renewed vigor and exchanged hugs as Aria and Dej left for the night. After their departure, Adam and Pavel retired to their respective rooms. Adam lay awake and stared at the ceiling, his thoughts halfway across the city with Adaptech, and then beyond the outskirts of New Metra City to the larger headquarters of Metra Corp. Would LaMont even be at the headquarters when they attacked? They wanted to move quickly, but they had just started to scratch the surface of the information contained in the datafile. Adam felt a deep, anxious pressure against his chest that they wouldn't be returning, that this was surely a suicide mission, the last bad decision he'd ever make. Maybe he'd get lucky and live to make more, but that didn't seem likely. They were going into the headquarters for the two most powerful companies in the Region. The last thought Adam had before drifting off to restless sleep was that this may be one of the last times he'd ever dream.

Rescue

Adam awoke the next morning with the weight gone from his chest, replaced by an exhaustion that had seeped into his bones. He struggled sluggishly against an unseen current from the moment he swung his legs out of bed. He couldn't remember dreaming during the night. *Figures,* thought Adam, noting that it was almost noon.

Pavel made Adam a breakfast of powdered eggs, smoked protein sticks, and coffee that gave a jolt along with a headache. The eggs looked like white folded cheesecloth, with no yolks, of near uniform consistency. The coffee offered Adam a vague aftertaste of burnt sand. However, the food woke him up, even if only a little. Pavel apologized, as he had at almost every meal, for the poor quality of the food. "I'm sorry, Adam. You know I can't venture too far from the house. The corner market isn't exactly overflowing with selections. You wouldn't believe how expensive it is, too. I won't tell you, because it would just make you angry."

"It's fine, Pavel. Thank you for the food," Adam said, as he had several times before. The food really was terrible, but it was better than some alternatives. Such as starving.

That afternoon, several hours passed in silence, Pavel hunched over the Lightcap formerly worn by Hana while Adam sorted through the mountains of information in LaMont's datafile. He found there was just as much, if not more, random junk as there was useful data. The man had digital receipts for dry cleaning from five years before, a hotel receipt from a year and a half prior, file after file of unimportant data. Despite the hunt for digital needles in virtual haystacks, Adam did find useful information.

It appeared to Adam that the Brain Sync acquisition was just for show, a formality, a way to add to the Adaptech balance sheet and increase its clout in the world market. He found notes going back over a decade showing LaMont had an intimate knowledge of the inner workings of Brain Sync, and access to its confidential intellectual property. At the very least, LaMont had someone on the inside. He found files suggesting the Mind Drive v5 had incorporated elements of Lightcap tech, specifically the components which helped to create a sense of docility, making the wearer more open to suggestion and less likely to experience intense emotions, even suppressing the capacity for self-reflection. The files explained a great deal, especially why no one seemed to mind that things kept getting worse. Between the mesh vid nodes, the lack of personal connections in daily life, and the high adoption rate of Mind Drive v5, people were too entertained to think and too preoccupied to care.

Adam found additional information suggesting LaMont had controlled Doctor Velim for quite some time. Daily log files going back more than five years, observations on his attempts to break her spirit while she wasn't wearing the Lightcap, which led to lower inhibitions during future Lightcap sessions. Adam was horrified to learn that after several years of almost daily use Sera Velim now sat quietly, awaiting commands, even when she wasn't wearing the Lightcap. LaMont noted Velim did occasionally resist commands against her personal moral code, such that he found her unreliable. LaMont had forced Velim to wear the Lightcap nonstop for the past ten months.

As Adam read through hundreds of pages of LaMont's notes, he found one recurring theme: LaMont trusted no one. Adam had sometimes thought he himself suffered from paranoia, a byproduct of an overly analytical mind and a tendency to see every potential point of failure or weakness in a given system. LaMont made Adam appear a careless exhibitionist. There were dozens of pages of rants—long, rambling pieces casting nearly every person within his social and professional circles as a potential spy or saboteur, including Adam. He found pages of data about himself; LaMont had compiled dossiers on each member of the programming team.

Adam came across a file simply labeled DT. *Damen!* thought Adam, immediately opening it. The file started out with the same background and biographical data the other dossiers contained. About three months into the project LaMont started making notes suggesting Damen was the subject of several tests, both physical and psychological. Nothing gave any specifics on what tests had been performed. Vague notes from LaMont indicated recovery times, brain inflammation, and cognitive abilities while carrying out different types of tasks. Adam could see clearly they were a team of lab rats, but it appeared Damen was chosen to be tested more thoroughly than the others. There were repeated references to Damen's young age, enough that Adam believed it was one of the main reasons Damen had been selected as a test subject over other people on the team. The last entry in the file was from the day Damen disappeared, input by LaMont. A single line read, "Terminated."

Adam passed the rest of the afternoon and early evening searching through the datafile, trying to find information about the types of tests performed on Damen and whether or not anyone else on the team had been subjected to similar testing. Despite Adam's efforts, nothing indicated what had been done to Damen. Eventually, Adam found a file for Dej, which he also immediately opened. It was the same as all the other biographical information on the rest of the team. Two things stood out. One brief notation read, "Secret messages". Another read, "Physical test: see RH". Adam needed to know more. He set out to find the file for RH, which he assumed was the dossier for Rosaria "Aria" Hines.

Just then, the front door erupted in a series of booms—three fast, two slow, the secret knock they created. Pavel lifted himself from the chair, took four steps across the room, and stopped to look through the door's peephole. He looked at Adam, his expression unreadable, and opened the door. Aria nearly jumped through. The sudden movement caused Adam to flinch. Her eyes and nose were red and inflamed. She had clearly been crying. Pavel closed the door quickly behind her, concern on her face.

Adam couldn't contain his impatience and asked, "Where's Dej?"

Aria shot him an angry look, her eyes full of pain, and replied, "He's gone. Same as Damen, although they at least had the foresight to have a message waiting for us when we got back from our Lightcap shift. The story this time is he was transferred to a new Adaptech field office in the Confederacy to head up a project for the next-gen autonomous car. Total bullshit. He would have said something to me—or at least to one of us. Right?" She turned pleading eyes at Pavel, who nodded his head sympathetically. She looked at Adam, who wasn't sure what to say. He couldn't remove the nagging idea things weren't as bad as they seemed to be. He didn't want it to be true, and the past several days had been a process of not only learning but persuading himself it was all as bad as it seemed. As a result, though he wanted to believe Dej was committed to doing what was right, there was also a part of Adam that felt a little envy at the idea of being able to get away, to start over, his slate wiped clean.

Dej was a talented programmer, as was Adam, probably enough so that either of them could have leveraged that skill as a way to be granted clemency for his crimes. As tempted as he was to confess and move on, Adam knew there was no going back, not with what he had seen, not with the Lightcap in the hands of a lunatic like LaMont and good people like Velim under his control. Adam was pretty sure Dej was the same type of person, though Adam also realized he had idolized Dej for years. The media portrayed Dej as a selfless genius passing hundreds of hours slumped over a notetab, racking his brain, trying to make the world a better place. Dej's was one of the few media stories praising altruism over vested self interest. How could they not portray him that way? By improving the autocar collision rate, Dej had prevented thousands of deaths.

Aria still looked at Adam expectantly. "I'm sure he's safe, Aria," Adam finally said. "He's too damned valuable. We should just assume we've got two people to rescue now, instead of one."

"*You* might have two people to rescue," hissed Aria. "I have one: Dej. I'll worry about him, you worry about the airhead who's probably in LaMont's pocket anyway—with or without the brain hugger."

Adam couldn't blame Aria for her anger. He was upset and he and Dej weren't even an item. Adam was afraid of making her mood worse, but he also had to tell her what he'd found in LaMont's datafile. "Aria, Pavel, I need to tell you both something," he said, as he turned his chair to face them both. "I've spent most of today trying to sort through LaMont's notes, and I found some troubling things. They've been experimenting on some of us."

"Yeah, no shit, Adam," Aria said. "We're all just rats in cages. We know." She seemed to be alternating between rage and fear.

"I think this is beyond what we thought," Adam said, trying to sound calm. "This isn't just testing the Lightcap but *us*. How we respond to different commands, or different levels of intensity. Damen was definitely a test subject to a greater degree than the rest of us, I think due to his young age. I wasn't able to figure out just what the hell they were doing to him, but I'm pretty sure it had a part in his death, whatever it was. Before I saw him get shot, there was already blood coming out of his ears and nose, as if he was experiencing an aneur—"

"Stop. Just fucking stop," Aria interjected, tears gathering at the corners of her eyes.

"Sorry. I wasn't trying to upset you. I need to tell you this, though. It's important. I found a file for Dej, and it looks as if they might have done some kind of testing on him too. And you. There was a note in his file that said something about physical tests, and it referenced a file for someone named RH," Adam finished, relieved to get it all out. They all knew she was the only one with those initials on the team.

Aria turned to look at Pavel and asked, "Can we be ready to do this by tomorrow? I don't want to wait. If we take too much time, it might be too late for Dej. We need to do this tomorrow, if at all possible."

Adam cut Pavel off before he had a chance to answer, exclaiming, "Did you hear me? I said they've been doing who knows what to you and me and Dej and Damen, and you don't even seem to care."

Aria snapped her head to look at him, then took three steps across the room and reached behind her back with her right hand. Adam forced himself not to cringe. There was a quick sound of metal scraping metal, *shiiink,* as Aria extended her hand upwards in a sweeping arc to draw a katana from its spot behind her left shoulder. The sword glinted in the light, the orb on the ceiling reflected against its folded steel. "Do you want to say that again? Tell me I don't care one more time. I am going to go get Dej tomorrow or die trying. You are welcome to come, but I'm going either way."

Adam had no idea how proficient Aria was with a blade, and he decided not to find out. Pavel affected his best diplomatic tone to say, "Now, Aria, I appreciate you being proactive and bringing your own weapon, but we do still need Mister Redmon's head connected to his shoulders. I understand you're frustrated, but you'll have a chance soon enough to rescue Dej and mete out punishment. We can be ready by tomorrow."

"Good," said Aria, her eyes on Pavel. She put the blade away with a pronounced *thunk* as the sword's guard met its scabbard, then glanced back at Adam. "Sorry."

"It's fine. I know you're upset. I am too. How are you going to get that sword into the building? I don't think they'll let you into 4C with it on your back." Adam rubbed his neck, almost glad they wouldn't.

"Right. You or Pavel will have to bring it in the chopper, and I'll have to get it from you once we meet up in the Metra Corp building. I'm almost done with the replica Lightcap, so I'll hopefully have my wits and not be some kind of mindless robot. I just need to print the final layers of the front module and double-check all the measurements. I don't think they'll be looking that closely. My biggest worry is I might not convince them I'm under the spell of the Lightcap. Fortunately, we got to observe you on the first day of the project, so I at least have some idea. Vacant expression. Short, emotionless answers. It won't be easy for me, because I want to go in there and start tearing heads off, but I think I can do it." Adam could see her struggle and felt impressed by her strength.

"Excellent," said Pavel, "because you're going to be on your own for about two hours. Once we get in the building, we'll have to make it down one floor and then find you. Feel free to attempt to disable the elevators and security system while you wait, it might reduce the amount of resistance we face. Only if you feel safe doing so, of course. We found diagrams of the layout in LaMont's datafile, but unfortunately there was no seating chart. We couldn't find any information about the insulation in the ceiling. Unless they've made an effort to soundproof, you should hear it when the retractable roof opens to allow the helicopter to land. Once you hear the roof, wait five minutes and then start making your way toward the door for the south staircase. We'll meet yo—"

"Won't someone notice if I get up and leave my desk?" Aria asked cautiously.

"It should be fine," Pavel said with a wave of his hand. "Remember, you're only rarely under direct one-to-one control while wearing the Lightcap. Most of the time you're on autopilot. Just act confident, and I doubt anyone will question you or even give you a second glance. There *is* a security station about twenty feet down the hall from the staircase, but we'll try and avoid notice. We couldn't find any data about how many Blues might be posted in that room. Adam is sure there are at least two on that floor, based on his memories of what happened to Damen. We should plan on as many as six or more. Based on the size of the security station, that's probably the maximum."

"Will we have weapons?" Adam asked. "Aria seems set, but I'd be just as likely to cut off my *own* head with something like a sword. Have anything that's a little more foolproof, like a gun or something?"

Pavel burst into laughter. His stomach bounced against his legs, and his chair swung back and forth, as if he were saying no with his entire body, not just his head. When his laughter subsided, he said, "Guns? If we had tried to get guns, the Blues would've already knocked down the front door. I am going to bring a small pistol, a thirty-eight special, two-shot derringer. It belonged to my father, and I've never had a chance to use it. Ammunition is so scarce these days I've never even fired the thing. The bullets have been in the chamber for almost twenty years now. Hopefully it still fires!" He chuckled. "I'm too damned old to swing a sword or get into a fistfight.

"For you," Pavel continued, pointing at Adam, "I'm going to give you the device Dej has been working on. It has one button, which accomplishes two things when pressed: it sends a command inducing panic in anyone wearing a Lightcap within a fifty foot radius. Then it kills the radio so no further commands can be received. It requires a substantial amount of power, so you only get to press that button twice and then it's worthless without a recharge. Try not to use it unless absolutely necessary." Pavel reached into a drawer next to his chair and pulled out a box, wide and short. He opened it and said, "I also got one of these for each of us. Ballistic vests made from woven nanotubes. Strong, lightweight. They'll provide protection to your torso from projectiles and bladed weapons, but they'll still hurt like hell, so don't get shot or stabbed." He pulled the vests out of the box and handed them over.

"Since I'll have my gun and Aria will have her sword, you can take these," he said. He handed Adam a small box roughly the same size as his palm. Adam opened it to find Electrodusters. Pavel saw Adam's surprise and said, "You wanted something you couldn't klutz up. This is it. Just put them on and punch. They deliver over nine hundred thousand volts as soon as they hit skin. Doesn't get much easier than that. They hardcode to the wearer's DNA so you can't zap yourself. The part that makes contact when you punch is a platinum tungsten alloy. Even without the shock, it still won't feel great. Try not to hurt yourself. To be honest, if any of us gets to the point of needing to rely on these weapons, it's probably already over."

The grim meaning of Pavel's words settled over the room. Pavel himself appeared dejected, as if he had already resigned himself to imminent death. Adam could only see anger in Aria's expression. He was a coder not a fighter, and felt woefully unprepared for a scenario requiring electrodusters and ballistic vests. He looked around the room, wondering how he appeared to the others.

The group passed the rest of the evening going over the logistics of the plan and making sure their supplies were accounted for, ready, and tested to the degree they could. Aria finished the replica Lightcap, and it was indistinguishable from Hana's Lightcap to the naked eye. Adam wasn't convinced their plan would work, especially the part when they somehow managed to infiltrate the top floor of the headquarters of the largest corporation in the Region. By comparison, their plan to gain access to the Adaptech building felt almost easy.

Pavel came up with the plan, and they sat in a circle as he went over the details. "The top five floors of the Adaptech building, mostly executive offices and conference rooms, are access controlled. Aria, you'll need to get to Adaptech before the rest of the programming team. Adam, you and I will sneak in through the back loading dock, where there's almost no security, and make our way up the stairwell to the 160th floor, where Aria will open the door so we can proceed to the roof. She'll then head to room 4C while we wait in the stairwell near the roof. Aria will fly over to Metra Corp on the JMR-Heavy with the rest of the v6 team. This assumes no one at Adaptech knows about her relationship with Dej and that the Lightcap replica doesn't somehow give her away. Once the copter returns from the Metra Corp building for its second run, we'll exit onto the roof, keeping low and running between the massive cooling units to keep out of sight, eventually making it to the raised dais of the helipad. A cargo elevator is used for loading supplies, so we should be fine in the stairwell until we're ready to make our move.

"A crew of two fly the chopper, along with another two guarding the landing platform. The helipad is roughly ten feet above the roof, which should give us ample cover from being seen by the guards. They load from the side facing the cargo elevator, and that's the direction I think the guards will be facing as they watch the workers who are loading the chopper. I believe the guard's primary task is to watch the employees during loading to minimize shrinkage, so they should pay us no mind." Pavel lifted up a pile of rope and metal. "I've also got these grappling hooks. We'll use them to climb the wall and get up to the platform." Adam felt slightly comforted by the amount of thought Pavel had clearly put into this.

The doctor drew paths across printed blueprints, indicating their planned trek across a plateau in the clouds. The trio synchronized its watches. Pavel and Adam offered aesthetic assessments to Aria in her counterfeit Lightcap, plans gone over second and third times to ensure consistency. They ended their night with a toast offered by Troyka, a vintage 1930s vodka that had belonged to his father. They drank to their departed friends and to their chances of saving those who still survived. The cool drift of alcohol spread out at the back of Adam's tongue and pooled into a warmth at the bottom of his stomach.

Aria left her sword with Adam, after giving him a hug and apologizing for drawing it on him earlier in a rare show of emotion. Pavel gave Adam a hearty handshake. "Sleep well," he admonished with a tone of fatherly concern.

Adam lay in bed awake until his frantic mind felt it had to be nearly dawn, though only an hour had actually passed before he fell asleep. He dreamed a memory from his youth of a weekend spent on an island with his parents, two days of laughter, embraces, and warm breezes carried over the lake. The sights and sounds of his father and mother smiling and joking with him over food and fire relaxed Adam's mind and, in his bed in Pavel's house, his body. A look of contentment passed across his face. Adam slept deeply and well, though for all any of them knew, it might be the last sleep any of them would enjoy.

It was a peaceful dream.

Calm

Pavel shook Adam awake early the next morning when it was still dark. Adam felt certain he had closed his eyes only minutes before, but the clock next to his bed proved to him several hours had passed. He rubbed his eyes blearily, then made his way to the common room, where their supplies were laid out. Weapons, ropes, and boxes ran the length of the table. Pavel loaded the grappling hooks and other materials into a backpack while Adam got ready. He looked as if he planned to go for a day of hiking, or maybe to some evening classes, not to stow away on a helicopter and infiltrate the headquarters of the biggest corporation in the Region. Two ballistic vests on the table reminded Adam that Aria had taken hers the previous evening. Adam put his on at the same time as Pavel, surprised by how tight it felt against his chest, his lungs straining against straps with each deep breath. Adam hit his own solar plexus, imagining a gunshot, and felt the nanotube weave of the vest tighten and disperse the energy of the impact. The blow still hurt, but not nearly as much as it would have without the vest.

Adam fitted the electrodusters on his right hand, covered them with a glove, and wrapped the katana handle and sheath in a blanket before he slung it across his back under the cover of his jacket. They had to avert suspicion on the subway. There would be no rescue if someone called the Blues before they made it to the Adaptech building. Pavel threw his backpack around his shoulders silently, and tucked the derringer pistol into his pocket, his jacket pulled down to disguise the telltale outline of the gun against his pant leg. The old man, his hair on end and stubble sprouting from his cheeks as on the day they met on the subway, turned to Adam and asked, "Are you ready?"

"Yes. Well, I think so," Adam said sheepishly. "I have everything I'm supposed to bring. I guess that means I'm ready." He silently cursed himself for sounding so unsure, so afraid. If there was ever a time for false bravado, this was it. "I'm ready. Let's go," he said with more authority.

Pavel nodded with understanding. He walked over to the door, swung it open, its bottom scraping against the cold tile floor, and left the house. Adam followed, closing the door behind him.

Adam had not been outside in many days, at the insistence of his caretakers. His requests for specific information had been answered by Pavel, Aria, or Dej. Pavel's part of town was even more dilapidated than where Aria lived, though it was just a handful of blocks away. Adam found the neighborhood dingy and aged, made worse by the grey slush gathered in the gutters and the dark earlymorning clouds. A rain not quite cold enough to freeze fell, and Adam occasionally heard the sound of snow piles sliding off rooftops, their barely audible scrapes followed by hollow thuds as they hit the ground.

Their faces obscured by scarves and hats, their remaining features blocked from the cameras by the ramble-jamblers around their necks, for all intents and purposes invisible and unknowable, Pavel and Adam made their way out of the ghetto to a functioning subway station. They avoided the platforms in this part of town since they were in various states of disrepair or enclaves for illegal activities, not wanting to use their weapons prematurely. As they neared the stairs leading to the underground rails of the nearest acceptable station, Pavel turned to Adam and said, "I think we should split up here. I don't foresee it being much of an issue, but people may remember your face from the news broadcasts after Montery and Slate were murdered. It's my hope they've forgotten you after Jared's execution. The winter clothes will help, anyway. We'll approach the Adaptech building from the east side, to avoid anyone who might know you, and end up at the loading dock. We'll meet there and go in together. Keep me in sight while we're on our way to the building."

Adam nodded. He stayed still and slowly counted down from thirty while Pavel walked away from him. When he reached zero, he proceeded in the same direction, shoulders down and hood up, pressed against the diagonal rain. He made his way down the stairs slowly, his feet placed on each step with purpose. Adam was fairly certain he could see the top of Pavel's head. He watched as Pavel boarded the car of a train that had just arrived. Adam reached the platform as the loudspeaker broke out with the sound of a pleasant male voice saying, "Please stand clear of the closing doors."

The doors usually stayed open for thirty seconds. Adam hadn't counted, but he was sure they'd been open for barely half that time. As the doors started to close, hidden pneumatic pistons hissing along their paths, Adam sprinted for the opening. He arrived just before the rubber gaskets touched, his left hand shoving between the gleaming steel doors. He pushed through the seam to find his progress ended by the blanket-wrapped katana diagonally spanning his back, stuck outside of the car. The doors were designed not to reopen, otherwise the trains would never be on time. The pressure wasn't getting any worse, but the doors didn't open to allow entry. Adam was stuck half in, half out. That was not a good way to go unnoticed.

Thinking quickly, Adam braced his feet against the floor, pushed into the door behind him with his back, then heaved against the door pressed down on his chest. The doors parted enough for him to angle his body inward, and he fell with a loud smack onto the dirty car floor, his right foot still caught in the door. Adam watched through the glass as his shoe popped off and landed noiselessly on the platform as his bare foot pulled through the doors. *Smooth*, Adam thought as he got to his feet. *At least I still have the sword.*

Missing a shoe and red with embarrassment, Adam found a place to stand. He was afraid a seated position would give away the outline of the katana under his jacket. Adam scanned the car for Pavel until his eyes came to rest on the familiar hood of the old man's jacket, his face partially obscured by shadow. A slight bow of the head indicated the doctor noticed him as well. They rode in silence, the passengers' heads stuck in readers, under domes, or asleep, all rocking in unison with the subway car as it screamed along the rail, linked by shared rhythm.

Eventually the wheels ground against their brakes and the train came to a halt at their stop. Adam watched to make sure Pavel left with the rush of those disembarking, then followed, distant but close enough to see the old man stepping around slower people ascending the stairs. He was surprised at Troyka's speed and agility for his age and his medium height. Adam's long legs struggled to keep up, despite long strides.

Up the stairs and onto the street, Adam managed to keep pace twenty meters behind, even as the aged man weaved between groups of slower pedestrians. Adam breathed with sharp pains as his lungs expanded, the cold air and moisture from the air replaced by heat from the core of his body. He watched a few breaths disappear forever. The rain fell stronger on his hood than it had when they left Pavel's. Every few minutes he'd pass someone carrying an umbrella being hit by rain. The sound of water against taut fabric reminded Adam of the sound of static.

Adam saw motion out of the corner of his eye as he passed one of the umbrella holders, a plump man whose shoulder he had brushed in his attempt to get through. The man grabbed him as he passed, asking, "Adam?" Adam turned to see the pink, round face of Nate Taylor, his old boss. "I thought it was you!" Nate said with pleasure. "How have you been? Still working upstairs?"

Damn it, Adam thought, aware he had to respond. There was no way to know if there had been rumors or even an official memo passed down to workers at Nate's managerial level. Adam cracked a smile, hoping his eyes didn't betray the raw panic he felt inside, and replied, "Sure am. You're coming in awfully early, aren't you?"

"Yeah," Nate sighed, "my team has to come in earlier these days. Roman has us pulling double duty, working mesh security for both Adaptech and Metra Corp. There have been a few blips lately that require the attention of my team, so I'm putting in some long hours myself. I'm salary. What can you do?" Nate asked with a resigned shrug.

Adam flicked his eyes across the backs of the crowd to look for Pavel, who was nowhere to be seen. They were almost to the building. Adam would have to find some way to extricate himself from the conversation with Nate. The plump man's pace was roughly half that of Pavel's, which had slowed Adam down considerably. He realized Nate had turned toward him as they walked. Before Adam had a chance to respond, the shorter man looked him up and down and asked, "Adam, did you realize you're missing a shoe?"

Silence. During times such as these, Adam wished he were a better liar. Since his lies were about as convincing as the pitch of a door-to-door insurance salesman, he decided to go with honesty. "That noticeable, eh? I was hoping to get away with it for the day, what with my feet under the desk and all. I was running late for the subway, thought it'd be a good idea to squeeze through the doors as they were closing. I made it, but one of my shoes wasn't as lucky."

They reached the corner where Adam had to split off to get to the loading dock. He still hadn't seen any trace of Pavel. He stopped. Nate did the same. Adam said, "I was going to go in through the back loading dock, take the stairs, try and prevent anyone else noticing my embarrassing footwear situation." He tried to laugh with carefree abandon, but his throat was so dry from anxiety it came out as more of a choking cough.

Nate looked at Adam inquisitively. "Oh, you have an access code for the back?"

Adam struggled to clear his throat, hoping it wasn't outwardly obvious he was shocked. The intelligence on the building from LaMont's files suggested the loading dock was the weakest point of entrance with abysmal security. Rather than lie, Adam opted for a half-truth. "Access code? Didn't know they put in an access code."

"Yeah, about two months back. Several memos were sent out, didn't you read them?" Nate seemed innocently amused.

No one ever read the memos. There were just too many, and there was too much other work to be done. In Adam's case, maybe they had given it to him when he was wearing the blasted Lightcap, or during one of the mind-numbing status meetings, if they had given it to him at all. His memory wasn't what it used to be. "Sure didn't," Adam replied. "Got a stack of memos on my desk almost a foot high, need to catch up. I know you understand that. Can you help me out? Our little secret?" He smiled grimly, pleadingly, convinced Nate would say no.

The look on the pudgy man's face was one of shock, as if he didn't immediately know how to respond. Adam was surprised, however, when Nate chuckled and said, "Why the hell not? I like you enough, and I know you're not the sort to do anything untoward. I was against the changes anyway, since all the floors where people work on anything confidential are access-controlled."

They walked the remaining steps in silence. Adam was sure this was some kind of trap, that Blues would be waiting for him when they arrived around the corner, but they made it to the other end of the building without being stopped. There was still no sign of Pavel, and Adam didn't have the luxury of waiting around for him to show up. The loading dock was completely empty, and they encountered no resistance on their way into the building. Having one of the managers from the security division probably helped.

The Security Software department was on the 5th floor. They took the stairs together, Nate's face even more red by the end, his breaths drawn in soft gasps. "Hey, thanks for doing me this favor," Adam said as they paused at the door to Nate's floor. "I really appreciate it."

"No sweat," Nate said, wiping his brow. "Well, maybe a *little* sweat." He laughed, then disappeared into the nondescript halls of Adaptech. An anxious silence settled over the stairwell after he left. Adam went up one flight of stairs, waited for about five minutes to ensure no one was going to ambush him, then went back down to the ground level.

Adam was relieved to see Pavel standing nonchalantly behind a shrink-wrapped pallet when he opened the door. Pavel jogged over to join him, then said, "I am glad you met a friend. Fortuitous circumstance. I figured I'd stay out of sight and see if he let you in, or if it was a trap. Glad it worked out." Adam wasn't sure what Pavel would have done if it had been a trap, but he felt it better to let the subject drop as they began their long ascent, his stomach churning.

Around the 30th floor, Adam began to wonder how Pavel kept going. Adam's legs were already on fire, and burned more with each step. *This is what happens when a cubicle monkey tries to climb a tree,* thought Adam, cursing his past excuses for not joining a gym. After the 60th floor, he made Pavel stop. Rather, the old doctor stopped because Adam was clearly distressed, his hands on his knees, his breath coming in desperate gulps.

"Need a minute. Knees hurt. Not happy," Adam said, between each sharp inhalation.

The old man smiled. Adam couldn't help but detect a hint of

pride in the corners of his eyes. Pavel seemed to be in much better shape. If the situation were reversed, Adam would probably have been proud of himself too. The younger man was too tired even to pant by the time they reached the 130th floor, and resorted to pulling himself up by the railing until his arms gave out then pushing himself up on the stairs until his legs gave out again. Adam switched back and forth in this way for the rest of the climb, which left him with arms and legs feeling like jelly by the time they stopped at the locked stairwell door on the 155th floor to wait for Aria.

Pavel and Adam sat down together at the stairway door that led to the access-controlled upper floors. Adam slid down the wall, put his hands on his knees, and took deep breaths until he felt strength returning to his limbs. Pavel cracked his back and fingers, then yawned. He had climbed the stairs with relative ease, though keeping pace with Adam had probably made the climb slightly less difficult for him. They waited in uncomfortable silence for several minutes, until they heard movement on the other side of the door.

The door pushed open toward them. It was Aria. Her eyes seemed sunken, set against puffy eyelids and dark circles on the underside. She looked as if she was very tired, had been crying, or both. Her eyes met theirs and she said simply, "Let's go." They followed her up the remaining flights of stairs. When they reached the top floor, home of room 4C, Aria turned to Adam and asked, "Did you bring it?"

"Yep," he replied, turning slightly to show her the diagonal line across his back, under the jacket.

"Good. See you there." With that she was gone, going to meet up with the rest of the team. Pavel and Adam walked up the remaining two flights to the roof access level, settled in, and prepared to spend the next two hours waiting for the second helicopter trip from Adaptech to Metra Corp. They tried to talk to one another, but even when they spoke in hushed whispers the sounds of their voices bounced around the polished walls of the stairwell, making them feel nervous at the risk of being exposed.

The time passed uneventfully. Adam jumped several times, alarmed by some sound from far below on the stairwell or from outside on the roof. He could not shake the foreboding feeling that each creak and groan was a prelude to capture, and the longer they waited, the more anxious he felt. He nervously cracked his neck and back, the pop of his joints amplified by the silence of the stairwell, and doubted his own ability to take much more waiting.

Pavel eventually looked at his wrist, his attention drawn by the soft vibration of his watch, its near-silent alarm alerting them that two hours had passed. Pavel's wrinkled face seemed to age fifty years in a moment, then he turned to Adam and said, "It's time." The old man stood, turned his back on Adam, and pushed against the crash bar. Wind and rain rushed into the stairwell as the door opened to the roof.

Adam immediately missed his shoe as soon as they stepped onto the roof, the gravel crunching under one foot but producing shocks of pain in the other. He let out an involuntary yelp. Pavel turned to look at him, then pressed his lips together disapprovingly and shook his head slightly. They continued, and Adam tried not to wince each time his right foot made contact with the ground.

The duo made their way across the roof, their view of the landing platform blocked out each time they ducked behind a large cooling unit. The helicopter was there, perpendicular to their line of approach, idling. On the other side of the helicopter they could see the legs of workers and wheels of carts carrying boxes of cargo for transport to Metra Corp. As they drew closer, Adam could make out the face of the pilot as he looked down and checked instruments on his panel.

When Pavel and Adam reached the wall separating them from the raised landing pad, Pavel shrugged his backpack off his shoulders. Calmly and efficiently, he opened the backpack and pulled out two hooks and a bundle of rope. With practiced motions, the old man connected the hooks to the ropes, handed one to Adam, then spun his own faster and faster until it emitted a slight whistle next to him. He aimed, timed, and released his hook, watching it sail in an arc and land with a *clink* against the edge of the raised platform. They heard it scrape against the cement platform's floor as Pavel pulled the rope taut, testing its grip.

Adam tried to repeat Pavel's movements, only to end up sending the hook on a line drive straight ahead. It hit the wall in front of them with a loud boom, thankfully obscured by the helicopter's spinning rotors. When Adam failed again on his second attempt, the older man grabbed the hook and rope. Adam, humiliated, watched as Pavel quickly wrapped them up and stashed them back in his bag, chuckling at Adam. Pavel then scurried up the rope and disappeared over the ledge for a moment, reappearing to extend his hand to assist Adam's climb.

Despite his skinny frame, Adam struggled to get up the rope, his muscles complaining loudly to his mind. Eventually he met Pavel's forearm with a grip. Pavel reciprocated, hoisting Adam up the rest of the way, then pointed at the rear of the chopper to their right. The older man waved his hand in the air, a silent command to proceed to that area. As they moved, Adam cautiously checked for indications the pilot had seen them, but they were outside his periphery. After a dozen paces, Pavel and Adam regarded the door to the rear cargo hold and opened it easily. The rain, already stinging them, began to turn to hail and rattled off the helicopter's skin with a metallic *ping*.

Pavel and Adam ducked inside the cargo bay and closed the door behind them. The hold's interior was pitch black, and the vibration of the rotors above replaced the sounds of the hail in Adam's consciousness. Pavel leaned in toward Adam, raising his voice to be heard, and said, "The ride takes about thirty minutes. These birds can fly fast, and have a top speed of over three-hundred kilometers an hour. It's going to be bumpy in here, so you should try to find something solid for support. We should be leaving soon." Adam groped in the darkness until he found a vertical piece of metal secured to the wall.

Several minutes later, true to Pavel's word, Adam felt his stomach lurch against the back of his throat as the machinery and cargo surrounding him shuddered, groaned, and lifted off the platform.

Storm

Adam's shoeless, throbbing foot felt almost a part of the metal floor beneath him. Pavel hadn't lied about the bumpy ride. Most of Adam's body hurt. It was then that he realized just how fragile he was, and that their chance of survival was so small as to effectively be zero. Though he was afraid of dying, he did not wish to continue living in a world where someone like LaMont would go unchallenged. Even if they failed in their attempt to rescue Dej and Sera, they had to try. His heart pounded nervously in his chest. He felt lightheaded for a moment, then a slow sense of downward movement.

As they dropped, Adam clenched and unclenched his left fist in an attempt to calm himself. They landed with a jolt. Adam's knees bent from the force of impact, his right hand tightening around the I-beam aiding his balance. He felt Pavel's hand on his shoulder as the old man leaned in to say, "Now we wait. They'll close the roof and unload from the main compartment. Once they've finished, we'll go."

Pavel once again proved to be clairvoyant. Adam heard the *swoop* of the rotor blades slow, along with a far-off noise of grinding metal. The sounds of hail against the outer hull of the vessel slowed and stopped. A final groan came from above as two alloy jaws locked together and the Metra Corp building roof slid closed above the landing pad. Adam could hear muffled voices and the rumbles of crates being moved out of the main cargo hold. After a few minutes the voices and rumbles ceased.

They waited until it had been silent for several more minutes. Pavel said, "I think it's clear. Let's go." Pavel and Adam found the door's handles and swung it open, a sliver of light appearing then widening to reveal an empty hangar. They stepped out, small bits of hail cracking under their feet as they walked. "This way," said Pavel, with a motion toward a nearby open hallway.

Adam took off the glove covering his electrodusters, dropped his jacket, unwrapped Aria's katana, then replaced the sword against his back. The short hallway ended with three doors. Pavel took the one on the left. Adam followed, trusting that the old man had some idea where they were going. The door opened into a stairwell. As he followed Pavel, the door behind Adam opened. He whipped about to see a guard emerging. Their eyes met. Adam charged without thinking, driving both his fists squarely into the man's stomach, causing the man to let out an involuntary cry, surprised by the impact.

Adam had intended to incapacitate the man with his electrodusters. As he watched the man struggle back to his feet, Adam realized they had not discharged. The man was wearing a Lightcap, and he would no doubt sound the alarm as soon as he had a split second to collect his thoughts. Not knowing what else to do, Adam remembered the blade across his back and drew it in one long movement. Adam brought the grip of the katana down with a crash against the front arm of the man's Lightcap, right where plastic met the bubble. The man appeared stunned for a moment, then slumped to the ground.

Adam turned back to Pavel, who wore an amused expression. The old man said, "Good job. Let's go," before starting down the stairs.

"Why didn't he get shocked when I hit him?" Adam asked,

following.

"Has to be skin, as I told you. Otherwise the damned thing would go off all the time," Pavel responded. "Details are important." They reached the bottom of the stairs, where they found a locked door, a keypad mounted in the wall next to it. Pavel turned to Adam and said, "There wasn't any mention of this in LaMont's datafile. There were a few numbers in there, but no notation to suggest their purpose." Pavel punched in six digits. The glass pad emitted a minor tritone and the red light near the top flashed three times. He tried another code with the same result.

"There may be an alarm set to go off if there are too many failed attempts," Adam warned. Pavel turned back, an annoyed look on his face, but his expression softened as he realized Adam was right.

"We'll need to find some other way to get in," the doctor said. "Some way to take the system offline or interrupt it." He looked Adam up and down and commanded, "Give me that sword."

Adam had no idea why Pavel wanted the sword, but obeyed, lifting the blade over his head and handing to the elder man, who grabbed it from him and raced back up the stairs. After a few moments of silence, Adam heard the door above swing back open and Pavel called down, "This is going to be a bit messy."

When Pavel reached the bottom of the stairs, Adam was aghast at what he saw. A six centimeter square of skin with blood dripping from one side and smeared on the other. Pavel's face was blank. His hand extended to return the sword. "Here, you can have this back," he said. Adam put the sword in place against his back as Pavel took the piece of skin and slammed its bloody underside against the glass keypad, where it stuck in place with a wet slap. "Use the electrodusters on this. Don't even have to hit it hard, just make contact." Pavel moved around Adam, grabbed the door handle, and applied downward pressure.

Adam wasn't sure why he did what he did, but he coiled his arm back and punched the square of skin with all the strength he could muster. The dusters smashed against the skin, producing a bright arc of electricity. The glass underneath cracked and popped. Pavel's hand moved as the handle gave way, the door opening along its path.

The room beyond the door was familiar. Rows of cubicles, each like the last, their bubbled tops giving the appearance of a room full of eggs in a large, open carton. Adam felt a chill of recognition as he realized this was the room from his dream of Damen's death.

Unlike the cubicle farms to which Adam was accustomed, in which there was a near-constant din of conversation, chairs moving, and phones ringing, this room was deathly quiet. Pavel and Adam ducked down one of the aisles, and Adam opened the milk-white door to the first cubicle in that row, sliding it along its track to find a man inside he had never seen before. The man wore a Lightcap and stared intently at the screen, where lines of code appeared at regular intervals.

A sudden sound of movement came from down the hall where they had just emerged, which caused Pavel to push Adam into the cubicle and follow behind him. The door could not softly slide back into place quickly enough to suit Adam. They heard rushed footsteps and muffled voices one or two rows away. Adam couldn't make out what they were saying but thought he heard the words "she" and "restraints".

The man in the cubicle did not stir or acknowledge Adam and Pavel's presence in any way, as if they weren't even there. Adam leaned over the man's shoulder in an attempt to read the lines of code on the screen, but Pavel grabbed his shoulder and said, "We should go. It seems as if they were headed deeper into the building, not where we came from. We need to find Aria."

Pavel nudged Adam out of the cubicle and exited closely behind, putting the door back in place. The motionless man remained, his eyes focused on his computer screen as he added more lines of code.

They went to their left, in the same direction the voices had retreated. Reaching the end of the row and emerging into a perpendicular hallway, a commotion on their right caught their attention. With their heads turned to their right, neither Pavel nor Adam saw the men who approached from their left until they ran past. Adam and Pavel both reflexively flinched as these two Blues entered their side view and continued beyond.

Adam and Pavel, stunned not to be confronted but ignored, saw that these two men also wore Lightcaps. The Blues turned and entered a door on their left, sounds of struggle coming through the gap where they entered. Pavel and Adam looked at each other, then ran down the hall to where the men had gone and threw open the door.

They found a small room with a lone table centered in the middle. Aria lay upon the table, struggling ferociously, one of her arms strapped down to it. Her free arm locked around the neck of a struggling Blue from behind. Four other Blues circled her, wary of her flying legs. The free Blues looked up as Adam and Pavel entered the room. Aria used the distraction as an opportunity to throw her leg into the air, where it connected with the closest man's neck. His throat emitted a sickening gurgle as he went down.

The Blue in front of Adam turned and threw a punch to Adam's chest. The glancing blow hurt, but the ballistic vest helped absorb most of the impact. Adam had reflexively tried to block it and mostly failed, but he found himself in an advantageous position to jab the Blue's face. A loud crack and sparks trailing over the man's skin from the point of impact indicated almost a million volts discharging in an instant. The man's head jerked back along the axis of his neck before he sagged to the ground.

Pavel had already handled one of the Blues, who now lay on the ground behind him convulsing, and blocked the attempted strike of another wielding a truncheon. Adam observed the practiced grace of the elder man, who grabbed the Blue's wrist with one hand and expertly delivered his other palm to the elbow with a nauseating crunch. The Blue cried out in pain, the sound of his shock bouncing off the walls of the room. Pavel slid his hand down to the man's wrist, grabbed the baton from his hand, then brought it crashing down on his temple.

"Nothing personal," Pavel said.

Aria still had one Blue from behind, his gasps growing more and more desperate, each attempt to remove her arm more futile than the last. Adam drew the katana and cut the bonds holding her right arm and leg. Aria took the katana from him, brought it to the neck of the Blue who struggled against her, and drew her arm quickly, as a cellist controls the bow across strings. The man sank to the ground, choking on his own blood and carved flesh.

"Thanks," she said as she turned to face them. "Let's go." A klaxon sounded as they walked through the door, and hurried footsteps came from every direction. A dozen Blues emerged from different rows and hallways, all wearing what appeared to be Lightcaps, and surrounded the three of them. Each Blue had a gun or baton drawn.

"Hands up!" said the closest one.

Pavel and Aria stood in front of Adam, who didn't think they had much of a chance to fight their way out of that. He reached into his right pocket, flipped open the cover of Dej's device, and drove his thumb against its button. Adam shuddered as the Blues' faces changed from dull sternness to wild abandon. Their hands opened and their weapons dropped to the ground. They began to run, banging into walls, each other, and any other obstacle they met. One of the workers broke through a cubicle door from the inside with a crash, its cheap plastic splitting with a crack as he unknowingly threw his body against it. Adam would have found this amusing under different circumstances, the mayhem reminding him of slapstick comedy.

"The radios are fried," Pavel said, "so they'll have to be repaired by hand. We need to find Dej and Sera." They had decided Sera would most likely be near LaMont, and they hoped Dej would be too. The executive suites were one level down, requiring them to go back to the staircase. The alarms still blared, but no more guards appeared. The trio pushed through the crowd of frenetic Blues and workers, the bodies bouncing against them and flying off at odd angles as they went down the cubicle row. No guard stood at the staircase door.

Aria took the lead with her red-streaked sword like a sharp-tongued guide. Adam followed behind her, with Pavel in the rear. After going down a flight of stairs they stood at the stairwell door, where Aria held up her hand. Adam and Pavel stopped. She opened the door, pushing it with enough force to make a half circle arc and end against the wall. They went through. Because of his height, Adam saw motion to his right a split second before Aria reacted to it. A Blue was raising his truncheon with the intent to bring it down upon her head.

Adam saw movement to his left as well and turned just in time to see a raised gun. He lurched toward the Blue wielding the pistol. A sudden bang assailed his ears as his stomach was pinched with a warm sting. Before the shot, Adam had started to swing, and his swing continued despite the shock to his abdomen. His fist connected with the jaw of the Blue, not hard enough to cause damage on its own, but the voltage discharged with a splitting snap. The Blue dropped with a thud. In his soreness, Adam could not help thinking he could get used to these electrified knuckles.

Adam turned to see Aria standing over the man who had attempted to beat her. He lay partially decapitated on the floor, slumped sideways against the wall, his mouth opened in surprise. Blood still gushed from his neck. She wiped her sword off on the dead man's uniform, leaving a thick red smear on his blue fabric and gold accents. Pavel still stood in the stairwell.

"This way. We have to find LaMont," Aria said as she led the two men down the hall.

The hallway reminded Adam of the hallway leading to room 4C in the Adaptech building, cold and white. They headed to LaMont's office, which lay at the end of the hall according to the datafile. Aria held up her hand as a signal to the men behind her to stop, then motioned to her right with her sword.

They pressed their backs against the wall to their right and Aria crouched down, her sword held steady in front of her. A heartbeat later, she charged around the corner. Pavel and Adam heard a shout of surprise, then the sound of Aria's blade slashing through flesh, sickening and wet, followed by a gurgle. A gunshot. Two thuds. The men lunged around the corner to see Aria bent over as she pulled her sword from two Blues. She had stabbed one through the neck, then used him as a shield and drove him into the other man, stabbing him in the head. The smell of blood mixed with gunsmoke hung in the air.

"Halt!" came a voice from behind them. Adam turned with Aria and Pavel to see two more Blues bearing down on them in a full sprint from the other end of the hallway. Pavel, closest to the Blues, reacted immediately. He pulled his gun from his pocket and fired a shot. The bullet hit the closest Blue on his upper right cheek, causing him to fall to the ground, carried forward by his momentum. The remaining Blue dodged to the side, leveled his weapon, and fired twice at Pavel. One of the bullets impacted against Pavel's left arm, causing the old man to spin and fall at Adam's feet.

The Blue advanced on Pavel, who lay motionless on the carpet, raising his gun as if to fire. Aria still struggled to remove her sword from the neck and skull of the two Blues she'd killed. Adam didn't know what else to do, so he rushed forward, prompting the Blue to turn the gun on him. Pavel swung his legs up, blurred against the dark navy of the gunman's uniform, and kicked the gun as it fired. Adam could have sworn he felt the bullet brush against the right side of his scalp before he tackled the Blue. Pavel had twisted his torso while he kicked, and wrapped his arms around the Blue's legs just as Adam's hit sent the guard crashing on the floor. His head bounced against the ground with a sound of cracking plastic, a disoriented look on his face.

Pavel and Adam got to their feet as Aria finally pulled her blade free. Pavel bled from his left shoulder. The bullet had entered just next to the ballistic vest, ricocheted off bone, and exited after traveling a straight path through the old man's bicep. Aria's eyes widened when she saw the blood, and she raised her sword to strike the Blue.

"Wait!" Adam cried. Aria turned to look at him. "You don't need to kill this man.," Adam continued. "Look, his Lightcap is damaged." He motioned to the man, whose eyes rapidly blinked, focused on nothing.

Aria, incredulous, asked, "Are you fucking kidding? Nothing wrong with having one less Blue around. Besides, it could just be temporary. Maybe the Lightcap will reboot, and then he'll come up from behind and shoot us in the back of the head. Is that what you want? Let's just kill him now and be done with it."

Pavel stepped between Aria and the fallen Blue, grimacing at the pain of movement. "Aria, we are supposed to be the good guys. Adam is right. There is no need to kill this man. He's no longer a threat to us. If you're that worried about it, I'll take his weapon." Pavel picked up the man's gun and stuck it into his waistband behind his back. Aria said nothing and lowered her sword. She remained silent while Adam tore off a piece of his shirt and tied it around Pavel's upper arm, then turned abruptly and continued down the hall. Adam and Pavel followed her.

They made it to LaMont's suite without further interruption. A monolithic slab of obsidian, shiny black with vertical handles of brushed metal, served as the door. Aria did not pause to make sure

Pavel and Adam were ready. She pulled the door open and they stormed into the suite. The door closed behind them with a hiss, driven back against its frame by hidden springs.

The trio was shocked to find themselves in an apparently unoccupied room.

LaMont

Aria slammed her fist on the empty desk. "Of course it would be empty! This was LaMont's office while he was third in line. With Montery gone, of course LaMont would take his old office. Probably bigger, or has a better view," she hissed.

They each went in a different direction to look for any clues. The suite, with a main room several times bigger than LaMont's office at Adaptech, looked as if it could have doubled as a luxury apartment. *No wonder he spends most of his time here,* Adam thought. A few chairs lined the wall along a bay of massive windows overlooking New Metra City far off in the distance. Adam caught himself looking out, his ghosted reflection superimposed over the glass, speckled with the light of the buildings outside. He heard a muffled noise from an adjacent room a few feet away and went to investigate it. Adam was unprepared for what he found when he turned the corner.

"Aria! Pavel! Over here," he yelled. Dej sat in an office chair, his arms taped down, his body slumped. Adam could see Dej's chest rise and fall almost imperceptibly, but could also see drops of blood falling from his chin onto his shirt. He ran up and began trying to free Dej from the tape, but it was secure and Adam had nothing sharp with which to cut it.

Aria got to them first, followed shortly after by Pavel. Aria cut the wraps binding Dej's arms to the chair with her sword. Pavel cleaned up Dej's face as Aria worked. Adam tried his best to stay out of their way. Dej stirred and groaned, but he did not speak.

"Dej," Aria said, as she crouched in front of him and cupped his face with her hands. "Wake up, love." She cried and wiped her face.

"We've got Dej. We need to get out of here," Adam said, then pointed back toward the door.

Pavel, who had spent his time examining the few things occupying the office, turned toward the others and said, "We may have a problem. It is clear they either expected us to come here or put Dej in this room for a reason—either as punishment or to get rid of him." His eyes jumped to Aria as he finished.

Aria didn't say a word, but she hoisted Dej by his left arm, her right arm behind his back to offer support. His head sagged, but Dej appeared to be able to put some weight on his legs. Adam rushed to grab Dej's other arm. The quartet made it back to the dark door, but it wouldn't open.

"Are you kidding me?" Adam demanded. "We walked right into a trap! That's great." He could scarcely believe they hadn't thought to prop the door open.

"It may not be as dire as you think," Pavel said, walking over to a glass touchscreen mounted in the wall to the right of the door. He touched it, and it lit up. "I'll take care of this, you take care of Dej," Pavel said, his fingers quickly moving across the screen.

They carried Dej to a plush chair close by the entrance. Aria snapped her fingers in front of his face in an attempt to wake him, but her action had little effect. Dej's eyelids were fluttering, but he had not opened his eyes or spoken. Pavel called Adam over to him.

"This is worse than I thought," Pavel said as he pulled up a file on the screen. "Control access is completely locked out, so the door cannot be opened from here. I was able to gain read-only system access, though, and it appears the environmental systems have been set to remove all oxygen from the room."

"What?" asked Adam, not quite believing what Pavel said.

"That bastard LaMont is trying to suffocate us," the doctor responded. "This door is a hermetic seal and the windows have no seams, probably as a protection against potential biological or chemical attacks. Based on the information I've been able to find, we have about ten minutes before we lose consciousness, and another ten, maybe fifteen minutes before brain damage, then death." He stepped aside side so Adam could see the information from the building's environmental subsystems. As far as Adam could tell, Pavel was right.

"Couldn't we just use the electrodusters like before to zap the system and overload it?"

"Probably not. Besides the fact the skin would have to come from one of us, I am not convinced it would have any effect, since control access to this panel has been revoked."

"Aria!" Adam shouted as he turned and looked back at her. "We have more important things to worry about than Dej right now. This room is slowly turning into our tomb."

Aria looked up at him, got to her feet, and said, "What do you mean?"

Pavel responded before Adam had a chance: "Environmental controls have been set to remove all the O_2 from the room. The doors and windows are sealed—no way for fresh air to get in. We need to find a way out."

Adam motioned to Aria to follow him and went back to the large floor-to-ceiling windows near where they had found Dej minutes before. He walked over to the side of the chair where Dej had been seated, then looked and her and nodded toward the window. Aria took the hint and positioned herself on the other side of the chair. They lifted their respective armrests and turned toward the window.

"On three?" Adam asked. Aria nodded. They both swung back. He counted: "One . . . two . . . three!" Their swings grew wider with each number, and they launched the chair toward their own faint reflections when the count ended. For a second Adam thought their plan had succeeded, as the chair smashed into the window with a loud boom. Steel and fabric met a tinted pane that bowed but did not break. At the moment Adam was sure the chair would pass through in a hail of shards, the glass bounced back and sent the chair hurtling across the floor. It slid with a screech and ended about a meter from their feet.

They tried again with the heaviest thing they could find, a large potted plant from the opposite corner of the office, achieving the same result. Adam put his hands on his knees and bent over, panting. Aria's chest rose and fell more quickly than usual as well. He wasn't sure if they were just tired or if it was an effect of the diminishing air in the room. Maybe both. Either way, they had run out of things to throw at the window.

"Any other ideas?" Aria asked.

"No," Adam said dejectedly.

Aria walked back over to where Dej was seated. His chin rested against his chest, which barely moved as he breathed. Adam went to Pavel, who still tapped furiously against the panel on the wall, attempting to find some way out of the room. He looked up as Adam approached and asked, "No luck? Me either. This system is locked down pretty good. They knew we were coming." Adam felt lightheaded. The old man looked as if he was fighting for breath, his chest expanding and contracting quickly. Pavel caught his breath and continued, "I don't think there's any way we're going to get out of th—" The panel emitted an urgent sounding series of beeps.

Adam's eyes widened as the image on the screen disappeared, replaced by two words in bold letters:

> **STAND BACK**

Pavel and Adam looked at each other dumbfounded, before realizing the message was likely directed at them. Adam ducked around the corner, Pavel close behind him. Seconds later there was a series of loud pops, followed by a low *whooshing* sound, then silence. They spent several seconds waiting for a rescuer or an executioner until they realized no one was coming.

Adam wasn't sure what he expected to see, but he eased his head around the corner. The door was ajar, the hint of light passing over its edges. Smaller text had replaced the words on the screen. Adam had to get closer to read it. When he neared the screen, he was shocked to see:

> You owe me, Redmon. If you make it out of that building alive, I'll be in touch.
> - Jon

"Friend of yours?" said a voice from behind Adam. Pavel stood there, reading over his right shoulder, with a look of grateful puzzlement on his face.

"More like a brother," Adam said with obvious relief and joy. "Jon Bays, my oldest friend. I haven't talked to him in over a decade. He disappeared after resigning from Adaptech. I assumed he had forgot all about me. Guess I was wrong."

"He picked a hell of a time to remember," came Aria's voice. Her body caught up and turned the corner with Dej slumped against her. "And I don't know about anybody else, but I would like to get the fuck out of this room now."

Back in the hall, they took a moment to collect their thoughts and breath. The oxygen must have been escaping the room prior to their arrival, because Dej took longer to revive. Eventually, however, he opened his eyes. "Aria," he said, his voice a whisper, "Thank you for saving me."

Aria looked as if she was fighting back more tears. She looked down and said to no one in particular, "I can't let anything happen to Dej."

Adam looked at Pavel, who nodded slightly. He then turned to Aria and said, "Take Dej back to the chopper. Get him patched up as best you can. The Doc and I will find Velim. We'll be right behind you. Stay safe."

Aria looked at both of them with surprise and gratitude. She picked Dej back up, and they were off down the hall. Pavel and Adam walked beside her for several steps, then made a sharp right turn at the intersecting hallway leading to Montery's old office. The Blue they had spared from Aria's wrath was gone, which gave Adam pause, but there was nothing he could do about it now.

Pavel and Adam walked to the end of the hallway in uneasy silence, greeted again by an unusually large slab of obsidian. Apparently Metra Corp executives preferred lavish surroundings over frugality, despite what the media had broadcast on the Spartan habits of the newly elected leaders. Adam wrapped his hand around the cold steel handle to pull open the door when Pavel said, "Adam, wait." Adam looked back and met the old man's gaze.

"I want to tell you that it has been an honor," Pavel said. "I know we haven't spoken much, and I know when we have it hasn't always been friendly. My mind has been weighed heavily with thoughts of this day for months.

"I knew I'd eventually have to make a move against LaMont, and that's why I started dosing you with Cloud, because I wanted someone on the inside I could trust and someone smart enough to find the truth. I am deeply sorry if my actions have created problems for you or caused any sort of lasting harm. I did the best I could, given the circumstances." Adam nodded, holding the door handle.

"I know we can't stand here and talk forever," Pavel continued. "The last thing I want to say is thank you for being so adamant about rescuing Sera. She is the closest thing I've ever had to a daughter, and I wanted very much to believe she had not sided with LaMont, but I cast those hopes aside as the delusions of a foolish old man. You have renewed my faith in the intrinsic goodness that can exist within a person. For that, I can never repay you."

Under any other circumstance, Adam might have got choked up. In this one, he held his hand out to Pavel and said, "Doctor Troyka, the pleasure is mine. I have read about you and your work since I was a child. To stand next to you now, to fight by your side . . . " Adam struggled for the right words, not knowing what else to say. That he owed Pavel his life? That Pavel opened his eyes to the truth? "*I* am honored," he finished, as Pavel gripped his hand firmly.

"Shall we?" The old man asked with a grin. Adam nodded and pulled the door open with all his weight. They stepped into the CEO's suite.

Montery's former rooms struck Adam as more extravagant than LaMont's old executive suite. They found themselves in a narrow hallway, lined with dark red mahogany bookshelves filled with aged manuscripts. The tattered bindings and the smell of musty leather gave Adam the impression they had been there for some time. This made sense, as LaMont did not strike Adam as particularly literary, but he was certainly the sort to keep any kind of decoration implying erudition, and everyone knew old books could be expensive and rare. *Also,* Adam thought bitterly to himself, *LaMont is probably the sort who'd collect trophies of vanquished foes.*

The hallway opened at a freestanding barrier, blocking the view of the door from the main area of the office. As they approached this wall, Pavel tapped Adam's shoulder, pointed at himself and to their right, then pointed at Adam and to their left. They went in their respective directions at the end of the hallway. Adam kept his shoulder pressed against the barrier as he approached its edge. The solid feeling of the wall gave him a bit of comfort as he lost sight of Pavel.

When Adam rounded the corner, his heart sank into his stomach. Two lines of Blues—one on his side, one on Pavel's—stood at attention, facing the room's interior. At the other end of the room, after the twelve armed men, sat Roman LaMont at a desk, wearing the same smug smile Adam had seen many times before. Velim sat at LaMont's right, silent, her hands folded in her lap. She gave no indication she was aware of what was happening. Everyone in the room, with the exception of Pavel and Adam, was wearing a Lightcap. Adam wondered what LaMont's was for.

"Gentlemen," LaMont said, spreading his hands out in a jovial welcome, "please have a seat." He indicated two large plush chairs facing his desk. Seeing no other choice, they sat down. "Welcome to my office. Can I get you anything? Pavel, my old friend, would you like a bandage?" He pointed to Pavel's bleeding arm. The doctor did not answer. LaMont turned to look at Adam and said, "Well, boy, I have to say I didn't think you had it in you. I thought you about shit yourself that day when I told you I would fire you if you stood up to me again, yet here you are. I must not be as intimidating as I thought." He chuckled.

Adam suppressed the urge to offer a witty retort and said, "I'm here for her." He motioned to Velim, who sat to his left, staring blankly. "I won't let you keep her as a slave."

LaMont leaned back and laughed, his head tossing as each staccato bleat punched against Adam's eardrums. Adam, who could feel his anger rising, wanted to leap across the desk and bash LaMont's face in, give him a good shock from the electrodusters, but he knew he'd be dead before he was halfway there. As his laughter subsided LaMont said, "Slave. That's rich. She's no more a slave than I am. You thought you were going to ride in here, knight on a white horse, and save the damsel in distress? Beat the big evil dragon and take home your prize? Speaking of slaves, where's the black bitch you're working with? I didn't expect her to be able to disable the elevator system and security cameras. Did she go back to the chopper with the Indian? I sure hope so, because she'll find a roomful of Blues ready to give her and the curry kid some new holes."

Adam was about to start yelling, but Pavel said with an even tone, "Bullshit, Roman. Absolute, utter hogwash. We know Sera is a slave. We know the Lightcap lets you play puppet master. We're here to end it. As far as Aria is concerned, I have no doubt she can take care of herself."

A look of shock passed over LaMont's face at unexpected boldness when he'd expected pleading. "We'll see how your friends fare," he said. "Sera's a slave, yes, but if she wanted to leave right now, she could. She's not always under control. When she's not, she has some degree of independent action." LaMont glanced at her with mock pity.

"Sure, but you neuter her sense of self, play up the obedience tendencies," Adam said angrily. "Don't act as if people have their full wills, or that she could get up and just walk out the door right now. She has to know somewhere in her addled mind that if she tries to escape you'll kill her. Is she even able to think on her own anymore? How long have you had that cap on her?" Adam could feel his voice rising, his control starting to slip away.

Pavel reached over and gently restrained his forearm in an unspoken warning or a show of solidarity, Adam wasn't sure which. He gripped the arms of the chair and attempted to calm down. There was no point in playing their hand too soon.

LaMont flashed his pompous smile, his face showing he knew he had got under Adam's skin. The smile parted, and he said, "Not as long as you think. She almost never wears it anymore. She's one of the most obedient assistants I've ever had." He sat back and tapped his fingers on his desk. "You don't really understand what is going on here," he added. "You think you have it all figured out, but you don't. Sadly, you never will.

"Sure, the Lightcap makes you a little docile, more open to guidance. Who says that's a bad thing? Look at those people out there," he said, sweeping his hand toward the window, where the lights of New Metra City sparkled in the distance. "They don't want choice, they want convenience. To be a part of something, to feel as if they have some kind of say. The poor bastards out there who work four jobs—you think they care about the shit going on up here? It's not even on their radar. They're too busy making sure they don't lose one of their jobs, because then they'd lose their house, and then they'd disappear. Gotta keep up appearances to live in a Corp Region!" He shook his head and exhaled as if faced with a difficult task.

"Did you know something like ninety percent of them have sold their voting share?" LaMont continued, his face wrinkling into a look of disdain. "A lot of them lie about it, and we make sure any official numbers get cooked before release. We keep modifying this great nation we've built. Our founder, Pennington himself, thought you had to give the poor their voting share. Now we know they just need to think they've got one. Appearances matter. Now more than ever. That's why there are over fifty million video nodes and counting, almost all of which are owned by Metra Corp, through TeleVice and its subsidiaries. Everyone can choose their own node, but they all come with a slant, a bent. Everything has a little truth, but it's all mostly false, all about appearances.

"Metra Corp is spun as being an umbrella group for the five founding corporations, when in reality it now owns them, plus many other companies here, in Cascadia, and the Confederacy. More and more each day, including Adaptech. Why do you think I was picked by Montery? Got named as third in line? It was part of my deal to allow the secret purchase by Metra Corp, absorbing Adaptech's assets."

Adam felt a flash of heat, then said through gritted teeth, "Yes, Montery. Slate. Hana. A lot of people die because of you, but your hands are never dirty."

"Oh, come on," LaMont said with a chuckle. "You can't possibly blame that on me. You're the one who did it. All we did was tell you Montery and Slate wanted to shut down the project, which was true, and that I wanted to expand it, which is also true. We asked you for the most logical way to make sure the project survived, and you said the obvious answer was to remove the two people standing in the way of me being in charge. It was your idea, Adam." He brought his hands back behind his head and leaned back in his chair. Adam had not thought LaMont's smile could appear even larger.

Adam opened his mouth to deny it, but before the words passed his lips he was struck with a disturbing sense of knowing. He knew LaMont's words were true. He remembered, vaguely, being asked how to handle the budget issue facing his project. By LaMont. And Velim.

Pavel spoke on Adam's behalf. "Adam is a good man. Sera is a good woman. You are not good, Roman. You never have been and never will be. You are corrupt—not just greedy but mad, terrible, and diseased. You have a sickness you seek to impose as the motive for the actions of others, but *you* are the one manipulating them and pulling the strings. I do not believe Adam would do this terrible thing of his own volition, even if you entrapped him into coming up with the idea."

"Guilty," LaMont replied, still laughing, holding his hands up as if caught by a Blue. "Adam came up with the idea, but he was no warrior, no assassin. We put him under control for the actual act, just so he wouldn't have to trouble his conscience. He had already expressed the idea, so why not let him see it through?"

"Because I'm not a murderer!" Adam cried. He was tired of this back and forth, but it seemed Pavel was trying to get something from LaMont. He kept waiting for some kind of signal from the old man, some indication it was time to throw the switch sending them all into a panic, then rescue the girl and make their grand escape, but Pavel had barely even looked in Adam's direction, his glances divided between LaMont and the floor.

The doctor then looked up at LaMont and said, "Roman, you have been nothing but a power-hungry maniac since the day I met you. Don't you realize what you're doing is not sustainable? You can't keep amassing power in the hands of the few at the expense of everyone else. They will eventually have had enough. Don't you understand your actions will lead to your own collapse? Look at the history you cite. The companies that eventually formed Metra Corp had to rebuild the entire society after Pennington and his cronies destroyed it."

"Oh, what do you know?" LaMont spat. "You're just an ivory-tower philosopher geek. I live in the real world. The fuck-or-be-fucked world." Stabbing his finger at the two men, he said, "If you're not taking advantage of someone then someone is taking advantage of you, or at the very least you've not maximized your efficiency. The world needs people like me, otherwise there would be no competition."

"So that's what it's about, Roman? A competition to amass the most before you go?" Pavel asked dispassionately.

"Sounds about right. Who cares about sustainability, being fair, or ethics? 'Screw you, I got mine.' That's been the rallying cry of humanity since the first grunter found a cave that was bigger and more dry than the other guy's, or went out and killed himself a lion and brought it back only to be surrounded by moochers. Go kill your own! You try to paint me as this unspeakable villain, but all I'm doing is what a billion other schlubs have done since the dawn of time, and that's look out for me and mine. Competition is what makes us better as a species." LaMont rested his hands in front of him as if he had just argued a case in court and won.

Adam moved his hand toward his left pocket, not enough to register movement, just a bending of the fingers, in the hope the old man would give the command to hit the button.

Pavel shook his head slowly, then said, "No, Roman. You are worse than any normal man. You have far more than enough, and it's anything but to you. You could have all the power in the world and still want more. I don't believe we need people like you to survive. In fact, people like you are making it worse. We'd be better off without you. You poison everything. Look at these men here," Pavel added, indicating the Blues. "Are they better off, Roman?"

LaMont leaned forward, shrugged, and shook his head, as if he couldn't believe what he was hearing. "Such dramatic language," he said. "You're just mad because I had the smarts to muscle my way into the top spot while you hid in the shadows." LaMont paused, then seemed to appraise Pavel anew. "Any way I can convince you to come back? You'd be under armed guard of course, but you'd be comfortable. You'd have to do whatever work I send your way, and if you tried to escape you'd be shot without hesitation, but if you say no I'll order these beneficiaries of my largesse to do that anyway." LaMont motioned to the Blues before turning to Adam and continuing, "Same offer goes to you, son. Better think fast, because I might change my mind and choke you myself." LaMont looked at his fingernails absently, relaxed.

Adam knew this was what Pavel had been waiting for. He did his best to put on a hopeful look and asked LaMont, "Is there any way I can just wear the Lightcap all the time? Maybe get a few days off here and there? But I have to know, what are you having them do? The coding, I mean."

LaMont looked at Adam shrewdly and said, "You know what they say about curiosity. It's probably not in your best interest to get too involved if you want to come back into the fold. But let's just say we've found a way to port some of the Lightcap features to v5. The v6 will have full Lightcap control tech built in to every unit. You never know, Adam. It's a busy world. Right, Pavel?" LaMont winked at the old man.

Though he felt sick, Adam tried his best to keep a calm face. He was fairly certain LaMont was bluffing, that there was no way he was getting out alive at this point anyway. Adam looked LaMont straight in the eye and said, "You can take your offer and go fu—"

"We accept." Pavel shouted, throwing both hands in the air. Adam noticed Pavel's left hand came back to the armrest with three fingers facing downward. The old man continued, "But only if we shake on it, money man." A finger flicked up on the last word. Two left.

"What did you say?" LaMont asked, his eyes wide.

"I accept your offer, but only if you shake my hand," Pavel said. "You know, to seal the deal." Another finger up. One left.

"But you . . . you called me . . . " LaMont trailed off, as though unsure he wanted to continue before he went on, "Never mind. Yes, let's shake on it. I'm glad you've come to your senses. I never really wanted to kill you to begin with. You can make me ridiculous amounts of money. You are on a short list of people whose lives are too profitable to end. Your buddy here is questionable, but I'm in a generous mood. Take those fucking zappers off first, though. I don't need that kind of headache today."

Adam took off the knuckles and dropped them. They hit the wood floor with a clatter. LaMont looked at Pavel expectantly, and the old man brought down his hand in a closed fist to push off against the armrest. Zero. Adam pushed against the armrest with his right hand, slid his left hand into his pocket, and flicked open Dej's device. Then he thrust his thumb against the button.

The Blues surrounding them immediately seized, then ran about in panic. LaMont looked completely shocked. As soon as his eyes left Pavel the old man drew the pistol from his pocket, raised it quickly, and fired. The noise bounced roughly off the walls and floor, final and ominous. LaMont looked down at his chest, a mix of pain and surprise painted on his face. There was no blood. He was wearing a ballistic vest.

Adam didn't understand why LaMont and Sera didn't seem to be affected by Dej's device. Pavel then drew the gun tucked in his waistband, the one he had taken from the Blue in the hallway, and pulled the trigger with a hollow click. He tried again with the same result.

LaMont laughed so hard his entire chest heaved, then caught his breath and said, "Biometric trigger. Gotta love 'em. Did you only bring one shot in your own? How quaint. Then again, I know ammo isn't easy to come by. Fuck, that hurt. I wasn't expecting it to hurt that much. I've never actually had to use this thing."

The armed guards still ran without purpose around the room, bumping into each other and everything else. Adam had to dodge one bouncing off the side of the desk, then pushed him back toward the wall. He turned back to LaMont and asked, "Why aren't you like them? Why didn't Dej's device work on your Lightcap?"

The CEO spat at the sound of Dej's name. "Little brown piece of shit. I should have known." LaMont opened a drawer, pulled out a small golden pistol, and pointed it at Adam before he continued. "I should shoot you right now for doing this to our men. We'll get it fixed though. The lady and I are fine because ours operate on a separate, dedicated frequency and use a different set of command functions. That's the case for all Metra Corp execs. Your team helped build it, in fact. Shame you don't remember, probably would have been useful information." He clucked his tongue.

"Now it's what's going to get you killed," LaMont said. "You, Adam Redmon, are going to witness just how powerful Lightcap technology is. Sera." He turned toward the woman seated to his right. She looked at him. "I want you to kill Doctor Troyka."

Sera Velim said nothing but reached into a bag slung over the back of her chair. She withdrew her hand, firmly wrapped around the handle of a knife, and looked to the floor as she stood. She started to walk behind LaMont.

"Sera, you don't have to do this!" Adam shouted. She continued, then rounded the corner of the desk toward Pavel.

Pavel stood tall and looked Sera in the eye as she drew within striking distance. Her hand swung back, the knife blade pointed forward, and Doctor Troyka said gently, "Sera, you have a choice."

Adam's eyes darted to LaMont, who seemed completely engrossed in what his puppet was about to do to the old man, neglecting both his attention and his aim. Without thinking, Adam dropped to the ground and grabbed the electrodusters, slipping them over the knuckles of his right hand again.

A Blue ran by. Adam sprung up to grab the panicked officer by the uniform and turned him wide to LaMont, using him as a shield. Adam heard at least three shots but felt nothing. He steered the struggling Blue into position, then tossed the man's body aside and threw himself across the desk. Adam is still not entirely sure how he did it to this day, but his right hand connected with LaMont's dimpled chin.

The punch alone would have left an impression, but the added boost of the electrodusters caused LaMont's head to pop back violently. The dusters' loud crack preceded the bumps and thuds of LaMont hitting the floor. The gun also fell and slid away from him, coming to rest a few feet away on the polished floor.

Adam rushed to Pavel, who lay at Sera's feet. She held a knife dripping blood, dark and arterial, her expression blank. "Pavel!"

Adam cried, sliding to a stop next to the old man. "Are you all right?" Velim did not appear to notice Adam's presence. She had stabbed the doctor in the armpit. Blood coated Pavel's shirt, the vest underneath, and the floor.

"Adam," Pavel gasped, "You have to take Sera and go. Don't try to order her to leave. There may be some kind of latent command that will make her attack you. Just take off her Lightcap and get out of here. I'll be fine; don't worry about me." As he spoke, his breath came in small starts. He applied pressure on the wound.

Adam knew he was supposed to be brave, to say he wasn't going to leave Pavel behind, but the man was bleeding on the floor and couldn't be moved. Adam knew he had to leave, then or never. He stood up and said, "Goodbye, Pavel. Thank you. Keep an eye on that knocked out bastard."

LaMont lay slumped on the floor behind his desk. Adam went over, bent down and picked up the gun, then walked back and gave it to Pavel. Adam moved behind Velim and removed her Lightcap. She started to drop, but he caught her under the arms and transferred her to his right shoulder.

"I'll shoot him if he moves," the old man said with a pained laugh. Pavel had taken his backpack off and was using it to support himself. He had also trained the gun on the unconscious executive. The Blues in the room continued to run aimlessly. One of them tripped over the doctor and fell into a thrashing mess on the floor. Pavel winced.

Adam nodded in agreement. The last time he saw Pavel was from behind, the man's bald spot slowly bobbing up and down as his arm rested on his bent leg, gun in hand, aimed at Roman LaMont.

Clear

Adam carried Sera from LaMont's office, the hallway somehow seeming longer and uphill, until he reached the turn to the right leading back to the stairwell. He had taken exactly eight steps when a lone Blue rounded the corner, coming from the direction Adam was heading.

At first, Adam thought he might be one of the Blues confounded by Dej's device, but his movements were too precise, too sure. The guard removed all doubts by drawing his weapon and commanding, "Put her down. Get on the ground," in an authoritative voice. The Blue wasn't wearing a Lightcap. *This must be one of the mercenaries working for LaMont*, Adam thought, men with murderous talent and not even a shred of conscience. Unsure of what else to do, Adam slowly lowered Sera's limp form to the ground. After he had gently sloughed her off his shoulder, the Blue yelled, "Now down on the ground." Adam complied, turning his view to the left as he spread his arms and legs out on the floor, face down.

Adam could hear the man's heavy boots moving closer. Adam held his breath and waited for a gunshot, the final sound of his existence. He heard a muffled pop from LaMont's office, then another. Pavel. LaMont's gun. He heard the Blue say, "What the . . . ?" but his question ended with a sudden crunch and a wet choking noise.

Adam looked up to see a blade stuck through the Blue's neck. Beyond these Adam saw Aria's set face, her jaw clenched and hand wrapped in a death grip around the grip of the katana. "Hi. You took too long, and there was no one left for me to kill. Let's go. The chopper's running and Dej is awake," she said, unable to stop herself from smiling.

They lifted Sera, who seemed unaware her existence had just been threatened, and made their way down the hall around the corner, to arrive at the stairwell door. "Thanks for saving us," Adam said. "Pavel didn't make it. Did you have any trouble getting back to the chopper?"

Aria peered around Velim's sagging head and gave Adam an incredulous look, but she said nothing in response. They made their way up the stairs to the hangar in silence. She kicked the next door open to reveal ten dead Blues strewn around the landing pad. The JMR's rotors idled, cutting through the air with a low *swoop* sound. Angry grey clouds hung silent over the open roof. Adam was thankful to notice the rain and hail had stopped.

Dej sat in the passenger section of the chopper. He gave them a weak smile and a thumbs-up sign as they approached. Aria hopped through the open door and hoisted Sera up, then Adam. She put Sera in a seat and quickly buckled her in.

Aria pulled Adam close and said, "We have to go. Come on." She dragged him toward the cockpit. She slid into the pilot seat on the left as Adam took the co-pilot seat on the right. Aria pointed to the headphones above his head, and he put them on. "We don't have much time," she yelled into her mic, the loudness of her voice from the speaker painful against his ears. "We're under fire."

Aria didn't need to tell Adam, because as the words left her mouth there was a telltale double ping sound, then more such sounds, suggesting bullets were peppering the helicopter. Adam then saw Blues at the door of the stairwell, their guns blazing at the chopper body. Aria grabbed something that looked to Adam like a throttle and pulled it toward her. The chopper shuddered and started to lift from the pad.

Adam also saw movement from above. The roof began to close against the cloudy streaks in the sky, the metal teeth of the skyscraper like those of a giant threatening to crush them. Aria saw it too and yelled, "Hold on." She pulled back and to the left on the stick as her feet worked the pedals in the footwell. The chopper pitched against the sky in the same direction and lifted higher, faster. Adam thought he heard the sound of metal against metal, but the teeth of the roof rushed past their view. They were free.

Aria pushed forward on the controls and took them southwest from New Metra City, issuing commands at Adam on the headset, providing him an impromptu lesson in basic navigation. She took the chopper to what Adam assumed was its top speed. After twenty minutes of the noisiest silence he had ever experienced, Adam asked, "Where are we going?"

"D.C." She replied. "I know a guy."

"Who?"

She gave no response.

Adam wanted more information, but her stony gaze did not invite further inquiry. He gave up and looked out the window, watching as several towns and cities of varying size passed underneath. They didn't speak again until Aria began to bark more orders at him to help her find a specific structure. He recognized the District of Columbia from pictures, but several of its buildings were different from what he remembered. Some were in a state of disrepair and some were fixed up, conveying a hodgepodge of modernity and dilapidation.

As if reading his mind, Aria said, "Some of these places haven't been touched in decades. Government got out in a hurry, whole place turned into a ghost town for a bit. But people came back. We always come back."

Adam could not believe the large steel fence and familiar façade, the semi-circle overhang surrounded and supported by a half-dozen stark bright columns. It wasn't until they'd passed over the building and he saw the large lawn that he knew. Adam turned to Aria, though it wasn't necessary since his voice passed through the mic to her headphones, and asked, "The White House?" He almost laughed at the absurdity of the situation.

Aria looked at him for an instant, then returned her attention to the craft, which she deftly landed on the South Lawn about ten meters from the stairs. Several men rushed from the building to the chopper. Adam was relieved to see they were unarmed. Once the craft had settled, Aria flipped several switches and Adam felt the thrum of the engines start to pulse with less urgency, its frequency dropping with each beat of the rotors against air.

Adam could not help gawking at the large house in his field of view. It stood, austere and imposing, but also marked with the scars of battle. The side to his right was charred, missing a large section of wall.

Aria shed her headset and got up. Adam followed. She stopped to kneel in front of Dej, who gave her a weak smile and mouthed the word, "Go." Sera sat unconscious beside him. At least her eyes were closed, Adam noticed. She looked peaceful, and color had begun to return to her cheeks.

Aria heaved against the door, which slid open with a grind and locked into position with a clunk. A smiling man stood on the other side, tall and mischievous, two unhappier-looking men on either side beyond him. Aria caught Adam off guard when she jumped into the man's arms and cried, "Nemo!" The man stumbled but caught her after his back leg anchored him on the grass. She hugged him for a long time, but eventually let go and looked to Adam, who waited uncomfortably. Aria said, "This is my baby brother, Nemo Hines." She turned back to her brother and continued, "Nemo, this is Adam Redmon. He's clumsy sometimes, but he's useful enough."

Nemo grasped Adam's entire forearm, placing his own against it. Adam felt obliged to reciprocate, and once he clasped Nemo's forearm, he found his own arm pumped with abandon.

"I am glad you could join us," Nemo said. He looked at his sister inquisitively to ask, "Pavel?" Aria gently shook her head no.

Adam said, "He didn't make it. He sacrificed himself to take down LaMont and save me and Sera." Nemo turned to look at Adam, who felt his face flush with shame for not carrying both Sera and Pavel to safety.

"It's fine," Nemo said. "I'm just glad you got Aria and Dej out safely." Adam wanted to tell him it had happened exactly the opposite way, that Aria had been the one to help them get out, but Nemo had already turned to her and continued. "And how is Dej? Let's go get him and this Sera person." It seemed to Adam that Nemo had said Sera's name with thinly veiled distrust, but he lifted himself into the helicopter before Adam had a chance to question it further.

Dej was in better shape than Sera, who was still unresponsive. Aria helped him up, his left arm slung across her shoulder and neck, and they exited the passenger compartment. Nemo moved toward Sera, and Adam helped him pick her up, thankful to have someone to help. Nemo jumped down to the ground and took Sera from Adam so he could climb down to join them. Adam then grabbed Sera's unsupported side. They walked together in silence, behind Dej and Aria, into the White House.

The two other men took Dej and Sera to the infirmary, where a doctor would examine them, leaving Adam, Aria, and Nemo alone. After several turns and a trip through a long hallway, they went through a door into an oddly shaped room.

Adam had seen the Oval Office in pictures, and he now found himself standing in a similar room in shambles. He remembered images of different desks, but folding chairs now sat in their place, cheap sheet metal resting on a blue carpet several feet away from an emblazoned eagle of Freedom. The eagle was covered in dark stains that were the color of dried mud. Four other men stood in the room. No one made introductions.

Aria and Adam spent the next several hours briefing Nemo on their time in the Lightcap project. Adam let Aria do most of the talking. He wasn't sure what he could add, given he barely remembered anything, and what he could recall was dream-like, disjointed, as if he had been an observer and not an active participant. Adam recounted everything he remembered, but he left out the nightmares and events he still couldn't discern as real or imagined.

Adam tried to look interested while Aria spoke, but had difficulty stopping his mind from wandering. Would Sera recover? Had Troyka survived? What about LaMont? Jon had let them out of LaMont's trap. Would they be able to find him, or would he fade back into the shadows he had called his home for more than a dozen years? What would happen to Adaptech and Metra Corp now that LaMont was gone? A part of Adam was afraid to learn the answers to these questions.

A sudden awareness that silence had settled over the room interrupted Adam's thoughts. Two sets of eyes studied him, wide and expectant. "I'm . . . I'm sorry, can you say that again?" he asked, his tongue stumbling on his words.

Adam was fairly certain Nemo rolled his eyes before he said, "I asked if you had anything else to add to what you and Aria have already said."

"No. Aria was pretty comprehensive," Adam said, relieved the briefing appeared to be coming to an end. Curt handshakes were given, and Nemo excused them. Nemo and Aria left together, followed by the men who had stood silently by Nemo during their meeting. Adam was left alone in the Oval Office, quiet and oppressive with its centuries of history. He sat for what felt like hours, looking out the window and reflecting on the combination of luck, coincidence, and stubbornness that had got them to this point. He was amazed they weren't all dead.

The exhaustion of the day began to catch up with him, and Adam found himself nodding off as he gazed beyond the window. He then mustered the strength to rise from the chair, fighting gravity itself, and walk out of the room, back through the hallways and up a set of stairs. Adam found himself next to Sera's bed in the infirmary. She looked peaceful, as if she were dreaming pleasant dreams. He pulled a chair next to her bed, sat there, and lay his head next to her hand. He fell asleep within minutes.

Adam stood atop a large hill. In the distance, he could see New Metra City, his home for most of his life. The city was burning, large columns of smoke holding the sky above the foundation of the earth. Adam was struck by the thought that he was responsible for this, that he was to blame. Life there had been irrevocably changed, and it was his fault. He was convinced cries of pain and anguish played against his ears, the almost-echoes of lost souls cursing him from afar.

Adam was startled by a high-pitched whine from behind him as two jets soared into his field of vision, headed toward the already decimated city. Four small flashes were followed by larger ones as their delivered missiles crashed into the sides of several buildings. Adam flinched against the bursts of light, his hand raising reflexively and his body turning to the side to shield himself from the terrible brightness. The hot heat of the explosions pulsed against his body, his hair blown by the wind of their fury. Adam turned to face the city and saw almost nothing left. Acrid air, the rush and stench of death carried by the breeze, pushed against his face and up his hairline.

He awoke to the feeling of movement across his scalp. Sera's hand lightly brushed against his hair. His head shot up to meet her eyes. She yawned as if waking from a nap, then opened her eyes fully and looked directly at him.

"Hello, Adam," She said. "I'm Sera. It's good to finally meet you."

Aftermath

The months that followed were full of activity for many people in Washington. Nemo, Dej, and Aria were constantly busy, either in meetings or working on special projects. Sera and Adam were provided neighboring apartments in Georgetown, an area of Washington relatively untouched by past battles. Their connected balconies overlooked the Potomac River. They spent their days talking about their lives, discussing technology, philosophy, and the meaning of existence.

Adam already felt an attraction toward Sera, but after spending the past several months with her, aiding in her recovery and listening to her mind and heart, he found himself thinking of her constantly. She seemed to have feelings for him too, but Adam also understood Sera was on a long road to recovery.

Sera had known who Adam was from the moment she awoke. She told them that after several years she had learned to be an observer while wearing the Lightcap and remembered a great deal more than Adam did from his time under the control of the device. This proved to be a source of both information and consternation, as Sera felt great self-loathing for the things she had done while under LaMont's control. She had begun seeing a therapist and making progress.

Adam made progress as well. His focus had returned, and he

could use a dome without issue. Dej had an entire team of engineers and coders go through each piece of hardware and each line of code to assure Adam his dome was only functional for controlling other devices. He couldn't help but feel an intense distrust of the technology, even with the assurances of a team of people who specialized in reverse engineering and neuron interfaces. Adam's first attempt at using a dome again had ended in a panic attack, but now he could use it for hours at a time with little effort.

The events of his tenure at Adaptech and rescue from Metra Corp headquarters seemed from a different lifetime, more so with each passing day. That's why Adam was surprised to hear a knock on his front door one Saturday morning, and even more surprised when he opened his door to find Nemo, Aria, and Dej standing on the other side of it wearing worried expressions. Nemo spoke first and asked, "May we come in?"

Adam stepped back and bowed slightly. They all took his unspoken cue and entered. Aria went to the balcony and retrieved Sera, who had been outside enjoying an iced tea and the warm day. As Aria brought her into the room, Adam noted Sera looked as confused as he felt as she took a seat next to him. Aria sat between Nemo and Dej, opposite Adam. Both Aria and Nemo looked at Dej, who cleared his throat and spoke. "So I know you guys haven't been very involved in discussions about plans. I don't know how attached you've been to the news, but things in Metra Region are a complete mess right now.

Adam and Sera shook their heads with helpless expressions to indicate their ignorance of current events. It had been difficult for Adam, but he had put aside his addiction to information while focusing on his recovery.

"Rupert Calloway took LaMont's place. He lasted about a month before being assassinated by a sniper while golfing at a private course. His replacement, Liv Daley, has been in office for two months, but who knows how long she'll last before someone takes her out. The entire Region is in disarray. Company stock value is the lowest it's ever been and there have been a substantial number of voting shares traded in the system. The votes will now be more consolidated than ever before. Those in power are amassing even more, and the proles are restless. To make matters worse, the Cascadia Region has gone dark."

"Dark?" Adam asked.

Dej looked at Nemo, who responded to Adam's question.

"Almost two weeks ago, our western outposts noticed there were no signals coming out of Cascadia. No public broadcasts, no mesh traffic, nothing. We're not sure if there has been some kind of catastrophe, maybe a natural disaster or coup, since their borders have been closed. We've also found evidence to suggest Jonathan Bays is in the Cascadia Region. We're not sure if he was there when he helped you escape the trap in Metra Corp headquarters, but we strongly suspect he's there now, possibly in Seattle or Portland. We also think he may know about or be involved with the production and distribution of Cloud. Of course, we don't have any way to reach him, so we've been working out the logistics of sending a team to Cascadia."

Adam looked at Nemo, then Aria. He said, "I want to go. I'm assuming Aria is leading the team?"

Aria shook her head. "No, but I'll be going," She said. "Nemo has put together a group, called Project Shadowcloud, and has someone who will be leading the team. We want you to join us. We still haven't decided if we should give you a weapon, but we definitely could use your smarts. We're leaving two weeks from Monday."

The meeting ended shortly after, with instructions given on where to be and what to bring on the day of departure. Adam and Sera sat in silence for several minutes after the others left, until she finally got up and walked to the balcony. Adam followed. She stood and looked out across the river, her hair blown back by a breeze.

Eventually, she said, "I'm coming too. It's better than sitting here and wasting away. No offense. I love our conversations and the peacefulness here, but I feel I'm doing nothing while the closest things I have to friends are out doing important work trying to make a difference. I'd rather do that than stay here, even though I know I'm still not healed." She looked at him searchingly. "I can be useful, right?"

Adam didn't say anything for several seconds. He had never seen her so vulnerable. At the same time, he knew she would not be dissuaded. Finally, he said, "You're right, of course. I want you to come. We could use you. And even though it's selfish, I don't want to be away from you." As Adam said these last words, he slipped his hand into hers. Sera looked at him and blushed, but squeezed his hand in response. He had been afraid she would recoil.

Adam experienced a moment of panic as the look on her face changed to frustration and pain. Before he could ask her what was wrong, she said, "Adam, look."

Adam followed Sera's gaze out across the Potomac and beyond to see several floating ad zeps dotting the skies. Adam had long before learned to ignore them, and he could even imagine them missing when looking at a particularly beautiful sunset or blue sky. This time, however, the usual flashing ads on hundred-meter long screens had been replaced by a black background and large, capital block letters in a sharp green. Adam gasped as he read the words:

TROYKA LIVES

ABOUT THE AUTHOR

Dan Marshall resides in Portland, OR, with his girlfriend, Great Dane/Dachshund mix dog, and two long-haired black cats. This is his first novel.

For more information, visit IAmDanMarshall.com.

NOTE FROM THE AUTHOR

Thank you so much for reading this book. I hope you enjoyed it. Please consider leaving a review on Amazon, Goodreads, or the review site of your choice. As a self-published and new author, I have no marketing department or professional assistance, so your feedback helps immensely. I enjoyed writing this book and hope to have more available soon, including a sequel to *The Lightcap*. I hope you find this story enjoyable enough to keep up with the doings of Adam Redmon and company. The next book will have a much broader scope and will show more of the other three Regions that make up the former United States.

Every effort was made to produce a work free of spelling, grammatical, and continuity errors. That said, there are 60,000+ words in this book, so it's possible some mistakes made it through the editing process. If you find any errors, please email me (Dan@IAmDanMarshall.com) and let me know. Thank you again for reading!

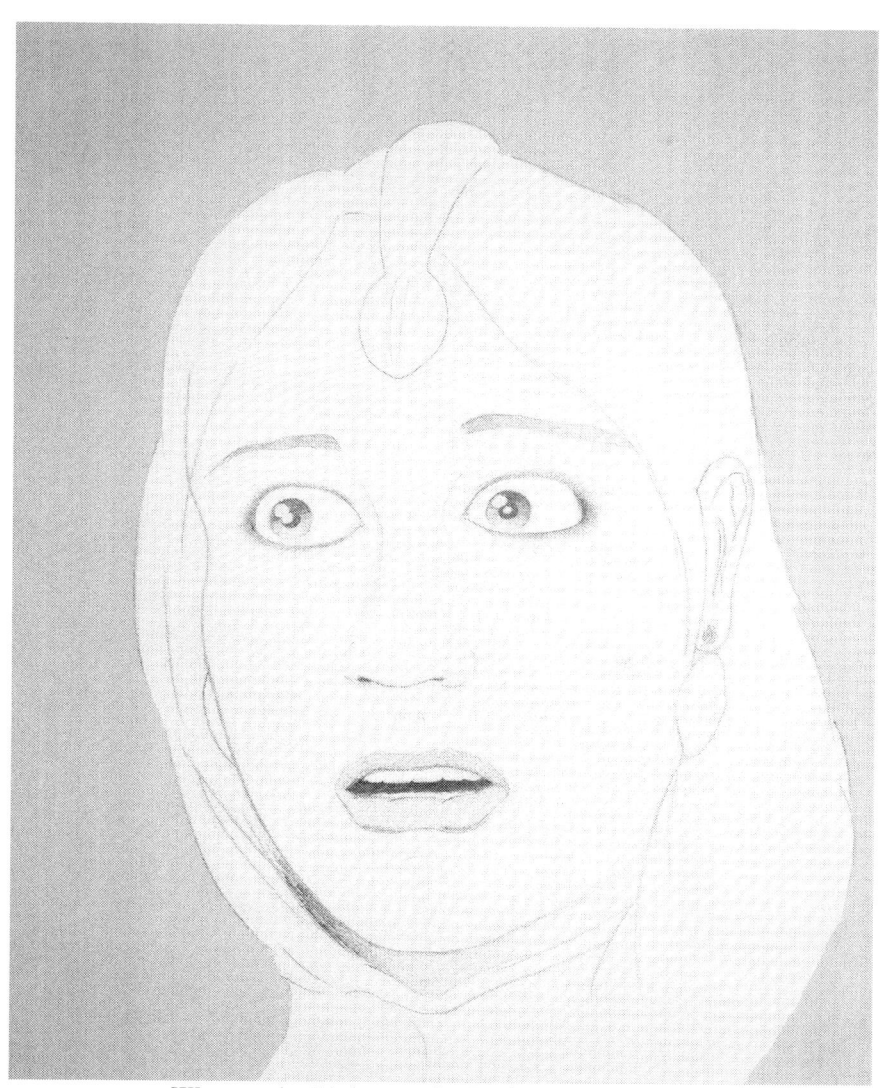

Woman in Lightcap, by Robert Peate

Made in the USA
Charleston, SC
04 June 2013